The Urbana Free Library

To renew: call **217-367-4057**
or go to **urbanafreelibrary.org**
and select **My Account**

LOVE IN THE TIME OF APARTHEID

LOVE IN THE TIME OF APARTHEID

Frederic Hunter

THE PERMANENT PRESS
Sag Harbor, NY 11963

For information, address:
  The Permanent Press
  4170 Noyac Road
  Sag Harbor, NY 11963
  www.thepermanentpress.com

Library of Congress Cataloging-in-Publication Data

  Hunter, Frederic, author.
    Love in the time of apartheid / Frederic Hunter.
    Sag Harbor, NY : The Permanent Press, [2016]
    ISBN 978-1-57962-444-6 (hardcover)
      1. South Africa—Politics and government—1948–1994—Fiction.
    2. South Africa—Social conditions—1961–1994—Fiction. 3. Social
    change—South Africa—Fiction. 4. Man-woman relationships—
    Fiction. 5. Fathers and daughters—Fiction. 6. Historical fiction.

  PS3558.U477 L69 2016
  813'.54—dc23   2016025195

Printed in the United States of America

For Donanne

CHAPTER ONE

JOHANNESBURG

Friday, February 3, 1961

As he opened his hotel room curtains on his third day in Johannesburg, Gat saw the tawny slag heaps on the edge of the city. Back in a mining town, he thought. How did I let that happen? It was after nine. He had not slept so late since his childhood. Or so badly. I must get out of this place, he told himself.

He had soaked in the tub for an hour the night before. Still he showered. Afterward, gazing at himself in the mirror, he saw a face that he did not think an employer would hire. Nor would a woman find it attractive. What woman would look beyond the jaunty beard and the sad eyes to see the man he really was? He could hardly stand to look at himself.

In Katanga where Belgians were midwifing the birth of a mineral-rich, breakaway province, trying to separate it from a newborn country called the Congo, Gat's commanders had decided he needed a change of scene. They had given him a round-trip ticket to South Africa, a thousand American dollars, a new passport, and a new driver's license. They had presented him a box of condoms, twelve dozen of them, and instructed him to use them all before he returned in four months.

But in his first two days in Joburg he had hardly left the room. If he ventured out, he supposed people would smell the taint on him. They would see him slinking along sidewalks like a man who had turned into a hyena. He had escaped the room only for meals, liquor, and exercise. And to buy newspapers. Their employment want ads had made him aware of how many jobs were available for which he possessed no qualifications.

He paced the hotel room, studying the slag heaps. They looked like huge lions lying just beyond the reach of civilization. Lions no longer roamed the mining towns of Katanga— Elisabethville and Kolwezi, Jadotville, Shinkolobwe—or this one, Johannesburg. Now they were places of other predators, places where rich men made use of men like him who were not rich. Gat stroked his beard and made a vow to himself: Today we leave this room.

He returned to the bathroom. There, as if by its own volition, his hand reached into the canvas bag he used as a shaving kit. It removed the scissors it found there. Gat began to trim his beard. The less hair there was on his chin the better he felt about himself. His eyes looked brighter; his body felt less burdened with weight. He scissored the beard completely off his face, the mustache too, leaving only stubble the way loggers clear-cut jungle leaving only tree stumps. He put a new blade into his razor and shaved so close that his cheeks, upper lip, and chin showed white below the brow browned by the Katanga sun.

Breakfasting in the hotel dining room on eggs fried too hard and cold toast, his upper lip still tender, his jaw red from the scrapings of the razor, Gat made another vow to himself: He would become a new man. He would put behind him the wreckage of his life: a career turned sour; no money put by; no connection to family; no woman. He would get himself new clothes and work more to his liking. Something he chose this time, not something he fell into. But how would he find that?

Two HOURS later in the men's department of a clothing store, he looked at himself in a three-sided mirror. Yes, the suit would do. Lightweight, dark blue. It would allow him to pass himself off as someone he wasn't. A businessman. Or an up-and-coming professional. One who spent a good deal of time in the sun. A man whose business was the land. He gazed at his image, threw off the hyena-slink set of his shoulders, and approved of what he saw. The suit helped.

He bought the suit, two dress shirts, three ties, two short-sleeved sport shirts, and a safari suit (trousers and tunic) for casual wear.

On THE streets of Johannesburg wearing his blue suit and tightly knotted tie, carrying his packages, the army captain began to shed his military identity. He strode along as a businessman might: erect, but relaxed, without the cocky set of the shoulders needed for commanding men, without the challenging glint in his eye. He felt less tainted now, almost fragrant with confidence.

He followed three white schoolgirls in light dresses, exulting in the freedom of summer to escape school uniforms. Feeling his eyes on them, they glanced back at him and giggled with pleasure at his interest. They hurried along like frightened birds, pleased by his gaze, all flattered, twittering modesty, their eyes lowered to the sidewalk.

Gat examined the Africans trudging toward him, balacla-vas pulled low on their heads. The men's bodies were thin and work-worn; the women's beneath folds of clothing had the shape of cigar stubs. Not a single African looked at him. All of them walked past as if he, a white man, had no more human characteristics than a lamppost.

Gat arrived at the Central Post Office. He had been instructed to check there for General Delivery. He found the proper counter, paused to remember the name in his passport, and gave it to the clerk. "A letter for you, sir," the clerk said on returning. "I'll need some identification." Gat offered his passport. The document claimed to have been issued in Brus-sels. In fact it had been issued in Elisabethville. It gave his name as Adriaan Gautier. That was false, but the photograph was authentic; it had been taken only a week before. The clerk checked it against Gat's face. "I've shaved," Gat remarked.

"Found you still had a chin, eh?" joshed the clerk. "Sign please." Gat signed. The clerk handed him the letter and the passport.

Gat went to the section of the post office marked "Nie-Blankes." No whites lingered there. He opened the letter; the stationery was parchment, embossed with the return address of a post box in Tervuren, the town east of Brussels where King Leopold II had built his Royal Museum of Central Africa. Folded inside the stationery Gat found ten crisp one hundred dollar bills. A second one thousand dollars. As a tip very nice. As blood money very meager. On the piece of stationery one word was typed: "Disappear."

ONE OF the first passengers on the early afternoon flight to Cape Town, Gat took his seat beside the window, settled into the persona the new suit afforded him, and opened his copy of the *Rand Daily Mail*. A treason trial of several dozen, mainly non-white defendants, had dragged on for more than a year; now it was drawing to a close. The state was seeking to prove that the African National Congress, apparently an African political party, was a Communist organization bent on establishing a Communist state. It seemed that South African whites were playing the same game that the whites farther north played, claiming that to cede power would only make a gift of Africa to the Communists. As if African nationalists would free themselves from the rule of white capitalists only to surrender it to white Communists.

"May I sit here? Do you mind?"

The woman was tall, slender, with an athletic figure, and blonded hair cut short. She clipped her words, spoke with an English accent, and indicated the aisle seat.

"Please do," he said. "By all means."

She dropped her large purse into the empty seat between them and smiled hello. She was a beauty and conscious of it, young middle age, forty or a bit older, probably had teenage children. She wore a dark blue suit, the female version of his own, with white piping at the edges of the lapels and the cuffs. Perhaps she was a businesswoman, he thought, but, no, her beauty made too vivid, too immediate, an impression for that. His eyes seemed involuntarily drawn to the blue-green pupils of her eyes, invited there by lines of mascara at the lashes and by eye shadow deftly applied to enlarge the sockets. She seated herself, exuding a vitality that made him glad that the Fates had set her beside him.

"I do hope we have a smooth flight. Don't you?"

Her smile showed perfect teeth, brightly white. She settled herself, crossed her legs with a sibilant rustling of nylons one against the other. He glanced at her legs. Beneath the hem of her skirt a knee peeked. Nice.

Once they were airborne, the woman smiled hello again as she withdrew from her purse a pair of glasses and a manuscript folder. While studiously staring at his paper, Gat was aware of her settling in to her study. He glanced over. The woman adjusted the glasses onto her nose and looked over at him as if expecting him to speak. Instead he smiled; her glasses were comically large. And yet they endowed her beauty with humanity and a whimsical quality; they suggested she had a sense of humor about herself. Gat reached over to her armrest to turn on her overhead light. It spilled yellow onto her. "That should be better."

"Thank you." She cocked her head to identify his newspaper. "You aren't reading that miserable rag!"

"Miserable? What makes you say that?"

"Every day the same scandal, that treason trial." Her eyes flashed mischievously as her voice exaggerated "scandal." "The horrors of the color bar and Bantu education. The misery of the townships. Do they think we don't know?"

"Maybe some people need reminding."

"Oh, posh!" she said. "In that sheet today's news is the same as yesterday's."

Gat smiled. "I didn't read it yesterday. So it's fresh to me."

She tilted her head and observed him over the top of her glasses. "You're not South African, are you? What's that accent I hear?"

"I'm Belgian."

"From the Congo?"

"From Brussels. Ixelles."

"Your people have had a rough go in the Congo! That creature Lumumba: he's a piece of work." Again the mischievous flash of the eyes.

He shrugged. For a woman her age she really was smashing.

"What brings you here?" she asked. "We're wearing practically the same blue business suit. So it can't be a holiday."

"I wish my suit had white piping."

They found each other attractive. She confessed to being an actress, not a very good one, though she had been at it long enough. She was flying to the Cape to do an industrial film. He carefully masked his identity. Because of his suit, she took him for a businessman. He said, yes, he was a Belgian manufacturer of sturdy, low-priced furniture, his uncle's profession in Britain. He was contemplating a move to South Africa.

On the flight to Cape Town they became pals. When he suggested they share a taxi into town, she offered him a ride in the convertible her producers were renting for her and drove him to the five-star Mount Nelson Hotel where she was staying. Flush with blood money, Gat took a room there because he and Tina Windsor had recognized something in each other. They agreed to meet for dinner. He watched her walk off beside the Coloured bellman: the athletic stride, the way the skirt of her suit fell from her hips, her tapered legs, her ankles, the long heels on her shoes.

AFTER CHECKING into his room, the cheapest available in this pink palace of opulence, Gat took a walk about the city center in order to assess the virtues Tina had claimed for it. Yes, he thought, Cape Town was more civilized, more relaxed, than the urban scabs around Johannesburg. There mining camps grown into cities reminded him strongly of the Katanga from which he was to disappear. Now and then he saw a "non-white," as the local parlance had it, in a suit like the one he himself wore, possibly a lawyer, doctor, insurance salesman. When two of them met, they greeted each other with laughter and shook hands. Moving along the boulevard, Gat found himself admiring women, the stylishness of their dress and the confidence of their strides. He felt more strongly that somehow only a woman could get him right with himself, only a woman could help him uncover the man he wanted to be.

Gat entered a square. Across it stood a large church with Gothic windows pointing to the sky above. A sign announced: Saint Mary's Catholic Church. Gat felt the lapsed Catholic's terror. How had his feet brought him here? He quickly started away.

"Gat!" The sound of the voice raised hair on the nape of his neck. "Captain Gat!" He walked faster. No one knew Captain Gat here. He was Adriaan Gautier, factory boss, manufacturer of low-cost furniture. But the footsteps drew closer. "Gat! That *is* you!"

Gat reached an alley. Ducked into it, fearing someone sent to eliminate him. A figure in military fatigues flashed past. Gat relaxed. The figure returned. It hesitated, peered at Gat. *"Salut, copain,"* the man said. He swaggered jauntily into the alley.

"Michels," Gat said, recognizing him. *"Salut."*

Michels moved to Gat and sharply slapped his shaven cheek. "You've shaved," he noted. "You look fifteen." The man was of medium height, rail thin, and very blond. His hair stuck like straw straight out of his head, not quite officer quality, even for the Congo's Force Publique. With his prominent nose and pointed chin, the wrists sticking out of his jacket, he looked like an Afrikaner yokel off the *platteland.*

Gat clapped the man's body in feigned friendship, patting for weapons.

Michels asked, "What're you running from?"

"From the bad dream of meeting you."

Michels had been sent out of Katanga just as Gat had with a mission to disappear. He chortled now, smelling of liquor. The set of his shoulders and the self-satisfied steps of his strut were even more pronounced than in Katanga where they attempted to give the slight body substance and a quality of command. "I knew it was you," he said in Flemish. "No two men walk the same way."

"How are things?"

"A lot better here than there. Why the suit?"

"Why the fatigues?" Michels was wearing camouflage fatigues without officer insignias, and a military bush hat, one side folded above his ear. "You going to a masquerade?" Gat could not help wondering if Michels had been sent to assassinate him. It was a crazy idea—Michels was a fuckup—but it was not crazy to be wary.

"You know what happens down here when I tell them what we did."

"Don't tell anyone," Gat said.

"Come find out," Michels invited. "I'm on my way to a bordel. White girls."

"That's a change for you." Michels was a famous patron of brothels in the *cités* of Elisabethville so raunchy that no fellow officers would accompany him. Force Publique doctors had stippled his buttocks with hypodermic shots of penicillin.

Gat looked about for a way to escape.

"I get it free there," Michels boasted. Gat regarded him skeptically. "No shit. I tell 'em what we did—"

"Don't tell. Not anyone." Gat pushed past Michels and started out of the alley.

"You look good in the suit," Michels said. "Like a fucking junior mining magnate from E'ville." They emerged from the alley onto the sidewalk where whites and blacks, Coloured and Malays, hurried past each other with no flicker of recognition except for their own kind. "Let's do something together," Michels suggested. "Where you staying?" Gat mentioned his hotel because it might be useful to keep tabs on Michels.

"You passing on pussy?" Michels stuck out his hand. Gat shook it. The two men parted, moving in different directions. Gat turned at the corner, hesitated a moment, then followed Michels for two blocks, studying his movements, the folds of his clothes. Was he armed? Gat thought not. Michels liked women too much to serve as a reliable assassin.

BACK AT the hotel he showered, put on the new yellow shirt and a blue tie with a yellow design in it, and at 7:25 went down to the dining room. Tina Windsor appeared at five of eight.

"You look amazingly gorgeous," Gat told her, partly because it was true and partly because he knew she would want to hear it. Her dress was basic black and displayed her figure well. It accentuated her vitality, her beauty.

They followed the maitre d' to a table and ordered sanely for what was to come: light on food, medium heavy on wine. Gat encouraged Tina to talk about herself and she was only too happy to oblige. Raised in Kenya, she fled the colony for Britain at eighteen, headed for university, so her parents thought, but was mad for the theater. She landed a part in a play, bequeathed her virginity on an actor less impressed in receiving it than she was in bestowing it, and began to live a glamorous life of parties and lovers. She unfolded anecdotes from her life as if they were scenes in a play: married a stodgy but very handsome South African, had children, took lovers, fell for a theater director who offered to share her with her husband, divorced and married the director and found now that, terrified at becoming fifty, he was chasing the friends of her late-teenage daughter. "Embarrassing for her and very tiresome for me," Tina complained. She gave Gat enough scenes from her romantic drama to assure him that he would be offered a role in it.

They had coffee in a parlor off the dining room. "Tell me more about the Congo," Tina requested. "Were you in Léopoldville during the troubles?"

"No," he said, improvising. He did not want to tell horror stories. "I've just been down there trying to straighten out a personnel matter. In our factory."

"What was that?"

"You can't want to know," Gat said. He wondered what he would tell her if she insisted.

"But I do!" she said. "You've heard all this boring business about my husbands."

"We had a Congolese—" He would model this character on Patrice Lumumba, the Congo's first prime minister. "Quite an extraordinary fellow really. Even if he had three wives."

"All at the same time? I can't imagine!" Tina laughed. "I've had my problems with two husbands, one at a time!"

"He was running our factory for us," Gat explained, improvising on Lumumba's situation. "There were problems, of course. That was to be expected in a shift to Congolese management. But it was nothing that time and a little patience could not have worked out."

"But who has either?"

"Right," he replied. "The inevitable problems arose. The Congolese was very capable. He had been told that he'd be running things. But he was supposed to understand, of course, that he would not really run them. A Belgian 'advisor' would."

"Oh, goodness."

"The Congolese caused problems. In fact, he fired the Belgian 'advisor' who happened to be the grandson of the company's owner. The grandson locked the Congolese out of the factory. The Congolese got the work force to walk off the job. It got very ugly. Threats were made. I was sent down to straighten things out."

"Were you able to?"

Gat paused, trying to work out the plot of his improvisation. "Well, the situation's resolved."

Tina looked at him. "What does that mean?"

"The Congolese refused to meet with the grandson. He insisted that threats had been made on his life."

"Had they?"

Gat sipped his coffee, playing for time. Then he saw how his riff on Lumumba's story would evolve. "The grandson was a bad lot," he said. "I didn't understand that at the time. He ran with a crowd that wanted to take revenge on Congolese. That was understandable, given what independence was like."

"What happened?"

"At the grandson's suggestion I set up a meeting with the Congolese. At night. In the factory office. He agreed to come because he trusted me. I sent a car and a driver for him." Gat paused.

"And?" asked Tina.

"The car was found the next morning. The Congolese was inside it. Dead." Tina gasped. "He'd been shot five or six times. The driver had disappeared."

There were silent for several moments. Finally Tina said, "That's going to happen here, isn't it?"

"I doubt it," Gat said. "If it does, you'll have gone long since."

"It'll happen here," Tina said, "and it's us they'll kill. I must get my children out of this country." Then she asked, "What's happened at the factory?"

"It's back at work. There's a warrant out for the driver's arrest."

"But he's disappeared."

"Probably gone back to his village. And here I am," Gat said. "Would you like to walk around the block? I need to settle my dinner."

After the walk they had a nightcap in her room. They joked about each wondering how the other would be in bed. "I didn't wonder," Gat assured Tina. "I knew you'd be fantastic."

Tina suggested, "Why don't you hurry down to your room for a toothbrush and anything else you might need?"

In his bathroom he collected the toothbrush, a change of underwear, and condoms. Examining his face in the mirror, he advised himself to give her a pass. He needed a woman to help him restart his life. Not a practiced courtesan, hungry for a tumble, so little aware of him she would not remember his name tomorrow morning. He recognized the advice as good, but military service had schooled him to seize the benefits that came his way.

When he returned to her room, she had changed to a negligee. He undressed as she watched, a little as if he were performing. They embraced.

In his opening move he kissed her shoulder. "Do you take offense easily?" she asked. The pucker left his lips; his mouth fell open. He had not expected talk. "I hope not," she said. "You a little nervous?" Gat cocked his head. No, he did not feel nervous. "I am," she confessed. She gave him an oft-used smile. He thought: No, lady, you are not a very good actress. For she was not nervous, just take-charge. "I want this to be amazing for both of us," she professed. "That's how it'll be if you let me give you a tip now and then along the way."

"A tip?"

"It's always— You know— The first time."

Gat felt the excitement in his groin drain away.

"A new lover can always use a little help, I think."

"I have done this once or twice," Gat said, keeping it light.

"Of course. But a little help can't hurt."

So she gave him tips: about which parts of her body to touch and when and with how much pressure. She cooed when pleased and emitted tiny whimpers when she was not. She warned, "Not yet! Not yet!" for what seemed forever. As Gat held off, he felt himself move out of his body to cross the room and look over at the two of them on the bed, writhing in the gymnastics of sex, wrestling for the purpose of joining their bodies in what was called love, but without possessing the slightest interest in one another. Then finally she cried out, "Now! Now!" and he pounded into her hard because he did not like her. "Oh, my god, now!" Then, "Harder!" And then, "Faster! Faster!" And then "Oh! Ohh! Ohhhh!!" Theatrical gasps of pleasure. She rolled away from him. They lay silently side by side.

She wound herself about him. He held her without pleasure. After a time she asked, "Did you get any black ass in the Congo? I assume that's de rigueur for businessmen from Brussels."

"I've had nothing as good as you in I can't remember when." That was the line he was supposed to say.

"But you must have wanted to try black ass."

"There's only one reason for that. You're in a hurry. A Congolese girl takes longer counting her money than giving you a pop."

She laughed, curled away from him, and brought her knees against her breasts.

FOR A long time Gat lay in the darkness. Usually he slept after sex, but now he was wide awake. Tina's backbone pressed against him, the vertebrae like silky nubs of fire. Gat felt depressed, drained, ready to leave. He stared toward the ceiling he could not see.

When he was very young, not yet twenty, he had tried to make a success as a planter in the region of the Congo called the Equateur. When he was failing, running out of both food and money, children from a nearby village found him. A village girl brought him food. The third time she brought it, she spent the night, sleeping on the mattress in the back of his pickup. They could hardly communicate. Still, bringing him food, sleeping with him, he sometimes thought of her as "saving his life." He thought now: How pure that girl's giving had been compared to this woman's!

Finally he moved to the side of the bed. He sat up. Before he could stand, Tina wrapped her arms about him. "Don't go," she said. In the quiet of the room her whisper sounded in his ears like a shout. "I really can't sleep unless there's a man within reach," she said. She twined herself about him. The air cooled his shoulder where she licked him. Her warm hand slid to his groin. "Come to me again," she pleaded. He said nothing and, even as her hand aroused him, he thought, I should have given this a pass.

Tina slid her body around his. She caused their bodies to join, rocked back and forth against him. She gasped. She clung to him. Tighter, tighter. "God, you are fantastic," she whispered. Her voice fluttered in what might have been a sob, might have been a laugh. "And I'm fantastic too. Aren't I?"

He said nothing. "I am fantastic," she said. "Let him screw twenty-year-olds."

She slid off his legs, stood, pushed him back onto the bed, and slithered against him. Finally she asked, "Who are you really?"

He said nothing.

"I've had manufacturers. Not one of them ever gave me that kind of pleasure." The minutes ticked by. "So who are you?"

He said nothing.

"Did you make up that story about the Congolese who got killed?"

He said nothing, wondering if the night would ever end.

"Or did you kill him?"

So . . . She suspected that he had killed men. He waited till she was deeply asleep, snoring. He slid from the bed, gathered his clothes, shoes, and the toilet articles kit, and walked naked through the halls of the Mount Nelson Hotel back to his own room.

CHAPTER TWO

CAPE TOWN

Saturday, February 4, 1961

Riding the bus south to the Cape of Good Hope, Gat watched sheer cliffs plunge into an ocean the color of blue ink. Seagulls soared and squawked overhead. Pungent salt air filled his lungs and left its taste on his tongue. The little towns seemed picture perfect, home to a settled, prosperous people. Or as the Afrikaners would say: the *volk*. If he were truly a manufacturer of furniture seeking enlarged opportunities, he wondered, would he actually contemplate emigrating here? The social problems waiting down the line seemed obvious: ethnic tension leading to sabotage, violence, and terror, possibly a race war. Could such a manufacturer discount them? Or assume they'd be avoided? If he found a companion like Tina Windsor, would he, too, be lulled into a stupor of affordable servants and creature comforts? Tina Windsor. He didn't want that.

He scanned the news in the *Cape Times*. According to it, Patrice Lumumba, termed "the Congo's hapless prime minister," was still being held incommunicado in an undisclosed prison in Katanga. Gat smiled tightly: deceit and half-truths. He read a squib reporting that Negroes in America were continuing to conduct "sit-ins" at drugstore counters and diners. Mentored by Communists and provocateurs, the report said, they were inciting violence, endangering the fabric of traditional life in the southern United States.

Gat laid the paper aside. He watched bleached cliffs and waves hitting them, white gulls, indigo sea, cerulean sky. He wondered: How could a land of such incredible beauty be a place of such cruelty and division?

At the Cape he skipped the tour and avoided the long-fanged, fluffy-haired baboons. They patrolled the parking lot, delighting urban tourists before snatching and devouring their sandwiches. He walked out to the end of the viewing plaza and stood in the wind. Grown cold, he went into the small canteen for a cup of coffee.

The place was empty except for the counterman, an African busy measuring coffee into a filter, his back to the counter. When the man turned, Gat felt a jolt of ice flash across his body. Had he seen a ghost? The counterman was perhaps six foot four, slender as a rifle barrel with the clipped mustache and the small goatee. Glasses shielded his intelligent eyes; his glance both penetrated and seemed oddly gentle. The man had cropped his kinky hair close to his head, incising a slit into the left side to suggest a part.

Gat immediately recognized the man's homage to Lumumba. His appearance communicated his solidarity, at least to those who actually looked at him. Gat felt an urge to signal his recognition. But would it unnerve the African? Gat asked for coffee. When he paid, he left a five-rand tip. "That's for you."

"Thank you, baas."

Gat moved to a display of postcards and feigned inspecting them while scrutinizing the counterman. If Gat believed in reincarnation, he would have thought that Lumumba was now working in this canteen. Gat bought a postcard and once more tipped the African generously. The man left the tip on the counter, tempted to pocket it but not quite trusting the impulse.

"You get many visitors here?" Gat asked.

"Oh, many, baas. Very many."

"From far away?"

"Oh, yes, baas. From very far."

They looked at one another. The man would venture no conversation beyond cheery, bland replies. Adept at roles, he chose obsequiousness as the safest with an unknown white man.

"I'm from America," Gat said. "I've been in the Congo for a while."

"We read many bad things about that place, baas."

Gat did not believe in ghosts despite his years of officering men who did. Still, just to be sure, he spoke a greeting in Lingala. The counterman looked at Gat with apprehension. He turned back to the coffee machine. Gat was satisfied that he was not an incarnation of Lumumba. Still, might as well be sure.

Gat made a couple of attempts to engage the man in conversation. But connecting with him was like winning the trust of a cat beaten by strangers. Finally Gat said, "I read that you were in prison in Katanga. I'm glad to see that you escaped and found a job down here. You make good coffee."

"Pardon me, baas. I don't understand what you mean."

"No? If you're not Patrice Lumumba himself, you look very much like him."

A moment of uncertainty between them. "I don't know what you mean, baas."

Gat gestured thumbs up. The man offered no indication that he understood. "There's no need to call me 'baas,'" Gat went on. "I'm an American."

A couple came into the canteen. The counterman quickly pocketed the tip Gat had left. After buying drinks, the couple left. Gat returned to the counterman and asked if he might have more coffee. The man refilled his cup. Then he whispered in a voice so low that Gat could hardly hear, "What will happen to Lumumba?"

Gat shrugged.

"They've already killed him, haven't they?"

Gat nodded that they had. That he should give that response surprised him.

The counterman looked upset. He glanced toward the door to see if shadows foretold the arrival of customers. He listened carefully. Then he ventured: "The Belgians thought the Congolese would accept a false independence, didn't they?" Gat nodded again. "They think Africans have just come 'out of the trees.'"

"I'm afraid it's going to be bad there for some time."

"It keeps getting worse here. The government thinks we will accept false homelands. We will not. Eventually Lumumba's ideas—"

Other members of the tour entered the canteen. "Lumumba" resumed his servile persona. "More coffee, baas?" he asked Gat. Gat held out his cup, nodded his thanks to the man, and went outside.

Sipping his coffee he was amused at pretending to be an American liberal. He rather liked the game. When he was first in the Force Publique, an experienced officer had taken him aside. "Let me give you some advice," he said. "Your men will perform better if you do not think of them as savages. Find something positive that each man can bring to the unit. They'll perform better and your superiors will think you're a leader. But don't tell them the trick." Gat had taken the advice and it worked. In E'ville he let his comrades think he was tougher than, in fact, he was.

Later as Gat stood at a railing watching waves crash against the promontory, he felt the presence of another person. He glanced over to see the African counterman. He nodded. The man moved nearer, wanting at last to talk, but anticipating a rebuff. Gat opened noncommittally: "Beautiful here."

"Very beautiful," came the reply. Then in a lowered tone, "Many interesting things happening in your country."

"Are there?" Oh, yes, he had claimed to be American. He knew how the State Department was interfering in the Congo, but little else. But wait a minute. A new president had just been elected.

"Our brothers in America are pulling down the apartheid of the South. *Gone with the Wind* is going, going, gone."

Gat smiled.

"Your new president. John F. Kennedy. What will he do?"

"He's younger than Eisenhower," said Gat. "Maybe that's a plus."

"African intellectuals say that America is trying to replace Belgium in the Congo. Is that true?"

"The Americans are obsessed with the Cold War." Gat reinhabited his pretended nationality. "We Americans, I should say. The people running my government are afraid that Africans will go Communist."

"We are not Communists!" the man whispered vehemently. "It is a trick to hold on to what is ours."

Gat shrugged. "I am afraid Americans must always have an enemy."

"When you go back home, tell people that we are not the enemy. We need your help! Look what happened in the Congo," the man whispered urgently. "The Belgians declared the country independent, then immediately landed troops in Katanga. Lumumba tried to stop the secession. But the UN refused to help him. You Americans wouldn't help. No one in the West would help. So he turned to the Russians. Does that make him a Communist?"

"It does if you are obsessed by Communism. Your government—"

"The government of *die boere* is *not* my government, sir," the man quickly corrected Gat.

"I'm sorry. The government here seems as obsessed about Communism as the Americans." Gat changed the subject. "What's this treason trial all about?" he asked. He was sure the man would have a different view than the actress.

The counterman's vehemence flared again. His whispers now had the sound of steam released under pressure. "The government arrested one hundred fifty of our leaders. More than four years ago! They said they would prove that these men conspired to overthrow the government." The man looked out at the ocean and shook his head. "There was no conspiracy. A state conspiracy! That's what it is."

"At least you are on the side of history," Gat said. It was the only comforting thing he could think to say.

"That itself sounds Communist," the counterman said. He was almost able to smile. He looked around to be sure that no one was monitoring their conversation. Then he spoke very quietly. "We will have to take up arms," he said.

"Will that work?" Gat asked.

"What else can we do? The government is pressing us every way they can. First it was Bantu education, pass books, and the treason trial. Then came 'separate development.' Very soon it will not be possible for me to talk to you like this. They will find a way to make a law against that!"

Seagulls were riding the air currents out over the waves. Gat and his friend watched them for some moments without speaking.

"May I ask you about something that perplexes me?"

"Go ahead," said Gat.

"Why are white people like this?" The man seemed genuinely baffled. "They are treacherous, greedy, deceitful. They hate us for the color of our skins. Why is this?"

"Not all white people hate you. I hope you know that."

"Perhaps. But it is the same story everywhere. White people go to America for religious freedom. And what do they do? They exterminate Indians. They enslave us to work their plantations and in their constitution they declare that we are three-fifths of a person. Why is this?" The man looked at Gat for an explanation, the Lumumba goatee on his chin moving as he clenched his teeth. "The Belgians go to the Congo and kill Congolese. The Dutch and the French and the English come here and kill us. The Germans go into South West and try to exterminate the Herreros. Like they later killed the Jews. And these whites all claim to worship a Christ who told them: 'Love one another. Love your enemies.' Why is this? Is it all treachery?"

Gat finally said, "I've stood in front of a mirror, looking at my white skin, and asked myself those same questions."

Finally the counterman looked at his watch and said, "I must go back." Then he added, "You are the first white man who has looked at me and seen that with my mustache and goatee beard I honor Lumumba."

"How can that be?"

"Because white people look at me and see nothing. I'm invisible to them."

"You're not invisible to me," Gat said. "And I wish you well." He extended his hand to the African. "Put your hand in mine to prove you're not invisible."

They shook hands. The man took Gat's hand in both of his. When he released it, he touched his right hand to his heart.

RETURNING TO Cape Town, Gat walked through the gardens of Parliament, thinking of the counterman. Whenever he passed an African, he tried to make eye contact so that each individual would know that for at least one white man he was not invisible. Met with Gat's nod, Africans glanced behind them to see who Gat was greeting. When they realized he might be looking at them, they hurried away. It was as if an unknown white man's looking at them could only bring them trouble. Still, Gat persisted. The command to "Disappear" gave him license to be different from the man he'd been in Katanga.

Down at the Foreshore he stood at the edge of Table Bay and looked out at the fog beginning to engulf Robben Island. Once a leper colony, now a prison, that was where the Justice Mr. De Wet, about whom he'd been reading, would send the treason trial defendants if, in fact, he decided to spare their lives. Gat suddenly felt as lonely and forgotten as the prisoners on that island.

The sun left Table Mountain and behind him the city began to clothe itself in lights. He wandered up into District Six. It was a section of labyrinthine streets that smelled of densely packed people of many races, their spices and their cooking, an area of Cape Dutch houses that seemed smashed together with a force that had squeezed them thin and elongated them. Some of the buildings had balconies. People sat on them, taking the air, calling to one another, singing along with their radios. There were young men on the streets, some pushing girlfriends against buildings to kiss them. There were women, too, Coloured and Bantu, as they were called here, and occasionally young white women, students or young office workers, tasting a teeming life of racial jumble from which marriage and maturity would separate them forever.

His soldier's eye told Gat that District Six would be a useful bastion from which to fight a revolt. The sheer numbers of residents militated against effective occupation or control. From the balconies and rooftops snipers could fire and escape, simply disappear. The streets and alleys could provide avenues of retreat and then be barricaded. No wonder the government was talking about declaring District Six a white area, tearing down the old buildings, removing the Coloured population to the Cape Flats, and straightening the streets.

Gat came upon a place in an alley with a sign announcing Hollywood Pizza. He went in and had pizza that was soggy and a beer that mostly failed to foam. The place was empty except for him and the two Coloured women who ran it. He tried to converse with them, but could not get beyond the "baas" that they insisted on calling him. Sitting alone he felt all the bad stuff of Katanga creeping back on him.

Wandering on he came to a jazz club. He went in, bought a drink, and listened to the music of a five-piece band of Coloureds. A young woman, her skin very yellow in the dim light, her face flat and cheekbones prominent, came to sit with him. She placed her hand high on his thigh and asked him to buy her a drink. He removed her hand. The woman left him. Other women tried their luck. Their enticements only increased Gat's depression.

As he left the district, moving along its sidewalks, his soldier's instincts gave warning: he was being followed. By whom? An assassin. Why not? After all, those who lived by the gun . . . Now it was his turn. He took refuge in an alley and watched the street. And shrugged. If that was his fate, so be it. If the assassin were professional, his work clean and quick, Gat would know only that he'd arrived at the next place. If that place existed.

He stood in the alley for long minutes. Nothing happened. Resuming his stroll, he received the same warning. How, he wondered, had the pursuer picked up his trail here? And who was he? Michels? A grim smile at the thought of Michels as an assassin. What a way to die! Michels made a mess of every assignment he undertook. Gat ducked around an entire city block, trying to shake his pursuer. The same warning came again. The pursuer was on his trail.

Moving toward the Mount Nelson Hotel, walking fast now, he came to a movie theater. He paid his admission. He slipped into the theater's darkness, into a seat in the back row. He kept watch. The movie had already started, a vehicle for Doris Day. He noticed an exit door at the side of the screen. If his pursuer entered, he would flee through there. No one came in. Keeping watch, Gat heard the movie's cheery prattle. He began to watch it. After walking through District Six with its jumbled vitality, its pungency and its music, he felt disoriented to move into the American dreamland of Doris Day. Did Americans really live in such affluence? What about the sit-ins and the southern states' apartheid the counterman had mentioned? Did none of that find its way into their movies? Were there really American women like this one, pert, relentlessly cheery, professionally virginal? Did they permit lovemaking? Were their bodies as scrubbed and lightweight as their brains?

After a while, still feeling on edge, Gat perceived the nature of his condition. The pursuer was inside him. Realizing that, he left the movie. He walked back to the hotel. He sat in the lobby, thumbing through newspapers. Ten P.M. He was feeling lonely, lost. Could he go to the actress's door and knock? Could he look bashful and say, "I think I left my toothbrush." Or he could phone her. Say simply, "Could I come up?" He truly wished he could disappear.

He made himself remain in the lobby. There he remembered the village girl who had brought him food when he was living in the back of a pickup in the Equateur. He told himself the story of their meetings. His loneliness increased. Well after eleven he went to his room. A note was waiting under his door. A woman's writing. An invitation to depression. He crumpled it without reading it and threw it into the trash. In his shorts and tee shirt he did pushups until he could rise no longer from the floor. He crawled into bed and waited for sleep, trying not to think about Katanga and what had happened there.

CHAPTER THREE

CAPE TOWN

SUNDAY, FEBRUARY 5, 1961

Gat sat up in bed. He was dreaming again, trying to run from Francqui Dam and the smell of gunpowder in the air. His body felt icy although it was soaking in sweat. He realized he was in the hotel. Alone.

He slid from the bed, found his way to the bathroom, located the sink, turned on the water. He filled the cup of his hands, drank, and bathed his face. He felt for the light switch, drops of water swimming off his face onto his tee shirt. Light on, he glanced confusedly about, looked for his toothbrush, pushed toothpaste onto it. In his dream, vomit rose in his throat. He had to scrub that taste away.

He shucked off underwear. He turned on the shower and entered it. Cold water jarred him awake. As it warmed, he regained his calm. He let the water stream over him, getting his bearings. He thought: What's the matter with you?

DRESSED IN the suit, the white shirt, and a tie he had not yet worn, Gat strolled through the Parliament gardens to an imposing church. He had decided to get with people. A plaque at the entry designated it the Groote Kerk, on the site where Cape Town's first church was built in 1678. Gat had hardly ever entered a Protestant church. So strong was his desire to connect with people, however, that he would risk attending a service.

Worshippers—whites only, of course—streamed into it, the men in black suits and broad-brimmed black hats, the women in summer dresses, heels, and hose. Gloves protected the women's hands; demure hats, some with veils drawn over their faces, covered their heads. Gat followed the faithful inside.

It was a Dutch Reformed service. The minister—the *dominee*—spoke in an Afrikaans that, Gat thought, must be an offshoot of a much earlier Dutch. His fluency in Flemish allowed him to follow much of the sermon. But instead of listening, he gazed at the fittings of the church and marveled at the piety of the overdressed congregation. He decided to venture out after the service to Sea Point to look for a cheaper hotel.

As he left the church, a man drew near him, a person of vigorous middle age with a well-muscled frame shaking hands and bantering with worshippers. Appropriately suited, his close-clipped blond hair turning to gray on a head too large for his short body, he held himself erect, almost military in bearing. By no means good-looking, the man was, in fact, square-headedly unattractive. Even so, he exuded self-confidence. His openness of manner and evident pleasure in being himself drew people to him. Reaching out for the hands of nearby burghers, exuding jovial charm, he moved with an infectious vitality and power.

Gat sensed that the man's assured self-possession included the certainty of his own moral probity. It was Gat's experience that such a quality engendered in some men a capacity for brutality toward others. In this Afrikaner it would be toward blacks and Coloureds, those whose otherness might threaten his view of public order. As the man drew closer, Gat heard those who shook his hand deferentially call him Colonel.

The man reached out for Gat as he drew abreast of him. *"Gooie more,"* he said. He extended his hand. Gat shook it.

"Good morning," Gat answered, resisting the man's charm.

"Good morning then," said the man with a laugh. "Did you get anything out of the service?" Gat smiled. "You're a visitor? I'm Piet Rousseau."

"Yes," Gat said. "In Cape Town for a few days." He now saw a woman, surely Rousseau's wife, standing several paces behind him. With her were a girl, perhaps twenty, quite attractive, and a young man several years older, no doubt their children. Gat introduced himself, saying that his name was Adriaan Gautier, but that people called him Gat.

"Welcome," said Rousseau. "Where are you visiting from?"

Gat looked more carefully at the girl. She was modest, dutiful, thinking her own thoughts. Gat thought she might prove interesting, even lovely, if someone lit a fire in her. If the man were truly a colonel, Gat calculated, he would welcome an opportunity to quiz Gat about events he had witnessed. And so he replied, "I've been in the Congo. In Katanga."

"How did you happen to be there?" Rousseau inquired.

"I'm a captain in the Belgian Army," Gat said. "Seconded to the Katanga Gendarmerie."

"Margaret," Rousseau declared, turning to his wife, "we must give Captain Gautier some lunch." Rousseau introduced his wife and the blonde daughter, Petra. She smiled perfunctorily in the way a child might curtsy. As Rousseau presented the young man—"This is Kobus Terreblanche," he said—Gat watched the girl examine him out of deep, brown eyes as if he were some exotic creature. "Our friend and Petra's friend," the colonel continued. Gat turned to shake the young man's hand. Tall, blond, with large, sturdy bones, he stood casually erect and was conventionally handsome in a way that suggested he lived an ordered life, possessed little imagination, and had no conception that the world might be complex. Rousseau took Gat's elbow to lead him from the church.

Gat looked again at the girl—casually, only a glance. But he noticed the girl's mother watching him as if he were a predator preparing to make a meal of her child. Gat nodded to the woman and made himself smile. The girl did not seem to notice.

Driving to the Rousseau house, Gat sat in the backseat with the young couple, Petra in the middle. Whenever he brushed her arm or leg, the girl leaned away from him as if singed by his touch. Coming from Central Africa where people in tight quarters—post office lines, for instance—crowded against one another, Gat found this behavior amusing. He began intentionally nudging her elbow. She moved away. Sensing her awareness of Gat, Terreblanche claimed his rights to her by holding her hand so tightly that his knuckles showed white.

"Sir, did I hear people calling you colonel?" Gat asked. "Are you army?"

Ignoring the question, Rousseau mentioned that his forebears had lived in the city for more than two centuries. Terreblanche leaned forward to look at Gat across the girl. "Police," he remarked with prideful respect. Rousseau called attention to the neighborhood, noting that as a boy he had walked to school along these very streets.

The family lived in a handsome Cape Dutch house on the upsweep of Table Mountain, not large but well maintained. The parlor welcomed visitors with the reserve of a museum.

Antique furniture stood on a polished slate floor. Ancestors in the dark dress of seventeenth-century burghers gazed out from large portraits. A grand piano festooned with sepia photographs in ornate silver frames occupied a corner of the room. Rousseau had small, stubby hands, Gat noticed. They might serve to deliver sharp blows, but did not seem likely to coax melodies out of a piano. He wondered if the girl played.

The party moved to a sunny, more intimate room—the "small parlor," they called it. It offered a comfortable pair of couches with matching armchairs. While Petra and her mother removed their hats, pulled off their gloves, and set them on a table overlooking a small garden outside, Rousseau explained to Gat that Petra had just matriculated from secondary school at Herschel.

The girl glanced at her father, miffed that he should unfold the landmarks of her life as if she were a child too shy to speak for herself. Gat watched her, amused at her predicament. She rolled her eyes to him as her father continued, mentioning that in another week she would leave for varsity, for "Wits," the University of the Witswatersrand in Johannesburg. It was pronounced "Vits"—for w's took a v sound in Afrikaans just as v's took an f sound.

Terreblanche threw off his suit coat, grabbed the sports section of the paper, and flopped down on the couch. He pulled Petra onto the couch beside him. Gat asked if he, too, were a student. "I'm at Stellenbosch," Terreblanche replied. "It's the country's best varsity, the very heart of Afrikanerdom. Wits is only so-so." He nudged Petra.

"They take a rotten apple now and then at Stellenbosch," she remarked.

"There may be news here of the Congo," Rousseau said, giving Gat the paper's front page. "Maybe you can find out what's happened to your friend Lumumba."

The girl glanced up at Gat with interest. "Is Patrice Lumumba a friend of yours?" she asked.

"That's irony, Pet," Terreblanche remarked from deep within the sports page.

Petra continued to watch Gat. "Have you met Lumumba?" she asked.

Terreblanche looked up from his paper. "Pet!" he chided with a patronizing smile. "Is it likely that Captain Gautier and Lumumba move in the same circles?"

Gat and the girl looked at one another. "Do you play that piano in there?"

"Doesn't Father wish!" she said, laughing. "He tried to make me learn. But every time the teacher came, she ended up running from the house in tears." She smiled defiantly at her father. "No one plays," she said, hesitating slightly, then added, "anymore. The piano's there to show off old photos."

A Coloured servant entered, pushing a cart that held a silver teapot and cups for them all. "We'll take it in the garden, Elsie," Margaret Rousseau told the servant. Rousseau opened french doors leading into the garden and they all went outside, Terreblanche taking Petra's hand and bringing along his paper. Rousseau inspected a bed of aloes and their long-stalked orange blossoms. Margaret Rousseau served the tea. Gat noticed the servant's small dwelling, attached to the garage at the rear of the property.

"You all have French names," Gat remarked.

"Petra's not a French name," the girl remarked challengingly.

"Neither is Kobus," added Terreblanche.

"None of us speaks any French," said Margaret Rousseau. "I'm the only one with a decent excuse. My background's English. My maiden name was Smith."

"Mother will let you think she came from the Smiths who gave their names to Ladysmith and Harrismith. He was a general or something—"

"Governor, dear," corrected the mother.

"But it isn't true," the girl continued. "Her father was a blacksmith. A white blacksmith, isn't that right? Or was he a black whitesmith? I'm never sure which." She glanced at Gat and bit her lip so as not to break into a smile.

"My great-grandfather, Petra," the mother again corrected. "You might as well get it right. And don't be so saucy." She turned to Gat. "My father was a small town banker in Natal. I'm an English speaker."

"And proud of it!" exclaimed the girl.

Gat wondered if she were showing off for him—hoped she was—even as Terreblanche kept holding her hand. But perhaps she was simply of an age to enjoy provoking her parents.

Rousseau gave his daughter a cautioning glance. He explained that French Protestants—Huguenots—had sought refuge in the Cape following wars of religion in France. "You've probably heard of the Massacre of Saint Bartholomew's?" he suggested.

"My history's a little shaky," Gat admitted.

Rousseau sat back, pleased to open the Afrikaner past to a visitor. "A century and a half after that massacre," he explained, "the Huguenots and the Hollanders, that is, the Boers— They had assimilated. All of today's Afrikaners descend from the eighteen hundred Boers and Huguenots living in the Cape in 1700." Petra yawned, permitting a demure sulk to appear on her face. Terreblanche folded his paper and leaned forward, his hands cupped before him as if to catch every insight that might spill from Rousseau's mouth, as if each word were a nugget of gold.

Margaret excused herself to supervise Elsie in the kitchen. Petra left the men to set a place for Gat at the table, wheeling away the tea cart as she went. Gat watched her depart. Rousseau continued his story. While many *trekboers* left the Cape for a wandering life farther north and east, the Rousseaus and

Terreblanches had remained in the Cape even after the British took possession of it in the early 1800s. Margaret came from English people who had emigrated to the eastern Cape in the 1820s. "She is only half-assimilated," Rousseau explained. "She refuses to speak Afrikaans. So I can swear in it whenever I want and she has no inkling what I'm saying."

Rousseau examined Gat. "Tell us about the Congo," he said. "You don't mind a grilling, do you?"

Gat watched Petra return from her woman's chore. She sat beside Terreblanche, who placed a hand on her knee.

"If I may speak bluntly," Rousseau probed, "you Belgians made a catastrophic balls-up in giving the Congo independence."

Gat shrugged, but said nothing. Petra saw that she was not the only one among them who could lay down a challenge, even if it were silent.

Rousseau prodded him. "How could your people let that Communist stooge Lumumba take power?" The garden went suddenly silent as if Rousseau's tone of voice possessed an authority that could be met only with a hush. Petra and Terreblanche watched to see how Gat would respond.

"He won the election," Gat said quietly. "Isn't that how the Afrikaners took power in this country?"

"But we weren't savages," said Rousseau mildly. "Didn't your people know what the African was like?"

"What is he like?" Gat asked. "Perhaps you know better than I do."

Rousseau smiled tightly. He regarded Gat through narrowed eyes. Petra looked from one man to the other, enjoying their maneuverings.

"He's a baboon!" exclaimed Terreblanche. "An ignorant monkey! How did you think he could run a country as rich as the Congo?"

"The Congolese are not savages," Gat replied quietly. His assertion seemed to suck the air out of the garden. Gat glanced at Petra. Her eyes shone with excitement. Obviously the opinions of her father were rarely challenged in her presence. "Lumumba was an extraordinary fellow. I heard him speak once."

"What was that like?" Petra asked. Kobus and her father glanced at one another, amused at Petra's curious interest in the Congolese with the strange name.

"I was commanding soldiers on riot watch," Gat said. "Lumumba had a way of casting a spell on a crowd. We thought there might be trouble."

Rousseau's eyes narrowed. "Was there?" Petra asked. "What did he say?"

"He told his listeners—"

"These were villagers without shoes, right?" asked Kobus. "Or education?"

"He told them they would be a free people, a great people in a great country."

Kobus guffawed. "With cars and fine houses and white girlfriends."

Gat gazed at Kobus as if he were an insect. "Lumumba was mesmerizing. He believed what he said. And why not? The Congo has tremendous resources. Why shouldn't they be a great people?"

"Were there riots when he finished?" asked Rousseau.

"We had matters in hand," Gat said. "There were some very excited blacks. And whites who went away worried. They had never seen this kind of Congolese before. He terrified them."

"You keep using the past tense," Rousseau observed. "Why? Is he dead?" Rousseau studied him as if suspecting he knew more than he was letting on.

Gat glanced at Petra. Her eyes watched him excitedly.

"Do you command—" Terreblanche hesitated as if only just in time he had caught the word "monkeys" from escaping his lips. "Do you command kaffir troops?"

"Yes."

"What are they like?" asked Petra. "Father has been in charge of—" She, too, hesitated and chose her words carefully. "Of African policemen. I wonder how you find them."

The trio stared at Gat. He felt the two men suspicious of him as unreliable, a liberal, while the girl seemed exhilarated by the presence of someone who did not parrot predictable clichés. "I could explain how I look at my job," Gat said with a glance at the girl, "but I'm afraid that would bore you all."

"Hardly," replied Rousseau. "You've been in a situation that may someday confront us. We want to know what you think."

"In my view," Gat began, "good military leadership requires that an officer win the trust, respect, and confidence of his men. Possibly also their affection, but that's not necessary. To win trust and respect the leader must assure that his men are well fed, clothed, housed, paid regularly, treated fairly and with dignity. They must understand the job they're to do. Hopefully their orders will be presented in such a way that they agree to them."

Petra watched Gat, fascinated. Rousseau and Terreblanche regarded him skeptically. Gat himself felt impertinent, pontifical, trying to impress the girl by marking out territory unlikely to be visited by her father and the swain.

Gat ventured, "I assume that this is what young officers are taught pretty much everywhere."

"Is this what the police commanders are taught?" Petra asked. It seemed like an innocent question, but since Gat had spoken of treating Africans with dignity, he thought she might be goading her father.

"The police and the army do different jobs, Pet," Rousseau replied.

"The basic job of my troops is to maintain public order." Gat turned to Rousseau. "A policing job. I stress to the men that the soldier's job is to serve the citizen, not to take advantage of him."

"What about bearing down on them?" Rousseau asked.

"Sometimes that has to be done," Gat admitted. "So do it swiftly, forcefully, but with restraint. Not capriciously. Not with cruelty." Gat regarded Rousseau, assuming that he could bear down very hard. He felt foolish, putting on airs in the presence of an officer of greater experience. But the girl seemed fascinated and he continued. "My observation is that if an officer assumes a malcontent is a savage, he is himself capable of—"

Petra smiled. "They make savages of each other, don't they?"

"Pet, you don't know anything about this," Terreblanche chided her. "This is men's talk." Petra looked annoyed with him. She glanced at Gat. Gat watched her.

Rousseau leaned back in his chair and stared at the ceiling. "From what I understand you to say, Captain," Rousseau began, his words now heavily accented by Afrikaans, "I take it that you regard your troops as your equals. Is that right?"

"I'm not sure what you mean," Gat said. "I'm their commander."

"You say that you treat these men the way you would want to be treated. You talk about their dignity."

"The African cherishes his dignity," Terreblanche said. "While wearing only a blanket over his nakedness." He chuckled. Petra again looked miffed with him.

Feeling defensive under Rousseau's scrutiny, Gat admitted, "Of course, most of what I've just said is out the window these days. Technically we are only advisors now. African sergeants have technical command of the troops."

"Our experience with the African," said Rousseau, "and we have three hundred years of that experience, tells us that in His wisdom the Creator of us all originated us for different purposes. The white race—whom He endowed with intelligence and adaptability, ingenuity and technical skill—was created for the purpose of leading mankind. He gave the black race strong bodies to chop wood and carry water, to dig in the earth for the resources He had hidden there." Gat knew from the way he spoke that every time Rousseau used a pronoun for the Creator, it was capitalized in his mind. "We believe that only trouble comes from confusing these destinies. Blacks and whites are not equal. Only confusion would tell you that they are. Our experience tells us that separate development is the only solution."

"Forgive me," Gat said. "My father was anticlerical, antiroyalist, and deeply egalitarian. His training may have distorted my perceptions. But it is hard for me to see Africans in business suits in Joburg, greeting each other like professionals, and then think that God meant them only to carry water and chop wood."

"I've never seen kaffirs in business suits!" exclaimed Terreblanche. "Anyway the chaos in the Congo proves that your approach—"

Gat raised a hand to interrupt. He was finding Terreblanche as annoying as the girl did. "There must be development," Gat said. "I'm not sure it must be separate. When Belgium bought the Congo Free State from Leopold Second, whose greed humiliated us, we accepted the civilizing mission.

Nation building. Certain infrastructural developments were made, but human development was almost totally ignored."

"Our separate development," said Rousseau, "envisions schools for our Africans appropriate to their life prospects, to their tribal orientation. We don't want to turn them into bad copies of white men."

Petra smoothed her skirt. Watching her out of the corner of his eye Gat lost the train of the conversation. Terreblanche was defending separate development.

"There is chaos in the Congo," Gat said, interrupting Terreblanche, "because Belgium ducked its responsibilities by rushing the colony to independence. I'm speaking as a Belgian myself. Our government proposed five years of preparation for independence. But once there were riots in Léopoldville, it abandoned that plan and announced independence in six months. Our government obviously assumed that it would maintain control over an independent Congo, especially over those aspects of the Congo that produced wealth for the metropole." He glanced at Petra and wondered how he could talk to her alone. He continued, "I can't decide myself whether that assumption was unconscious, based on the notion that Africans would accept the form without the substance. Or if it was malicious, motivated by greed. By greed, I think."

Margaret Rousseau appeared at the door of the room and asked Petra to help with lunch. The girl rose and left the room. Gat watched her go. As did Kobus. When Gat returned his eyes to the girl's father, Rousseau was watching him.

As PETRA walked from the small parlor, allowing her hips to sway languidly, she wondered which men were watching her. Kobus no doubt, asserting his proprietary interest. But was Captain Gautier? Possibly. Of course, she could not look back. The captain had gazed at her frequently while they were talking. But perhaps that was his conversational manner, including everyone as he might when addressing troops. The raw recruits under his command were probably about her age. Would he consider her like his recruits: no longer quite a child, but not yet an adult? Certainly not yet a woman.

She found her mother standing outside the powder room in the main hall. "Are there things I need to do?" Petra asked. "I thought Elsie had—" Her mother's conspiratorial smile caused her to stop speaking. She asked, "What? Why'd you call me out?"

"I thought you might want to separate yourself from Kobus."

"Dear Kobus! Possessive and dismissive, all at once." Petra slipped into the powder room to inspect her face in the mirror.

"You know you needn't sit next to Kobus when you go back," remarked her mother. Petra checked her lipstick. Margaret watched her daughter self-absorbedly examining her face, apparently not fully conscious of how attractive she was, of the beauty that Kobus wanted every other man to understand was his. "What do you think of the officer?"

Tempted to tell her mother that she was, in fact, much more interested in what the officer thought of her, Petra fluffed her hair. "It's rather exciting to watch someone disagree with Father, don't you think? Kobus certainly never disagrees with him."

"That's why he's so fond of Kobus," Margaret said. Petra turned from the mirror to face her mother. Had she really made that observation? Her mother beamed at her. "Of course, you won't tell your father I said that, will you?"

Petra turned back to the mirror. "I wish I knew more about Katanga," she said, studying her face. "I really ought to read the papers."

"Not that they carry much news."

"I feel such a schoolgirl. If the captain asks me about myself, what do I tell him? That we studied *Macbeth* for our O levels?"

"That might interest him," Margaret encouraged, amused. "Macbeth was a soldier, after all." She added, "When he looks at you, darling, I don't think he sees a schoolgirl. He sees a very attractive young woman."

Petra was not quite sure what to make of this remark. Since her eighteenth birthday her mother had begun to talk to her as if she were an adult. She had even shared confidences as if preparing her for the fact that, now that she was almost ready for varsity, she had become a woman. Petra studied her figure. "I do wish Kobus would stop putting his hands all over me."

"He does that, Pet, to let the captain know that you belong to him."

"I do not belong to him! How dare he! He can be so tiresome!"

"I'm afraid we of the weaker sex—"

"Posh on that weaker sex business, Mother!"

"—we women are condemned to watching men play out their rivalries as if we were their cause. The truth is that they are simply competitive with each other." Margaret added, "We are not the weaker sex, my dear. Our strength is letting them think we are. It plays on their vanity and vanity is their weakness."

"That sounds so manipulative," Petra replied, still studying her face.

"And nurturing one's beauty: that's not manipulation?"

"That's hygiene, Mum." The women laughed.

"Manipulation lubricates daily life," Margaret Rousseau declared. "Just like white lies. And having things we never talk about." She studied her daughter in the mirror and placed her hands lightly on the girl's shoulders. "You will be meeting all sorts of new men in Johannesburg," she said. "That will be good for you. Some of them will make you wish Kobus were around. And some will make you glad he's not. And it will be good for you to meet both kinds."

MEANWHILE IN the small parlor, Rousseau asked Gat, "Have you seen combat in Katanga?"

Gat shrugged, then decided to tell the story, a story for men. "Another white officer and I were acting as advisors to three African lieutenants. We led a company of African soldiers into northern Katanga. Our mission was to show the Baluba people the muscle of the Katanga government—that is, the alliance of the Lunda and Bayeke tribes. There was to be no blood shed. The troops would simply show the Baluba— who've remained loyal to Lumumba's government—that the secession would succeed. That was the mission.

"When we reached Baluba country, I was apprehensive about the men. They'd never seen combat. They were unusually edgy. I was concerned about discipline."

"With good reason, I imagine," said Rousseau.

"As we moved into the first village, I realized that many of them were afraid. And angry to feel that way. Some were kids, wearing their first boots. They swaggered, but they also smelled of fear. If a truck door slammed, they ducked and looked for snipers. When we entered that first village—"

"They rampaged," Rousseau said. He smiled knowingly.

"They went berserk," Gat acknowledged.

Rousseau nodded his head as if he could have predicted this situation.

"It was like trying to control a tornado," Gat confessed. "I don't know how the firing started. Who began it. Who ordered it. Or if there was an order. They met no resistance. That made them jubilant. They shouted. Laughed. Shot at anything, everything. Killed women, children, old men."

In his mind Gat saw huts burning in a fog of smoke, felt the flames singe his skin, heard again their roar and the cries of women running with babies in their arms, the screams of children, the crackle of gunfire. In his mind he smelled again the acrid smoke, tasted in his mouth the dust and chaff from the flaming huts. He recalled men holding a screaming girl while another raped her. He pulled the man off her. They turned to attack him, recognized him, ran off. "The African officers egged them on." Gat shook his head. "I still have nightmares about that day."

"They're savages," Rousseau explained.

"I don't excuse their behavior," Gat said. "But they expected to die and they didn't. They felt powerful, invincible."

"They're savages," Rousseau repeated. "This business of 'one man, one vote' and 'all men are created equal.' It's fine as metaphysics. But every day of the year I deal with facts. We understand the African here. We are making sure here that our way of life, our civilization, is not destroyed by that very tornado you could not control. It cannot be controlled. We will never let it get started."

Terreblanche asked, "What happened when you returned to your base?"

"We were heroes," Gat admitted. "I wanted to punish the officers. For that I got into trouble. The politicians wanted to stir up tribal hatred. They instructed the officers to shoot up the villages." Gat shook his head. "It will take years to build a nation of one people out of all those tribes."

"If you've had enough of that," Rousseau said quietly, "we need people like you in South Africa. To help us hold the line here."

"Thank you, sir," Gat said. "I'm committed up there."

Petra returned to the room, her skirt rustling. She started past Terreblanche for a chair opposite Gat. The young man reached out, grabbed her wrist, and pulled her beside him on the sofa. Rousseau smiled at Terreblanche's possessiveness. "And lunch?" he asked.

"Almost," Petra said. She smiled at her father and at Gat. Terreblanche took her hand and placed it in his lap. "Have you decided whether Lumumba is dead or alive?" she asked.

"He's in a Katanga prison," Terreblanche informed her.

"Is he?" The girl looked challengingly at Gat. "Or did someone throw him out of a fifth-story window. That's what they do here."

"The police do not throw anyone out of windows," Rousseau said.

"But conspiracy suspects do land on the sidewalk outside police headquarters. Don't they, Father?" Petra had mastered the art of asking subversive questions with an innocent, inquiring voice. "With their heads cracked open, brains and blood spilling out? Isn't that true?"

"You're being tiresome, Pet," Rousseau admonished mildly. He turned to Gat. "As for your Mr. Lumumba, I think it's rather unlikely he's still alive."

Gat sensed that Rousseau, the patient paterfamilias, had observed his share of African political suspects being tortured, had supervised African police affixing electrodes to suspects' testicles, had heard the screams of men shot through with electricity. Glancing at the girl and her young swain, the two students, Gat understood that they had no real notion of what Rousseau's job entailed.

"The Katanga authorities contend Lumumba's in prison," Terreblanche said. "Do you think they've eaten him? Roast liver of Lumumba?" He scoffed.

Rousseau allowed himself a tight smile.

"Are there cannibals in Katanga, Captain?" Petra asked.

Gat turned to the girl and winked conspiratorially. She was remarkably pretty when she was being provocative. "I've never knowingly supped with one."

"You might have lost a leg if you had, eh?" Terreblanche gave another hearty laugh. "You must be glad to be down here where it's civilized."

"Yes," said Gat. The girl was watching him. "Belgians can be very boring." In her presence the men would make no mention of what Gat had told them. It was not a matter for a woman's ears. "Belgium's a small country," Gat prattled on, kidding the girl. "Katanga is even worse: too small to be a country, too large to be a mining compound. Which is all it really is."

"So now and then you have to get out," Petra said. "Is that it?"

"Get out or go crazy," Gat agreed.

"Do you think what happened in the Congo is likely to happen here?" the girl asked. Gat could not tell if she wanted his opinion or was simply tweaking her father and the boy-friend. But it did not matter because Margaret Rousseau appeared to call them to the table. As they rose, Petra persisted, "Do you think it will happen?"

Gat said, "Talk to me in twenty years."

As THEY sat down to a clear soup, Margaret Rousseau declared, "We do not talk politics at table. Certainly not on Sundays!"

They talked instead about family matters. Rousseau and Margaret were going the next day to Pretoria, the country's administrative capital, for meetings he must attend. When they returned, they would drive Petra up to Wits and get her settled at varsity. While they were gone, she would spend the week in Stellenbosch with Rousseau's sister.

"She's going to help me set up my place," Terreblanche explained. "I'll be reading law there as soon as the school year starts." He boasted once again about his university. "Stellenbosch turns out the best of South Africa's men."

"You aren't going there, Petra?" Gat asked, teasing. "Doesn't an intelligent young woman want to be where 'the best of South Africa's men' are turned out?"

"Here, here!" exclaimed Rousseau.

"I'm not going to varsity to catch a husband," Petra declared. "I may never marry." This seemed to be news to Terreblanche. "I may join a convent."

"You won't be joining a convent going to Wits!" Rousseau remarked.

Gat and Petra looked at one another. Petra had never had a man, who was clearly no longer a boy, gaze at her with such intensity, with such a recognition that she herself was no longer a girl. Her body grew warm. She smiled at Gat as she turned toward Terreblanche. "I'm not going to do varsity studies in a tribal language," she said, "as they do at Stellenbosch."

"It is *not* a tribal language, Petra," Terreblanche scolded. "It's the language of the future in this country."

"I'm going to study in a world language, Kobus. English. Aren't we speaking English now? That's the future."

"I wanted Petra to go to Stellenbosch," Rousseau explained to Gat. He spoke again as if Petra were a child for whom he answered. "But I've agreed she can try Wits for a semester. If it's too liberal, she'll—"

"Father, living in this century is too liberal for you!" Petra grinned at this impertinence and Rousseau laughed, wagging a warning finger at her.

"In this country it always turns to politics!" Margaret said.

After dessert they drank coffee. Rousseau turned to Gat and said, "The Congo offers an object lesson for us here in South Africa." He made a confession. "Last year there was an unfortunate incident for us at a place called Sharpeville—"

"An unfortunate incident?" blurted Petra. "A massacre! One hundred Africans shot in the back."

"Nowhere near one hundred!" insisted Terreblanche. "The press exaggerates everything."

Rousseau held up his hands like a teacher calling for order. "They were burning their pass books," he reminded his daughter. "That was illegal. They were playing with fire and got burnt."

"That is a little harsh, darling," Margaret said. "Captain Gautier will think we're not far from the way we're portrayed. Heartless monsters."

"I could never think that," Gat told her gallantly, "after that lovely lunch."

Petra's flashing eyes scolded Gat for being so obvious. To restore her estimate of him, he turned to her father. "What's this treason trial I keep reading about?"

"Yes, explain that, Father," challenged Petra. She smiled at Gat. "It's lasted more than a year, you know."

Rousseau rebuked his daughter with a glance. "African enemies of the state have been charged with conspiracy. Their aim is the violent overthrow of the government and the establishment of a Communist state."

"They have links to the Soviet Union and Eastern Bloc countries," Terreblanche blurted out excitedly.

"The defendants will be convicted," Rousseau declared. "Unfortunately, we have a judge who is—" Rousseau paused to search for the right word.

"Unreliable," said Petra. She looked at her father, then at Gat.

"His mind is tied up in legalisms," said the colonel. "It is clearly in the interests of the country that these African nationalist leaders be put away. What's at stake is the South African way of life. If these men are not dealt with, the terrorist threat will only grow. There are already acts of sabotage. How a judge cannot see that the way of life he enjoys could well be destroyed is something I cannot understand."

"We Afrikaners are like the children of God in the wilderness of this continent," Terreblanche added. Gat turned to the young man, wondering if he actually believed what he said. But he spoke with unpretentious conviction; Gat could not doubt him. "Some Europeans smile at that," Terreblanche went on, "but we have a unique culture, language, and mission, perhaps divinely ordained, to rule this land and the people we found here."

"In any case," Rousseau continued, "these events—Sharpeville, the treason trial, the State of Emergency lifted last year—they've made it clear to enlightened, like-minded people that we have our work cut out for us. Our mission is to preserve white civilization in the years ahead. We're determined to succeed."

"I decreed that there would be no discussion of politics at table," said Margaret Rousseau, "and as usual you have ignored my decree."

IT WAS arranged that Kobus and Petra, who were off to meet friends, would give Gat a lift to the Table Mountain cable car. Before she set off, Petra went to the kitchen with her mother to thank Elsie for the meal. The servant stood washing dishes at the kitchen sink. "The dinner was a marvel, Elsie," Petra told her. "Kobus certainly packs away your food when he's here!"

"I don't think that officer has eaten so well in months," said Margaret. Elsie smiled, looking away from the two white women so as not to seem impudent. It was deemed unseemly for a kitchen servant to look her mistress in the face. "When you finish with the dishes, Elsie," Margaret said, "you're free to go home to your people. For four days. We won't need you again until late Thursday."

As the two women moved out of the large kitchen past the pantry, Margaret said, "You won't need to get to Wits to meet men quite different from Kobus. The captain looks at you as if he hadn't seen a woman in quite some time."

"I don't know what you mean, Mother," Petra replied. She knew exactly what her mother meant, but would not be caught admitting it. "I must seem like a child to him. That's how Father and Kobus treat me."

"I assure you he doesn't consider you a child."

"He seemed very nice to me."

"Of course, he did!" said the mother. "They always seem 'very nice' when they gaze at you as if they might throw themselves at your feet. Men used to look at me that way. Sometimes I wish they still did." Then she counseled, "A beautiful woman can have great power over men."

"Mother, stop it. I'm not beautiful."

"That's for the men to decide. You'll learn all about that at Wits."

Petra smiled slyly at her mother. "Isn't that why I'm going there?"

Margaret held her daughter's hand. "I'm not trying to overprotect you," she said. "But do be careful. I made mistakes. Don't you make the same ones."

The women parted. Petra moved along a hall to rejoin the men in the garden. Gat had used the small bathroom off the hall. Now he waited there for Petra to pass by. When she did, he moved out behind her. She stopped, turned. They looked at one another. "What will you study at Wits?" Gat asked.

Petra contemplated him, her eyes narrowing in challenge. "You were in there waiting for me."

"Was I? Are you worth waiting for?"

"My mother says you gaze at me as if you hadn't seen a young woman in a very long time."

"I've never seen a woman like you."

Petra grinned, then hid her mouth with her hand. "Oh, please!" she said. She rolled her eyes. "Kobus doesn't even say things like that. You can't be cornier than him!" They looked at one another. "How long has it been?"

"Too long." He smiled, not giving a damn how corny he was.

They gazed at one another, both feeling on edge. Petra cocked her head. "What am I going to study at Wits? How to escape my background."

Gat laughed, beguiled. "You do put it to your father."

"Why not? Father doesn't care what I think. I'm just a girl. He thinks women are for breeding. As if we were cows."

"Does he expect you to breed with Kobus?"

"Can't you tell?" They looked at one another and all the house seemed silent.

Gat gazed at her. "If you keep standing there, I'm going to kiss you."

"Are you?"

He kissed her. She did not move. Electricity shot through both of them. Gat put his arms about her. She broke the kiss, backed away. They looked at one another, their lips burning.

Gat took her arm, moved to kiss her again. She glanced toward the garden.

"Meet me somewhere," Gat said.

They heard the door from the garden open.

He whispered, "Just tell me where."

"Petra!" It was Terreblanche. "Let's go!" His footsteps approached.

Gat released the girl's arm. She moved off, talking, saying anything. "I really wanted to go abroad to study," she prattled as if they'd been chatting. Gat put his hands behind his back. When she was several paces ahead of him, he shuffled after her. "Maybe America. University of California."

"There you are," said Terreblanche, appearing at the end of the hall. "We need to move!"

"I might as well have said the moon," Petra continued, facing Gat and walking backward, ignoring her friend. "I suggested England. No! France. No! No!" She grinned and turned to face Terreblanche. "Captain Gautier was asking how I ended up at Wits. I'm explaining how I was at my Wits' end." Gat laughed. Petra giggled, slapped Terreblanche on the chest, and turned to Gat with a flirtatious smile. Terreblanche swept her off the floor as if she were property needful of guarding. "Let me down! Let me down!" she cried, hooting and kicking her legs, flirting with Gat while playfully slapping Terreblanche's face. Terreblanche carried her out into the garden.

Outside the house Gat shook hands with the Rousseaus and thanked them for lunch. He climbed into the rear seat of Kobus's 1955 Chevrolet convertible. As they moved off, Petra waved to her parents. Gat watched the girl: the curve of her neck, her small ear, her blonde hair blowing in the wind.

As the convertible neared Table Mountain, Petra turned to Gat. "I wish I were going to be here to act as your guide," she remarked. "We want you to take back a good report to Katanga."

"Here, here!" agreed Terreblanche. He understood she was only being polite.

Gat gazed at the girl. She smiled because of the wind and plopped an open palm on her head to stop her hair from blowing. Gat asked, "Where would you be tomorrow night if you weren't going to Stellenbosch?"

"The Table Bay cruise is rather fun," Terreblanche offered.

"There's a new coffeehouse," Petra said. "It's called San Francisco. Modeled after the beatnik cafés everyone has heard about in California. I might be there. People read their poetry and play jazz."

"Maybe I should go tonight," Gat suggested to test her reaction.

"All entertainments in South Africa are closed on Sundays," Terreblanche said.

"So that the population may contemplate religion." Terreblanche rebuked this impudence with a light poke to Petra's shoulder. The girl smiled flirtatiously at Gat.

As the convertible pulled up to the Table Mountain cable car station, Petra said, "I must ask you again, Captain: Do you think what happened in the Congo is likely to happen here?" Gat could not tell if she wanted his opinion or was merely tweaking the patriotic boyfriend.

"Why should it happen here?" asked Terreblanche. He seemed annoyed that Petra should ask such a question just at a time when Gat should be leaving. "We're giving our blacks a system that works for them."

"Do you think separate development will work, Captain?" Petra asked.

Gat watched the girl with a straight face, but with secret amusement. She was putting Terreblanche through his paces.

Gat suspected that in this game the only victory came from saying nothing, for Petra played to annoy, not to win. Terreblanche folded his arms across his chest. "Do you think it will work, Captain?" Petra repeated.

Gat grinned at her, watching the lips he had kissed. If she wanted his answer to that question, she would have to find some way to see him again. "San Francisco Coffeehouse?" he asked. "That's the place to be?" Their eyes locked.

The girl nodded. "On Kloof Street. Almost to the top."

"Maybe I'll look it over tomorrow night then," he said.

"You might like it," Petra told him.

Gat left the car and shook hands with both of the young people, holding Petra's longer than necessary. He stepped away and waved.

As he drove off, Kobus said, "Katanga must be tough duty. That guy really looks old."

"How old do you think he is?" Petra asked, glancing back at Gat.

"At least thirty. Maybe older."

GAT RODE the cable car to the top of Table Mountain. Happy to stretch his legs, needing to keep them in shape, he made a tour of the mountaintop, looking at the city, the bay, and a formation called Lion's Head. He climbed toward a series of outcroppings designated, not surprisingly given the strangely Biblical anchorings of Afrikaner society, The Twelve Disciples. He thought about Petra Rousseau. Impudent young virgin! Kissing her. That had been pleasant. And, strangely, it excited him more than did spending the entire night with the actress.

He strolled down from the mountain, thinking about Petra. How could he see her again? Could he find the house? He did not even know the name of the street. In the Kobusmobile he should have been watching for street signs; instead he couldn't take his eyes off her.

He boarded a bus, unmindful of its destination, and rode it out to Sea Point. He got off there and walked around. Hotels more in line with his budget fronted on the beach. He entered one and made a reservation for the next night. He took a bus back into the city, thinking that if he saw Petra again he must be on his good behavior. After all, he'd met her at church. That idea amused him. Moreover he had talked about military command as if he and his men were seeking the Holy Grail. Rousseau himself was not fooled, but she might have been. Thinking about her, he could still feel her kiss on his lips.

CHAPTER FOUR

CAPE TOWN

Monday, February 6, 1961

The police driver arrived promptly for Colonel Rousseau and his wife. He carried the luggage set beside the front door to the trunk of the car. "Margaret!" Rousseau called, irritation in his voice. He hated to wait and had the forbidding air his police uniform bestowed on him. "I hope we don't have to wait for you like this next week," he told his daughter. Petra stood with him in the front hall in pedal pushers, a blouse, and sandals.

"I'm ready to go right now, Father."

Rousseau started up the stairs, shouting, "Margaret! The planes don't wait, not even for the police!" He returned to his daughter, detected a rebellious set of her chin provoked by his badgering her mother. Before she could chastise him, he said, "Behave yourself in Stellenbosch."

"What does that mean?"

"Don't let Kobus put his hands where they're not supposed to be." Petra jeered scornfully. "Young men are often carried away."

"Father, I could slink toward Kobus totally naked and he'd keep his hands behind his back." Rousseau narrowed his eyes, a rebuke to her for talking in such a worldly way. She added, "He treats me like a porcelain doll."

"He respects you."

"He respects you, Father."

"He expects to marry you."

"I can't tell you how boring that is!"

Rousseau smiled. "You're a good girl, Pet. You wouldn't want it otherwise."

"Pish-posh," pouted Petra.

Rousseau chuckled, confident that his daughter was, indeed, a good girl. And even better, if passion threatened to overwhelm young Terreblanche's respect for her, his awe of her father would intercede. There were worse ways to protect a daughter, he thought.

Margaret hurried downstairs, carrying a small valise. She handed it to her husband; he took it to the car. She kissed Petra lightly, pressed her cheek to hers, then looked deeply into her eyes. "Are you sure you're all right here?"

"Mother, you and Father want me chaperoned every minute?"

"He feels your wild streak coming on."

"I don't have a wild streak. I wish I did!"

"You know. The one you inherited from me."

"Yes, Mother, you're a very wild woman. A regular Tess of the D'Urbervilles. Thomas Hardy ought to write a novel about you—except he's dead. Of boredom, I think." The two women smiled together.

"He loves you very much," said Margaret. "And so do I."

"I love you both," replied Petra, almost by rote. "Except when you smother me with all this care!"

The women went out onto the stoep together. Petra watched her parents drive off in the chauffeured car.

Once back inside the house, she walked meditatively to the kitchen. She poured herself some coffee, tasted its rich bitterness on her tongue, its heat radiating inside her. She returned outside, kicked off her sandals, and marched across the yard. She stopped, holding the coffee cup in both her hands, feeling its warmth. "Elsie?" No reply. "Elsie?" she called again. She approached the servant's small dwelling attached to the garage. "Elsie?" She moved closer, knocked at the door. "Elsie?" No answer. The servant had gone to her family. Well, she had to make sure.

She hurried back to the kitchen, leaving her coffee cup on the counter, and through the house to the telephone alcove in the hall. She stared at the squat black instrument and wondered: Am I really going to do this?

She dialed the number quickly. When Kobus answered immediately, she groaned, her voice croaking, and asked, "Are you all right?" He assured her that he was. "You didn't eat anything at that braai that made you sick?" No, no, he was fine. "Well, I feel absolutely crappy." She heard the intake of his breath at her use of the vulgarism. "I don't know any other way to put it." She groaned again. "I have never felt so completely, totally crappy."

He told her how sorry he was; he would come over immediately to be with her. "No, don't come," she said. "I just vomited. All over myself." She knew that description would rattle him. "I don't want you to see me this way," she went on. "I've sent a message to Elsie. She'll come be with me. I've called my aunt to say I can't come today." To sound convincing, she struggled with a cough. "You go out to Stellenbosch, start fixing up your place. When I'm better, I'll take the train out." She added, "I'll probably be better tomorrow," because if the Belgian officer didn't show up at the coffeehouse, she wanted Kobus in reserve.

He pleaded that he was worried about her; he must see her. "No, no. I'll be all right," she assured him. "I can probably sleep it off." Trying to get him off the phone, she said right now she needed to sleep. He told her he loved her. She rolled her eyes. They left it that he would drive in from Stellenbosch to fetch her when she felt better.

As soon as she hung up the phone, she whirled around the parlor, plotting her campaign against the officer, trying to decide what to wear.

Gᴀᴛ ᴡᴏᴋᴇ to the sound of pounding. Who was knocking now? The man with tea had wakened him some time before. He rubbed his eyes and looked at the door. Hit from the other side, it rattled in its mounting. Gat left the bed, crossed the room in his tee shirt and shorts, and flung open the door. Gabriel Michels stood across the threshold, his fist ready to strike the door. "You're still in bed?" Michels said, surprised. "You alone?"

"What time is it?" Gat asked.

"Time to come have breakfast with me. If you're alone." Michels had combed his hair and trimmed the blond beard. He wore a light blue safari suit and shoes so new that they squeaked when he walked.

Gat nodded for his colleague to enter. "You look like you're headed for Sunday school."

"I bought a suit of pederast-bird's-egg blue so they'd let me inside this pink elephant of a hotel. When I came by yesterday, they threw me out." Gat laughed. Michels looked about the room. He went to the window, opened the shade, and peered into the garden. "This must cost you."

"There's cold tea there if you want it," Gat said.

Michels swept the pastry from the tea tray into his mouth and poured red-brown liquid into the waiting cup. He took his tea to the bed and stretched out on it. "This beats what I've been sleeping on! What's it cost to buy a woman in this whorehouse?"

Leaving the hotel, the two men walked through the warm summer sunlight toward town. They found a milk bar and bought coffee and rolls. They ate for some minutes in silence. "You had a woman since you've been here?" Michels asked at last. Gat nodded. Michels studied Gat. "Bullshit," Michels tested. Gat shook his head. "How'd you find her?"

"She found me."

"Bastard. Was she good?" Gat fluttered a hand levelly above his rolls. Michels stirred his coffee, staring into it. "I've been paying for it," he said at last. "I know I told you I was getting it free. And all over town. But you know— What's a little bullshit between comrades?"

"You said you were telling everyone what we did."

Michels nodded. He took a swallow of coffee.

"That didn't get it for you free?"

Michels shook his head. "Cape Town whores don't give it away. Hell, every guy that visits them boasts he's killed a kaffir. And if it's been in the papers? Shame, as they say. They don't read the papers."

They fell silent. Finally Gat asked, "What have you done down here? Been to Cape of Good Hope?"

"No Good Hope for me. I've been having bad dreams. B-K dreams." Michels watched Gat as if expecting him to acknowledge the same Belgo-Katangese affliction. Gat chewed his rolls and sipped his coffee.

"I'm having trouble handling this," Michels said. "I spend my days wandering the streets. I'm looking for something. Not sure what. Women? Drink? Dope? Some place to crawl away and hide in? Maybe all of them."

Gat said nothing.

"When I wake up in a bad dream," Michels went on finally, "I like to wind myself around a warm woman. You know? I need something besides a pillow to hold in the night." Gat nodded. He sipped his coffee, looking through the milk-bar window at people passing on the street. "When we got back to E'ville that night," Michels asked, "you get laid?"

"I was busy vomiting."

"I got drunk," Michels related. "Went to the Princess. You know that place?" Gat nodded. "You know Nadia? Long black legs, no body hair?" Gat shook his head. "Bought her for what was left of the night." Michels gave Gat a piteous glance. "I couldn't function. Front door, back door. In her mouth. Nothing happened."

"You still having trouble?"

"No," Michels answered quickly. "Just that night. And the next day." Michels took the last roll and chewed on it. "I'm back in form. But it's not much fun."

"Whores stop being fun. That happens."

Michels finally said, "Had a strange dream last couple of nights." After a pause, he said, "White guy in a mask. He comes up behind me. Puts the cold snout of a gun right where my head meets my neck." Michels put his hand on the spot and rubbed it. "Then he shoots me. So now I'm wondering: is it a dream or a warning?"

"What kind of warning?"

"That they're sending someone to assassinate us."

For a long moment the two men did not speak. "Why?" Gat asked.

"So we don't go back and assassinate them." Michels looked steadily at Gat. "When I saw you on the street, I thought they'd sent you to do me."

"So you chased me through the streets? Why assassinate us?"

"To keep the lid on it." After a moment Michels said, "You know what pisses me? We do what the colonel calls 'our duty.' And that makes us expendable. He betrayed us." Michels examined Gat, wanting reassurance.

"Somebody up the line betrayed him."

"You think so?"

"The rich exploit the poor," said Gat. "The strong exploit the weak. The powerful exploit the powerless. Senior officers exploit junior officers. It's the way of the world. We got caught in it."

Michels asked, "You tell the woman you slept with?" Gat shook his head. "Walking into your hotel," Michels said, "I half expected to see an assassin in the lobby."

"I'm moving to a cheaper place this morning."

Michels taunted, "You come here with Kasai diamonds smuggled up your ass?"

Beneath the table Gat opened his legs and put his hand to his groin. "The only jewels I brought with me are in my hands."

HAVING CALLED her aunt to say that she felt poorly and would come tomorrow, Petra stood in her closet, examining her clothes. She heard a car pull in to the driveway. She went to look out the window. Kobus was leaning into the rear seat of the Chevrolet convertible, removing a large bouquet of roses. Petra ran to her bathroom, shucked off her clothes, tossed on her nightgown and robe. The doorbell rang. She disarranged her hair and examined herself in the mirror. Her face looked fresh, pink-cheeked. She took mascara and quickly shadowed her eyes. Not much of a job. Kobus rang the doorbell again. She tore open the bed she had made only minutes before and grabbed a pillow. The doorbell rang yet again.

She answered the door, the pillow held before her, wisps of her hair straggling into her eyes. She gazed disconsolately at Kobus. He smiled at her wretchedness, shoved the roses at her, and immediately took her into his arms. "You're so cute!" he exclaimed. He kissed her voraciously and tried to open her lips with his tongue.

She broke the kiss and turned away. "I smell awful. Taste worse."

He continued to press her to him, kissing her face and neck. When she pushed him away, he grinned at her with sappy affection. "I love it that you call to ask if I'm okay when you're the one who's sick." He lifted her into his arms and carried her upstairs. At the top he sat her on the banister and nuzzled her hard, pushing against a newel post. He was more aroused than she had ever seen him. That stirred her. Also dismayed her. Did her weakness arouse him? Her womanly frailty excite him? She was not frail! She did not want him around. Not now!

He carried her into her room, set her gently on her bed. She thanked him, slid quickly under the covers, the pillow and the roses held before her. She laid the bouquet beside her, buried her nose among its roses, and pulled the bedcovers up to her neck. She laid her head against a second pillow, croaked, "Thank you, Kobus," in a sickly way and closed her eyes.

Suddenly he was lying beside her, one arm crooked behind her back. The other reached across her to pull a rose from the bouquet. He kissed her yet again. He laid the rose beside her cheek, reached under the covers to pull away the pillow, and tossed it behind him. He put his hand beneath the covers and fumbled to open the robe. He slid his hand onto her breast, kissed her deeply. Kobus had never been so ardent. His hand slipped down her body, trying to pull up her nightgown. Petra felt excited. Her body tingled, but she said, "Don't, Kobus, please! I really am feeling sick," because if she was aroused, she was also alarmed. She felt ready for this to happen, but not with him. If it happened with him, he would feel he owned her, that she had given him the deed to herself. He would treat her in a manner that would tip off her parents to what had taken place in their absence. She would never live down their disappointment in her.

"Don't," she implored. "Please." She turned away from him.

"I love you," he said. She nodded. He had said this often before, but now he seemed to mean it more than ever. Finally he sat up on the side of the bed. He stroked her forehead. "You aren't feverish," he said. She placed her hands over her face as if she would cry. "Can I get you anything?" he asked. She shook her head. "Tea?"

Again she shook her head, thinking of her father's warning. Could he know Kobus better than she did? "Thank you for carrying me upstairs," she said. "And for the roses. I'll try to sleep now." She closed her eyes.

Kobus got off the bed. He knelt beside her, kissed her forehead, the smell of his shaving lotion strong in her nostrils. She heard him stand, felt the love-look in his eyes descend on her like a warm blanket on a hot night. She was afraid he'd insist on staying. Then she heard him tiptoe from the room, the unwanted heat leaving with him. She forced herself to keep her eyes closed until she heard the motor of his car and the hum of it pulling out of the driveway. She slid from the bed, crawled to the window, and peeked outside to watch his Chevrolet moving off down the street.

THE MEN returned to the hotel hardly speaking. Gat did not think for a moment that Michels's dreams constituted a warning. Still they agitated him. His guts tightened. His eyes scanned the Monday morning streets on the lookout for danger. Having shared his apprehensions, Michels felt calm enough to whistle most of the way back. As they walked down the hall, Gat said, "In case there's an assassin in my room, you enter first."

Gat went into the bathroom to pack his shaving kit. Michels followed behind him. He looked around, sat on the toilet lid. "Did I tell you about the other night? After I saw you?" Gat said nothing, putting his toothbrush into a plastic container. "I was half drunk and horny. About midnight a woman came up to me on the street, offered herself for practically nothing. She pulled me into an alley. It was black as a kaffir. As I'm pumping into her, hands clap me on the shoulder. Start pulling us apart."

Gat jeered. "Serves you right. Alleys are for pissing." He glanced in the mirror and told himself, Ditch him. He's what you're trying to escape.

"It's the fuck police," Michels said. "Honest to God, they have such a unit. So the fuck police arrest us. At the station house the top dog informs me that this woman is forbidden to me by law. She's Coloured; I'm white. Never the twain shall fuck."

Gat returned to the room. He tossed the canvas kit onto the desk beside his suitcase. He heard Michels pissing in the bathroom. "You're acting like you never left Katanga," Gat called to him. "I'm trying to act like I never was there." He added, "Be sure you flush."

Michels flushed and returned to the room. "I spent the night in jail," he said. "In the morning I explained to the top dog that all I wanted was a little fun. I thought she was white. I didn't know it mattered if she wasn't white. Turns out there's an Immorality Act. These people are serious about separation."

Gat carefully folded his suit and laid it in the suitcase. He gave the same attention to the new shirts and the ties.

"I told him what we'd done up there." Gat shook his head. Michels shrugged. "It got me leniency. A mere fine: a hundred rands. And a warning. 'If you dip your dong in black or yellow, don't do it where we can find you.' So I paid. I'm pretty short now." Gat realized he needed money. "It was that or spend the weekend in jail, then be prosecuted. These are hard people."

Yes, Gat thought. Hard people. But Michels ought to stay out of alleys.

As soon as Kobus was gone, Petra shed her nightgown, slipped into her day clothes, and went to the phone. "What's going on?" her cousin Hazel demanded. Petra had asked what she was doing that evening. "I thought you were going to Stellenbosch with Kobus."

"Can you keep a secret?" Petra asked. Silence from Hazel. "Well, can you?"

"Not forever," replied Hazel. "How long?"

"Just don't tell Kobus."

"Oh-oh. What's going on?"

"I may be meeting a man at the San Francisco Coffeehouse."

"What!!!" screamed Hazel. "How old is he?"

"He might be thirty." Silence at the other end of the line. "He doesn't know I'll be there," Petra explained. "And I don't know that he will. If he does come, it'll need to look like we kind of ran into each other."

"And you can't go there alone," Hazel said.

"So you go with me. If he is there and comes over, then you leave."

"Doesn't he have a friend?"

"He doesn't know anyone in South Africa." Petra hesitated, then added, "Except me." The girls giggled. Petra explained how she had come to meet Captain Gautier. "He looks at a woman the way she wants to be looked at."

"You're not a woman," Hazel said. "We just completed O levels."

"Of course, we're women!" Petra insisted. "Plenty of *platte-lander* girls have babies at our age."

"Are you going to have a baby with this man?" Hazel asked. The girls squealed and agreed that Hazel, whose parents were more lenient about her driving than were the Rousseaus, would fetch Petra at nine that evening.

WITH MICHELS in tow, Gat moved into the Protea Hotel in Sea Point. The men bought bathing suits and swam in the ocean. Afterward lying on the sand on towels taken from the hotel, Michels asked, "You ever think of going to Canada? Or America? Mexico?"

"Africa's the only place I ever wanted to go," said Gat. He gazed out at the surf, recalling how at thirteen he had determined that one day he would leave tiny, crowded, small-minded Belgium for enormous, underpopulated Africa. There a man could stretch himself to more than his full size and accomplish great things.

Beside him Michels gaped at girls so intensely that Gat found it embarrassing. He hoped that his own eyes had not looked that way at Petra Rousseau. "How can I get to Canada?" Michels asked. "I'm dying here. Running out of money. I couldn't borrow some from you, could I?"

"Not if you're going to Canada."

"You think I could find a job here?"

"Be a miner. Mine owners always need good men."

"The next mine owner I meet I may shoot."

Back in their safari suits they walked into Green Point. When they came to a bookstore, Gat went inside to browse. Michels drifted off to find a bar. Gat was looking for books that might explain what was happening in Africa; he wanted analyses different from those he read in *La Libre Belgique* or *De Standaard* or was told by mine owners and Belgo-Katangese apologists. But works suggesting that change was blowing across the continent were not available in South Africa.

Leaving the bookstore Gat searched for Michels only long enough to assert truthfully that he had done so. He walked to the foreshore and bought a sandwich and a beer at a place overlooking the ocean. He watched cranes loading ships, possibly for Canada, and assumed that Michels would turn up at the Protea Hotel during the night and beg to sleep on his floor. He took a bus up out of the city, located the San Francisco Coffeehouse on upper Kloof Street, examined wares in a bicycle shop, and browsed again in bookstores.

He bought a novel about Algeria, found a park, and read. Now and then he wondered if he and the girl would actually meet. If they did, what would happen? Wouldn't her meeting him signal— Maybe not. She was very young. And if that happened . . . Would he be taking advantage of her? He would not exploit her. He needed her to value him. Meeting him would risk her innocence, admiration, her trust. He would not betray her trust. Gat and Petra would value one another. They would form a bond if even for only one evening.

When sunset reddened the sky, he went to the coffeehouse. Few people were there. Petra Rousseau was not one of them.

PETRA SPENT the early afternoon wondering how she should dress for a meeting that might never take place. What would appeal to a man of Gat's age? How old was he anyway? Maybe she should just dress like the schoolgirl she was, the almost varsity student. That was all she'd been yesterday and the man had kissed her, hadn't he? In any case, Hazel would be dressed the way she always was, excessively casual. Hmm.

As Petra stood in her closet, it suddenly occurred to her that it would be foolish to spend the day worrying about the appearance of her exterior if the captain, should he be at the coffeehouse, were to discover within ten minutes of conversation that she was a carefully dressed ninny, that her interior was an empty void. What if he asked her opinions of trends in Africa? What if he discovered that she could talk only about school and the fact that she had played Banquo in her class reading of *MacBeth*? He might find Hazel more interesting.

Petra grabbed a school notebook and drove her parents' Ford sedan to the library at the University of Cape Town. Settling down with encyclopedias and news magazines, she began to study current events—even taking notes!—so that her arsenal of manipulation would include an informed mind.

She read impatiently, chewing her pencil's eraser. She scanned colonial history. No, no! What about Lumumba? He was the one everyone talked about. She finally found material about the run-up to independence.

Petra's head soon swam with the unfamiliar names of parties and politicians. How would she keep them straight? She laughed aloud at the notion of rattling off the names of these politicians to Kobus. She wondered what the captain would do if she spouted them. She smiled at that idea.

Petra remembered hearing talk about the Katanga secession and Lumumba's problems. Many South Africans were happy about chaos in the Congo. It seemed to prove that Bantus could not rule themselves.

She read that Lumumba's government asked for United Nations assistance in ousting the Belgians' neocolonial invasion and ending the secession. Although the UN sent troops

and advisors, Lumumba found himself increasingly powerless. When the UN refused to help him deal militarily with
Katanga, he sought Russian planes to ferry troops to Katanga.

Petra wondered: Was Lumumba a Communist? Had he
intended to allow Russians to use the Congo as a base to
penetrate Central Africa? Her father thought so. As did the
Americans. But did that make sense? Lumumba was an African nationalist, wasn't he? Why would he want his country
taken over by Russians?

Petra read through her notes. If she were writing a varsity
paper, she asked herself, what sort of conclusion would she
offer? That Lumumba was a monkey, as Kobus claimed? Or
a savage, as her father said? Perhaps Lumumba was a person
of ambition—he was clearly that—caught in a colonial cage.
Maybe he was even a man of intelligence stunted by lack of
opportunities. How many Bantus, she wondered, were there
like that in South Africa? She recalled Captain Gautier telling
her father about Africans in business suits, professionals, greeting one another on Johannesburg streets. Were such people
the ones enmeshed in the endless treason trial?

Whatever his qualities, she realized, Lumumba had been
impulsive and unwise. In the Cold War atmosphere—which
he did not understand—he could not seek Russian aid without terrifying the Americans. They had their own race problems; most of their leaders probably considered Lumumba a
cheeky black.

Petra wondered what had happened to him. Was he lan-
guishing in a prison or army camp in Katanga? Might he be
released? Or was he already dead?

Driving home she thought: All this information! It was
like cramming for a test. If Captain Gautier were at the coffeehouse, would she tell him she'd spent two hours stuffing
her head with facts about the Congo? She burst out laughing.

Not on her life! He might run away. She would do what she did with exams: she'd try to relax.

BACK HOME, Petra snacked on what Elsie had not taken from the refrigerator. She bathed, using the soap and shampoo she smelled on her mother when her father had been away and returned home amorous. She brushed her teeth, buffed her nails, did her hair. She applied her makeup sparingly and so carefully that most men would think she used nothing but lipstick. She slid into a girdle, pulled on hose, and fastened them to garters. She donned a lightweight skirt that fell well below her knees. It was the skirt of a woman, for the school uniforms she had so long worn had to be three inches above the knees. She chose a blouse that understatedly emphasized her breasts and decided to complete the outfit with a navy blue beret and a light sweater to match.

When Hazel arrived, she approved Petra's choices with a low whistle. "He'll have no idea how much thought you've given this," she said.

"Too studied?" Petra asked.

Hazel sniffed the air, detecting the scent of the aphrodisiac soap, and smiled wickedly. "What do you want from this fellow anyway?"

"I want a change from Kobus Terreblanche," Petra declared. "I want an evening with a man who does not want to end up like my father."

"While there's still time."

ONCE INSIDE the coffeehouse Gat ordered soup and coffee and thumbed through mimeographed chapbooks of the poets who read their work at the place. All in all, they reinforced

Gat's assumption that he did not understand poetry. He said as much to the waitress who refilled his coffee; she turned out to be one of the poets. She promised him that poetry "connected better" when performed aloud. She also assured him that readings would start shortly. He went to the men's room to relieve himself of the coffee he had drunk and returned to drink more. Musicians performed. Poets read their work.

Gat sat where he could watch the patrons' comings and goings. He saw a young woman who looked very much like Petra Rousseau. She entered with a friend. She wore a navy blue beret cocked over the side of her head. In an understated way she was deliciously gorgeous and she was definitely Petra. Gat felt suddenly shy, no older than Petra herself. He sat unable to move, his legs trembling. He wondered what he should do: Declare himself immediately? Play it casual for a time? Pretend not to notice she'd arrived? But what if another man got to her before he did?

The girl with Petra, who looked more intelligent than beautiful, Gat thought, began to scan the room. For a moment he wished Michels were with him. He had not considered that Petra would bring a duenna. But, of course, she would not come alone. But obviously Michels was not the right companion for a woman of any intelligence.

The girls were shown to a table against the wall. They sat and ordered. Gat watched them. If Petra caught sight of him, she gave no evidence of the fact. Nor did she glance about to see if he were there. She and her friend watched the musicians as if others in the room were of no interest to them. Gat made himself wait till their coffees were served. Then he crossed the room. "Hello, Petra," he said when he reached their table. "As you see, I took your advice about coming here."

"Hello, Adriaan Gautier," Petra said, feeling adult and very desirable. "This is my school chum Hazel. Hazel, this is—."

"Please, call me Gat. Everyone does." As Hazel and Gat shook hands, she observed him carefully. "May I join you?" Gat asked.

"Please do," Petra replied.

"I'll just fetch my coffee." Gat went off.

Hazel cocked an eyebrow wickedly and nodded her approval. The girls giggled briefly, then suppressed their amusement lest Gat catch sight of it.

Gat and the two young women drank coffee together. They listened to music and poetry and tried to make conversation that included them all. Gat was conscious that his companions considered him different from them. It was a stretch for them to feel his social equal. After all, he was almost aged. That might be exciting (for he had experience), but was more likely to prove boring (for he might pontificate or want flattery). Still, to be with an older man made the girls feel daring and sophisticated.

Gat told them that he expected to be in the country another week. He thought he might buy a bike and pedal to Durban. "What should I see along the way?" he asked. They offered suggestions, some serious, others facetious. These latter caused the girls to snicker to each other.

Hazel took cigarettes from her purse and offered them around. When Gat declined, so did Petra. Hazel smoked, inhaling into her mouth, but not into her lungs. Then she threw her head back in a gesture she'd seen actresses use and released the smoke above her head. Petra watched Gat for clues as to how she should behave. He carefully affected casualness. He hardly glanced at her. He watched the poets and musicians for he feared that looking at Petra would betray his needfulness. That would certainly scare her. When he smiled at her, he did it quickly for Petra's friend examined him relentlessly with analytical eyes. He did not want the friend taking Petra to the ladies' room to adjudge him a geek.

"Petra says you disagreed with her father," Hazel commented during a break in the music.

"Did I?" Gat laughed. "Oops!" He did not remember challenging Rousseau. He made a roguish face. "That's a no-no, I take it."

"Very few people contradict a police colonel in South Africa," said Petra.

"Is that why you're here?" Gat asked.

"Possibly." She smiled. She and Gat regarded one another. He moved his knee against hers and she did not move hers away.

"Petra's here because her Stellenbosch plans changed," Hazel said. The girls nudged one another and suppressed the urge to giggle.

Gat bought cake that they all three shared. "What's Katanga like?" asked Petra, ready to put her afternoon study to use. "What's this secession all about?" Her mother contended that a man was happy to talk if you got him on his subject.

Hazel asked, "Do you have a girlfriend there?"

"Several dozen," replied Gat.

"Black or white?" persisted Hazel.

"Some of both."

"Which do you like better?"

"Depends on my mood," Gat said. "If I'm in the mood for a companion who tells me how marvelous I am, how handsome, a woman who will oblige my every whim, then I seek out one of my black girlfriends." Gat cocked an eyebrow. The girls glanced at one another and rolled their eyes. "But if I'm in the mood for an intellectual companion who lists everything that's wrong with me—"

"Then you're looking for a white girl, aren't you?" Hazel said.

Petra slapped the back of her hand against Gat's shoulder and pushed her knee against his.

"Funny," remarked Hazel. "When we want intellectual companionship, we always go to kaffir boys, don't we, Petra?"

"Intellectual companionship?" queried Petra. "I don't go to anyone for that!"

Suddenly Hazel asked, "Is there a future for white people in the Congo? Or in Katanga?"

"No," said Gat.

"Which one?" asked Petra.

"No," said Gat.

The girls watched him. The expressions in their privileged, innocent eyes had grown serious. "Is there a future for white people here?" Hazel asked.

"What do you think?" Gat replied.

But instead of exploring the matter further, they pushed the last piece of cake around the plate, the girls leaving it for the man, the adult leaving it for the children.

"I think it's terrible that we whites live so well on black labor!" Petra said.

"But if we weren't here," observed Hazel, "they'd still be living in grass shacks and killing each other." Petra took a look at Gat to see if he would attempt an answer. He said nothing. "Instead they're living in tin shacks and dreaming of killing us. That's what you think, isn't it?" Hazel stared coolly at Gat, challenging the outsider. "You think they're going to kill us all." Gat said nothing. Petra pressed her knee more strongly against his. "Maybe not us," said Hazel. "Our children."

"I don't want to talk about killing," Gat said.

The girls excused themselves to go to the loo. Petra came back through the mist of cigarette smoke alone. She sat beside

Gat and once again pushed her knee against his. "Hazel went home," she said.

"Good," Gat said. Petra blushed and turned away. When she turned back, Gat looked at her a long moment, thinking how pretty she was. He thought, too, that she seemed more a woman without her chum, less a schoolgirl. "I'd been hoping all day that you'd be here," he told her.

"Have you? I don't believe that."

"All right. Not all day. Just most of it." He smiled at her and she lowered her eyes. He put his hand on her knee and pressed it against his own. He thought to himself, It's been a long time since I wooed a girl so carefully.

The musicians were playing again. Because of the noise, Petra leaned close to hear him. "Did your friend say that I look at a woman as if I hadn't seen one in a very long time?"

"She said you were too old for me. That you probably really do have both white and black girlfriends in Katanga and that I should go home with her."

"Why did you stay?"

"Because this may be the one night of my life when I can escape people like—" She shrugged.

"Thank you for staying," Gat said. "You are very beautiful."

"And you are very corny."

Gat stared at the musicians. His entire being was focused in the palm of his hand that held the girl's knee.

"Do you know why you kissed me yesterday?"

Gat cocked his head and gazed at her. "Maybe you should tell me."

"You were competing with my father and Kobus. They presume to own me. So you shoplifted a kiss from them. It was men playing games."

"You mean I'd 've kissed Hazel if she'd been Petra Rousseau?"

"It had nothing to do with me."

Still holding her knee, Gat placed his other hand on Petra's shoulder and kissed her. They broke the kiss, looked at one another. "And my shoplifting now: that had nothing to do with you?"

"Do you have a wife in Katanga?" Gat shook his head. "A girlfriend?"

Gat shrugged. "I'm not a priest."

"Is she white or black?"

Gat gazed at her, kissed her softly. "Does it matter?" Petra shook her head, realizing she need not worry about the differences between political parties. If there were to be talk of Katanga, it would be of this kind. "There's a woman I used to see," Gat said, "a secretary at Union Minière. She's white. I saw her only because Katanga can be very boring." The girl said nothing. They listened to music. Then Gat explained, "In Katanga all whites stick together. They sit around scorning the blacks because not being black is the only cement that holds them together. It's a relief to be away from there." Petra nodded. Gat said, "I look at you the way I do because— Well, you *are* beautiful. You're young and fresh—"

"Don't—for God's sake—say innocent!"

"You are innocent—of all that Katanga poison. The hate and uncertainty and duplicity. The deceit." They said nothing for a time. Then Gat asked, "Are you going to marry Kobus Terreblanche?"

"No. My father thinks I'm going to. And so does he. But I'm not."

"Your mother knows this?"

Petra nodded.

"Well, we've got all that straight," Gat said. "So . . . Are you going to marry me?"

"Is that a proposal?"

"Just a minute. I'll tell you." Gat leaned over and kissed her tenderly. Her lips tasted sweet. She pulled away before he wanted her to.

WHEN THEY left the smells of coffee and cigarette smoke and got outside, the air was fresh. It was just beginning to lose the warmth of the day. "How do I get you home?" Gat asked. "Are there taxis around here?"

"You could walk me home," Petra suggested.

"Is it that close?"

"Half an hour."

They walked through the quiet streets, the air fresh and cool on their arms, their hands not touching but longing to touch. Gat knew he should feel at peace. Instead he wondered: What was he doing in this strange city? With this teenage girl? He was looking for a woman. But he was moving through the quiet night beside the overprotected daughter of a senior police official who was inexperienced and undoubtedly a virgin.

Yet as their footsteps clicked through the darkness, illumined now and then by streetlights, he felt again the presence following him: Katanga and what he'd done there. As they passed beneath the leafy overhang of a tree, he took the girl's arm and turned her toward him. They kissed, tentatively, his hands clasping her shoulders, her hands at her sides. The kiss was so sweet that Gat felt the presence retreat. Now he held her body close to his and kissed her more forcefully. The presence retreated even farther away. He and the girl looked at one another and started walking again, his arm around her waist.

They reached her parents' house. He walked her to the stoep. They looked at one another and kissed again. Gat felt partly outside himself and looked at the two of them with amusement. He was being as virginal as the girl, holding her hands in his, gazing into her uncertain eyes. He knew that she wondered what came next. And did he? "Is this good-bye?" he heard himself ask. "Are you going to Stellenbosch tomorrow?"

"Would you like to come in?" she asked.

He entered the house with her and felt Katanga shut away outside. In the darkness of the entry he kissed her. Then again slowly. She opened her mouth to his and in the quiet of the house, its night sounds like contented breathing, he tasted her sweetness. "We're alone here," Petra said. Gat kissed her again, deeply, and held her, clung to her, feeling safe with her body against his. They embraced tightly in the dark. She asked, "Why are you really here?"

"To be with you."

"You're holding on to me as if—"

"As if my life depended on it?" He kissed her forehead.

"Do you have to be so corny?" Still he held on. "But why are you?"

"Things in Katanga are so— Ghastly. I've known I couldn't go back until—"

Petra snickered lightly in the dark. "I didn't think you really wanted to marry me. Do you?" They laughed and he continued to cling to her.

Gat whispered, "I need you to save my life."

"I thought I'd seen too many movies," Petra told him. "But you're the one." She broke from his arms and walked through the dark parlor with its antiques and forebears' portraits, on into the parlor that overlooked the garden. She turned on a light. "Is there nothing to do in Katanga but watch movies?"

Gat followed her, thinking that her ancestors, those Netherlands burghers, would certainly not approve of their being alone together in the house, yet feeling the presence of Katanga waiting just beyond the door. He wanted to hold her again. He checked himself—like an eighteen-year-old. Play it at her age level, he counseled himself.

"Can I get you something to drink?" she asked. "Not coffee."

"No, thanks. I'm fine."

"I'd offer you my father's Scotch or vodka," she explained. "That's probably what you'd like, but he keeps it locked up because otherwise he's sure Elsie gets into it." She smiled. "He can't allow himself to think that I would."

"Do you?"

She gave him a crooked smile, then looked at the ceiling, her mind trying to visualize the contents of the refrigerator. "I think there's Appletizer."

"Whatever that is, fine." He paced while she was gone.

She returned with two tall glasses of golden liquid, beads of condensation sweating on the glasses the way Gat felt himself sweating inside, wanting her. They clicked glasses a little awkwardly and drank. Gat smelled the aroma of apple juice and felt the coolness move into his body, calming him. Petra went to the tall radio-phonograph, turned on the radio, and dialed to a music station. She gestured Gat to a couch and sat on an overstuffed chair beside it, uncertain of what would happen if she sat beside him on the couch. She gazed at him a long moment, then repeated what he had said, " 'I need you to save my life.' Why do you tell me that?"

"Because it's true."

"How can it be true?" Gat shrugged. "I don't know what that means," she said. "Boys don't talk to me that way."

"I'm not a boy."

"Is that a Belgian officer's way of getting a girl to—" She shrugged.

"No." Gat told himself to proceed carefully; the girl obviously felt out of her depth. "I'm sick of what my country has done in the Congo," he explained. "I'm ashamed. It's not pleasant to be ashamed of your country when your job is to defend it." Gat left the couch to sit on the end of the coffee table. He slid his hands beneath Petra's skirt, lodged them behind her knees, felt the weave of her hose. She looked uncertain. "I want to be with someone who has no taint of the Congo on her. Or Katanga." She shifted her legs, crossed them. Gat withdrew his hands. He stood and paced. "Katanga is right outside that door." He pointed toward the door into the garden. "I want it to stay there. And that's how you save my life."

Petra said nothing. She stared into her drink.

"I've frightened you, haven't I?" He looked at the girl. She refused to look at him. "Would you like me to go?"

She nodded, still staring at her drink. He stopped pacing, stood looking at her with his hands in his pockets. He started toward the door. She stood, put her drink down. He watched her a moment, then moved through the formal parlor into the entry hall. He heard her trailing after him. At the entry door he turned toward her. She watched him from the formal parlor. "I'm sorry I'm so young," she said.

"I'm sorry I frightened you."

"Did something happen in Katanga?"

"Yes," he said.

"And being with me keeps you from—"

He nodded.

This man might need her for solace; that idea had never occurred to her. "I dreamed about you last night," she said. "Thought about you all day."

"I did some thinking about you."

They smiled at each other.

"I feel like such a child," Petra said. "That's how my father treats me. And Kobus. How old are you?"

"I'm thirty." Gat smiled gently. "Does that seem older than time itself?"

"I don't want to feel like a child anymore." They looked at one another without moving. "As soon as my parents left this morning, I called Kobus. I told him I was sick, couldn't go to Stellenbosch. Because I hoped you'd be at the coffeehouse tonight."

He moved back toward her. He did not touch her because he knew that this was what she hoped he'd do and it was too early yet. "You knew I'd be there, didn't you?"

"I worried all day about working this out," she admitted. "Called Hazel. Wondered what I should wear. I even went to a library and read up about the Congo so you wouldn't think me a ninny."

"You're not a ninny. You're lovely. When you walked into the coffeehouse, my heart jumped into my throat."

"I hoped you'd walk me home. I daydreamed about it. I wasn't sure what I'd want to happen if you did. Not this, you about to go." She looked forlorn. He smiled at her, loving the child in her that was trying to become a woman. "Why don't you kiss me or something?"

He smiled at her, wanting her to want him. The music from the radio swirled into the room. "Dance with me."

She moved to him in the entry hall. He took her in his arms, held her close. She trembled as they moved to the music, her body against his, he feeling the pressure of her breasts against his chest, she pleased by the warmth of his cheek against hers, by the swelling in his groin as he pushed against her. She tasted the apple juice sweetness on his lips. He smelled her hair, the perfume of her mother's soap. They clung together as the music wrapped about them.

When the music ended, he gently pulled the beret from her head. She shook out her hair. He ran his fingers through it. He kissed her deeply, slid a hand to her breast. "I want to sleep with you," he whispered. "You must have known that when you first saw me look at you."

"My mother knew before I did."

"Let's leave her out of this." She smiled and watched his hands begin to unfasten the buttons of her blouse. She let it fall to the floor, allowed him to unfasten her bra and pull it off. He cupped her breasts, bent her backward to kiss them. She felt a quiver surge through her body as his lips lightly bit a nipple.

He raised her skirt and half-slip to her waist, felt the garter belt and hose, the panties and girdle. "So much stuff between me and you!" he said. She retrieved her blouse and bra, led him back into the small parlor, extinguished the light. "Don't look at me," she said.

"Of course, I'm going to look at you."

In the darkness she removed her clothes. He admired her, crouched beside her to kiss and caress her body. She felt dizzy as his hands moved over her. Finally she stopped those hands. She said, "I don't know what a man looks like."

He put her hands on his groin. "That's what he feels like," he said. "I'll take off my clothes upstairs." He lifted her in his arms and climbed the stairs, carrying her. She thought, I'm becoming a woman. Two different men have carried me up to my room today.

When they reached the top of the stairs, she whispered, "I'm a virgin," looking shame-faced. "It's a nuisance, isn't it?"

"Do you want to stay one?"

She shook her head and pointed to her room. He entered it with her still in his arms, the smell of Kobus's roses perfuming the room. He kissed her and let her down. "If you want to stay a virgin, there are things we can do, things that—"

"But you won't enjoy it, will you?"

"I don't want to take anything from you that you—" He shrugged. "You may not be ready for this. It could hurt a little at first."

"Can you make sure I won't get pregnant?"

He nodded. She looked uncertain. "I'll show you when the time comes." He looked at the bed. "That's awfully narrow."

"There's a double bed in the guest room." She led him there. He smiled, watching her move with her arms held before her breasts. While she opened the bed, he eased off his loafers and began to undress. She took the tunic of his safari suit and draped it on the gentleman's stand that her English grandfather had used. He removed his trousers and handed them to her. As she folded them over the stand, a thought occurred to her. "Will I bleed?" she asked.

"Some probably."

She hurried to the bathroom and returned, carrying the guest towels. She spread them across the center of the bed. "Do you mind if I do this?" She turned to receive his permission for the towels and found that he was naked. He let her look at him. "You're so big," she whispered.

"That's why a virgin bleeds." She looked into his eyes, a little fearfully, then back at his groin. It fascinated her. He took her hand and guided it to him.

"It's so hard."

"It doesn't work unless it's hard." She looked up at him, still holding him, and he wrapped his arms about her. She put her arms about his firm soldier's body, loving the feel of his skin against hers. "You're so warm," she said.

PETRA CRIED when Gat entered her. But he kissed her so tenderly, kissing the tears away from her eyes, that she endured the pain, even enjoyed it. And it did not grow worse, but eased as he moved against her and away and against her again. She clung to him and he to her and it was like a rocket blast that shot both of them somewhere neither of them had ever been. Afterward they clung to each other wrapped about one another and Gat felt safe.

CHAPTER FIVE

CAPE TOWN

TUESDAY, FEBRUARY 7, 1961

A s Gat left the bed, he was aware of the rise and fall of Petra's breathing. He washed quietly in the bathroom. Since all towels were spread across the bed, he used a washcloth to dry himself. Now, returning to the bedroom, he heard no sound at all. She was awake. He tiptoed to the bed, settled onto it, and gazed over at her. She had pulled the sheet and summer blanket up to her chin.

"Are you all right? You cried."

"It hurt." She sat up. "But I liked it."

He reached out, touched her face. "I should go."

"Why?"

"It's the chivalrous thing to do."

"Is it? I'd think the chivalrous thing would be to stay." He stroked her face. "Are you going to leave me all alone in this house, thinking I've given my virginity to a man I'll never see again?"

He moved to her, slid his legs about her body and his arms about her head. "I can't leave," he whispered, "because

I don't know where the hell I am." She rearranged herself so that she could embrace him. "Do I just walk downhill?" They kissed for a time. "If I leave, when can I see you again?"

"Stop talking about leaving. I don't want you to leave!" She said, "I'm a mess. I did bleed." She slid off the bed, leaned down to stare at the towels, and began to pull them off the bed. Gat got up beside her. They collected the towels and started toward the bathroom. "Don't come in here with me," she said.

"I got you dirty. Let me wash you."

"You're a pest!" She stood in the bathroom doorway and took the towels from him. "There's a linen closet in the hall. Go get a couple of towels."

He walked naked into the hallway, found the closet and fetched the towels. When he returned, she had left the bathroom door open, was running water into the tub. Gat crouched beside the tub and flicked droplets at her. "You *are* a pest!" she said again.

He helped her into the tub, then followed and gently poured water over her from the cup he made of his hands. She stood and let him wash her. She washed him. Then they lay down together, her back to his chest. They refilled the water to keep it warm and finally left the tub, each rubbing the other dry, and returned to the bedroom. Petra lay down on the bed. Gat put on his shorts.

"Why are you doing that?"

"My friend here is going to swim into you again unless we keep him under wraps."

"I want him to swim into me again."

"But not unless he wears a raincoat."

"Do you have another one?"

Gat lay beside her and whispered that he did. He pulled the sheet and summer blanket over them and they held each other. After a while Petra reached down and pulled open Gat's shorts. They caressed one another. They made love again, Petra putting Gat's raincoat on him. They slept, wound about each other, and Gat felt again at peace.

AT HIS hotel in Pretoria, while dressing, Colonel Rousseau received an early morning phone call. "Sorry to bother you, Colonel," said the duty officer in Cape Town, "but you're to be informed about serious crimes committed by non-whites against whites."

"What's happened?" asked the colonel.

"A Belgian tourist—probably a tourist—was killed outside a brothel in District Six. Gates of Heaven. You know that place?"

"Know it. Never patronized it, though." Rousseau smiled at that comment.

"Heard the girls are so-so, but never tried them out." There was a crackle of static over the line from Cape Town. "We've got the victim's wallet so it doesn't look like he was killed resisting a robbery. More likely a knife fight. Apparently the victim was an officer—lieutenant—of the Congo's Force Publique."

Another officer from the Congo, Rousseau thought. He wondered if the victim knew— Gautier. Wasn't that the name? Had they come to the Union together? Gone whoring together? "Name?" asked the colonel.

"Gabriel Michels, age 28."

"Got a suspect?"

"Not yet. Michels was known at the brothel. Obstreperous, a braggart. Refused to pay. They threw him out. According to the madam, that was before the body was found on the street. It's likely that perp's run off. We're betting he was cut up pretty bad."

"Anything else?"

"Victim was carrying eighty American dollars in a money belt. We'd sure like to know where he got American."

Yes, thought Rousseau. Those boys weren't paid that well. And never in dollars. Must have been up to some mischief. He wondered if Gautier was involved. "Close down the brothel," the colonel instructed. "Until I get back, hold the madam, her bouncer if you can find him, and every girl Michels patronized."

"Anything else?"

"Check with immigration. Find when he entered the country. And see if another Belgian officer—Gautier—entered with him." Rousseau spelled Gautier's name. "That's it," the colonel said. "Thanks for calling."

"Yes, sir. Have a good day."

The colonel hung up the phone, finished buttoning his shirt, and reached for his tie. He threaded it under his collar and began to knot it before a mirror. His wife watched him. She knew better than to inquire about phone calls. But she had heard her husband mention Gautier and wondered what the connection might be.

Brushing her hair at the vanity, Margaret Rousseau observed, "Petra was quite taken with Captain Gautier."

"I noticed," replied the Colonel. "Good thing she's gone to Stellenbosch."

WHEN PETRA woke Gat, light filled the room. He went to use the bathroom and returned to the bed. They lay against one another, enjoying the feel of each other's skin. They listened to the sounds of early morning, a rooster crowing far off, the first cars in the streets.

Petra said, "Now I know why people are always whisper-ing about this as if it were something extraordinary. It is."

Far away in the hall downstairs the phone rang.

Gat held Petra so that she would not move. But she had no intention of moving.

"It's— Let's see," she said. "Maybe it's Kobus calling to see if I feel better. I could tell him the doctor is with me now."

"His root remedy . . ."

"Yes, works wonders." The phone continued to ring. "Or," she said, "it's Hazel wanting to be sure I got home."

"Let Hazel wonder," Gat said.

"If I talked to her, I'd have to tell her you're here."

"Why do that?"

"To hear her scream." They laughed together. "She'd ask, 'What happened?' and I'd have to tell her because I'd want to hear her scream again." Gat chuckled. Petra screamed gleefully herself. "Or it's my mother. And I don't want to talk to my mother."

Finally the phone stopped ringing. Petra gazed at the ceil-ing and finally asked, "Is there any reason you have to stay in Cape Town?"

"To see you."

"Then why don't you drive me to varsity?"

Gat raised himself to his elbow. "Your parents seemed keen on doing that."

"I want you to do it." Gat gazed down at her. "We'll toss my things into my car— The car I use— Get your things at the hotel and be on our way."

Gat stretched out beside her, took her in his arms, and held her gently. "You don't know anything about me."

She pulled back her head to look at him. "All I need to."

"It's not enough. There are things you should know."

She kissed him, held him tight.

"I came down here because— I executed a man in Katanga. Three men actually."

She said nothing. When her hold on him loosened, he held her more tightly. "Are you on the run?"

"It was an official execution."

"What does that mean?"

"I was acting under orders from the State of Katanga. Which means from the mining bosses at Union Minière. I got rid of people they found inconvenient." He added, "Which is inconvenient for me because I became a soldier to protect people, not to execute them so that rich people, who never dirty their own hands, can get even richer."

The girl sat up, feeling suddenly naked in the presence not of her lover, but of a stranger. She covered herself with the sheet. In bed with an executioner? She had given her virginity to a killer? In the night he had gently opened a closed part of her body, freeing her. Just this morning his body had shaken her with joys she had never imagined possible. That such convulsions, such pleasures, resided inside her had never . . . Now the opened part of her body ached.

She hunched forward, wondering what would happen. Gat lightly laid his hand on her back. She recoiled. He began gently to caress her back, rubbing warmth into it. Finally she began to relax. These aren't the hands of a killer, she thought. She turned to look at him, her brown eyes large and wanting to trust him. "But you were under orders, you said. So—" Her voice trailed off.

He drew the sheet around her shoulders. "But the State of Katanga does not exist in law," he said. "So even if there were orders, the killings—" She gazed at him, not understanding. "They might be seen as criminal acts. Murders."

She scrutinized him, surprised at the word.

They watched each other, Gat wanting to hold the girl, but fearful of frightening her. Executions. He regarded them as murders. "If the Katanga secession fails, I could be hauled before a jury."

"But you were under orders."

"But not written orders." They watched each other. "Could I have refused to act without written orders? No. So it would be my word against that of the rich men. The Belgian mining magnates and Katanga politicians, they will all say, 'No one was to be executed. Gat acted on his own.' If that happens, I will pay the price."

Petra stared into Gat's eyes. He drew her to him. He was staring now at Petra's blonde hair, but he saw in his mind the face of the men he had killed, their eyes resigned but imploring. He smelled the odor of gunpowder, heard the gunshots reverberating, felt the chill of the night air and the presence behind him of the state dignitaries watching the murders. With his arms about the girl, he felt emptiness inside him. He tried to let his skin think for him, tried to feel only the girl.

"I can't believe you'd murder anyone," Petra said.

"Because you know nothing about me. I did it. I executed them."

"Who were they?"

"I can't tell you who."

"Men I'd heard of?" Gat said nothing. Finally he released Petra, lay on his back, and pulled the blanket to his waist. "That's why it would have been chivalrous to leave in the middle of the night."

Petra said, "I don't understand any of this." He had been so gentle with her, leading her so safely where she wanted to go, into womanhood. "Why did you come here?"

"My commanding officer ordered me to take some leave."

"Why not Europe?"

"It's winter there. I didn't want to be any colder than I was already feeling."

"It bothered you then."

"Of course, it bothered me! I've been used by industrialists who want—at any cost—to preserve their wealth. I'm not the only one who's bothered. There's another officer down here. He's sure they'll send someone to assassinate us."

Petra felt a cold shiver of fear and turned to snuggle against him. "Why?"

"So we can't tell anyone." She turned him toward her. "I don't think that's going to happen," he assured her. "It infuriates me to be used that way. And I may have used you. For that I'm sorry."

"How have you used me?"

"Ever since this happened, I've felt dead inside. I needed to act out the processes of—" He hesitated. "Of making joy with someone like you. I've needed to hold on to someone like you. To get my life back."

"You didn't use me. I wanted it to happen. For all you know I used you."

"Anytime," he told her. "Available anytime for that."

"Drive me to Joeys," Petra implored. "I couldn't stand it if I never saw you again." She smiled mischievously. "Anyway I want to tell the girls in the dorm that it was my lover, not my parents, who brought me to varsity."

WHILE GAT showered, Petra put on a robe and went to the small parlor to retrieve the clothes she shed there. As she was returning back up the stairs, the phone rang. "Petra, are you feeling better?" Kobus asked. "I called earlier. Were you asleep?"

"I must have been in the bathroom. I'm a little better." She realized her voice sounded healthy. "Maybe I should stay in town. You go out to Stellenbosch. I'll—"

"But when will I see you then?"

She really did not want to see anyone just now, she said. She had been up a good part of the night and parts of her body were feeling in ways they never had. It delighted her to spin not-quite falsehoods and hear Kobus's concern, his voice cooing with sympathy. She insisted that she could not see anyone just now and hung up as soon as she could.

When Petra returned to the guest room, Gat helped her out of the robe. When she went to bathe and put on a summer dress, he took the boxes that she had packed for the move to varsity and put them into the back hall downstairs. Then he took the towels soaking in the bathroom sink and their bed sheet down to the service porch off the kitchen. He scrubbed the blood out of them and left them soaking.

When he entered the kitchen, he found Petra pushing burnt eggs out of a skillet into the sink with a spatula. "Do you know how to fry eggs?" she asked.

Gat suppressed an urge to laugh. "Yes, I do."

"I'm sure you think I should know. I've watched Elsie, but I've made a mess." Gat could not keep from smiling. "Don't laugh at me!" Petra commanded. "I'm trying to get breakfast for my man."

"That's why we leave in the middle of the night," Gat said. He laughed heartily.

"Don't patronize me!" Petra retorted, amused herself. "You think I'm a useless rich girl, don't you?"

"Splendidly useless." She hit at him with the spatula. He grabbed it, still laughing, to keep it away from his clothes. He wrenched the spatula from her hand and retrieved the skillet from the sink. "You need to grease this thing," he explained, still amused. He wiped the skillet dry.

The doorbell rang. They looked at one another. "We won't answer it," Petra whispered.

"Do you have some butter?" Gat spoke in a tone so low she could hardly hear him. He pantomimed spreading butter on toast. She took a plate of it from the refrigerator. He sliced a bit of it and placed it on the skillet to melt.

The doorbell rang again.

Petra and Gat looked at one another. He whispered, "After the pan's greased, you put in the eggs. How many do you want?" She raised a single finger. Gat broke three eggs into the skillet and whispered, "You try not to break the yolk."

"And you didn't!" she replied gleefully, whispering. "Aren't you smart?"

The doorbell rang yet again, quite insistently.

"It must be Kobus," Petra said, disconcerted. "No trades-man would ring like that."

Gat tossed salt and pepper onto the eggs. Petra stayed his hand on the pepper. "Do I turn yours?" Gat asked. "Or leave it looking at you?"

"Looking at me, I guess," Petra said. She held her breath, listening. "I think he's gone." She smiled. "Whew!"

Gat pulled her to him "Are you paying attention here?" he asked. "When you spend the night with men at varsity, you'll want to know how to cook their eggs." She elbowed him.

A knocking, very loud, came at the back door. Petra froze. She looked toward the window in the back door and saw Kobus Terreblanche staring at her and Gat. "Petra!" he cried. "Open the door."

Petra seemed unable to move. Gat went to the door, unlocked and opened it. Terreblanche burst into the kitchen, confused by what he saw. Even so he breathed out righteous indignation. "What's going on here?" he demanded.

"I'm teaching Petra to fry eggs," Gat said. "Do you want to learn?"

"I know how to fry eggs," Terreblanche retorted. "What are you doing here?"

"There are three eggs here," Gat pointed out. "Would you like one?"

Terreblanche looked at Petra. "What's he doing here?"

Petra told him, "He's driving me to Wits."

"Your parents are driving you to Wits!"

"Change of plan," said Petra.

Terreblanche blurted, "You don't even know him!"

"Plates?" asked Gat.

Petra opened the cupboard and reached for breakfast plates. "Are you having an egg, Kobus?"

"I'm very good with eggs," Gat assured him.

Terreblanche glared at Petra. "No, I'm not having an egg!" he said with a voice that sliced the space between them. "And you're not sick!" Petra turned her back to him, took two plates, and handed them to Gat. He served the eggs. Terreblanche scrutinized him. "You haven't shaved!" Then it dawned on him. "You spent the night here!"

Petra got out forks. Gat put the plates on the table where Elsie usually ate.

Terreblanche took Petra by the arm and whirled her toward him. "Did he spend the night here?"

Gat took a fork from Petra and began to eat his eggs. "It's getting cold," he reminded her. Petra pulled loose from Terreblanche's grip and sat down to eat.

"What's going on here?" Terreblanche cried. "You don't even know him!"

Gat and Petra ignored the man. But he would not be ignored. He leaned over the table and put a large open hand over each plate. "Answer me, Petra!"

Petra got up from the table to face Terreblanche on her feet. "You always treated me like a child, Kobus. He treated me like a woman. Now get out of here. My life isn't any of your business."

"Does your father know about this?" Terreblanche asked.

Gat stood and looked at Terreblanche with all the patience he could muster.

"I should beat you to a pulp," the young man said.

"He's an army officer, Kobus," Petra said. "He can beat you around the block."

Gat and Terreblanche glared at one another. The young man was taller than Gat and well-built. But he was a student of the law, not warfare. At last he turned his back on Gat as if he would not stoop to the indignity of a fight. He went to the sink, washed his hands, and left the kitchen without a backward look.

Once he had gone, Petra sat down and covered her face with her hands. Gat knelt beside her and stroked her back. "Will he telephone my father?" she asked. "What will he do?"

PETRA DROVE up before the Protea Hotel in the 1957 Ford sedan, the Rousseaus' second car, the one she was allowed to drive (though not at night). She examined the Protea's façade and turned at Gat. "This is certainly not the Mount Nelson. No wonder you preferred to stay with me."

"I knew the bed would be better." He thought it unnecessary to tell her that he'd spent nights in places infinitely worse than this, had been billeted in brothels, had slept for months in the bed of a pickup, had rejoiced on occasion to find shelter in a mud hut. She gazed at him both fondly and uncertainly and answered his grin with one of her own.

While Gat went to shave and fetch his luggage, Petra waited in the Ford sedan. She knew she should be wondering who Gat was. Instead she thought about the notes she had left at the house. One was for Elsie, explaining that her cousin Hazel had spent the night in the guest room and had had "an accident" that the two girls had made unsuccessful efforts to clean up. She wondered if Elsie would be suspicious of these falsehoods.

The other note told her parents that attending university in Johannesburg was a chance for her to assert her independence. So she had driven there with a friend. She would return the Ford as soon as she could. Reading that, her father would sink into one of his black moods, especially if Kobus Terreblanche felt impelled to inform him who the friend was. If her father learned that, it would be very hard for her mother to control him.

When Gat entered the hotel room, he saw no evidence that Michels had slept there. He wondered where his buddy had spent the night, where he was now. But Michels would have to take care of himself. Gat shaved, packed his belongings, made certain he had left nothing, and checked out.

Outside the hotel he found that Petra and the Ford were gone. Perhaps she had panicked, he thought. He should not have said so much about Katanga. He took his bags to the awning-covered verandah, bought a *Cape Times* in the lobby, and settled down to read it.

He scanned for news from the Congo. There was none. Glancing through the paper, his eye caught a report, no more than a paragraph, headlined: Tourist Murdered in District Six.

He skimmed the piece until he came to the words "Gabriel Michels, 28, an army officer from the ex-Belgian Congo." He read the piece carefully. It reported that Michels's body had been found outside a bar, apparently after a knife fight. That was all.

Gat read the paragraph three times. A"knife fight"? He recalled that occasionally Michels had boasted of taking care of business that way. But he boasted of so much. Had he been carrying a switchblade? Or had he been "eliminated"?

Gat thrust the paper aside and stared across the road at the ocean. Had an assassin been sent to South Africa to eliminate men Belgian officials had ordered to disappear? That seemed a likelier explanation than that Michels, with his dream of Canada and his penchant for stumbling into trouble, had gotten caught in a situation he could not control.

Gat was certain that Colonel Rousseau would learn of Michels's death. He would pair the Belgian officers together. Fortunately he had not mentioned Michels to the girl. He resolved to tell her nothing of what he'd learned. But it was just as well to be leaving Cape Town. At that moment Petra parked the cream-colored Ford sedan before the hotel.

Gat grabbed his bags and hurried toward her. "Going my way?" he asked jauntily, shoving his bags among the pile of her belongings in the rear seat.

"Did you miss me?" she asked.

"Didn't think of you once."

"Oh, really? Why the grin?"

"Facial tic. You driving some place I might want to go?"

"We could find out."

Gat watched her, thinking: Christ, she's pretty. So fresh. Desire tickled his groin.

Once in the car, Petra told him, "I have a present for you. But you can't have it yet." She smiled mysteriously. "And I have something in mind for me. I'll tell you when I give you your present."

She drove them east out of the city, turned off the main road toward Hermanus, passed through the tiny dorp and out onto a road that skirted the ocean. "My grandmother grew up out here," she told Gat. "I used to come here with her." She parked along a deserted stretch of beach. She pointed off toward a small bay several hundred meters from where they were parked. "I love this beach," she said. "I want you to see it."

"Let's take a swim."

They walked barefoot to the beach, carrying their swimsuits and the towels Petra had brought. Gat held up a towel while Petra changed, peeking over it most of the time. "Don't look at me!" she implored.

"But I love to look at you. You have a wonderful body."

She turned her back to him and placed her left arm over the cleft in her buttocks. Gat laughed at her and put on his suit without benefit of towel.

They ran into the surf and swam as lovers do, splashing one another, dunking each other, pretending to be whales, spouting water into the air and at one another, swimming underwater to catch each other's legs, doing back somersaults, floating, embracing. Eventually Gat treaded water close to her, his hands below the surface. Finally one hand rose above the water holding his swimsuit. "There's no one around," he said. "Why not?" Petra scanned the shore, saw no one, and struggled out of her suit.

Gat swam to her, "This is better!" he said, holding her to him, the taste of salt in their mouths, the feel of their wet, chilled skin against one another in the warm sun, their heads bobbing under the surface as Gat tried to tread water vigorously enough to keep them both afloat. At long last they left the water, Gat still holding their suits. He threw them onto the towels.

Petra hugged him then, her pelvis thrust into his body. "Can we here?"

"No," he said. "Never near sand." He kissed her very hard.

A few miles farther on they found a small hotel and had lunch on the patio. As they were finishing, Gat suggested, "What if we took a room for the afternoon?" Petra blushed, grinned mischievously, and blushed even more deeply.

Gat went to the office to ask if he and his wife could have a room for the afternoon. He explained that they were on their honeymoon. The bottom half of the hotelier's face smiled obligingly while the upper half, the eyes, examined him carefully. Petra entered and spread her hands on the office counter. She was wearing a wedding ring. The hotelier saw it and agreed to give them a room.

They climbed the stairs to the room in silence. As he unlocked the door, Gat asked, "Where'd you get that ring?"

"What a sweet room!" Petra exclaimed. She put her valise on the table under the dormer and opened the window onto its view of the ocean.

"Where'd you get that ring?" he repeated, beginning to undress.

"I went shopping this morning," she said, pleased with herself. "I have one for you." She withdrew a small box from her valise and gave it to him. He opened the box and gazed at the band of gold. "It won't bite," she said. "I had to guess about the size." She watched him look at the ring. "The rings are my present to you," she said. "Your present to me is to wear yours." Gat's eyes shifted from the ring to Petra. "At least in the hotel," Petra said.

Gat looked back at the ring without speaking.

"I don't know what happens in the rest of the world," Petra told him, "but this is South Africa. There are Puritans here, especially among Afrikaners. My father's one. So is Kobus. A nice girl does not have a lover. She doesn't even use that word. She doesn't go to a hotel with a man who's not her husband." Petra implored him with her eyes. "My reputation may not mean anything to you. But—" Her voice faded as her emotion rose.

Gat gently touched her face. He liked her very much and was afraid that he might hurt her. Not wanting to be a child did not necessarily make a girl ready to be a woman. Yet he had made her one. Moreover, pleasure like this, coming to a hotel for sex, was for adults. "We're having a good time together," he told the girl. "But we don't know each other very well." He kissed her lightly and tried to smile. "And you're pretty new at this."

Tears began to well up in her eyes. "Can't you just wear it in the hotel?"

"Yes, I can do that," he said, but he did not move. She took the ring from the box and slipped it on his finger. "The fit's pretty good," he allowed. Then he looked at her. "You understand what's happening, right? You're on your way to university and I will be going back to Katanga. That means we can have a good time with each other and then we'll say good-bye."

She nodded.

"I'm a little worried that I've taken you along a path you aren't ready yet to travel." She shook her head and wiped away her tears. Well, he thought, the damage had been done. He kissed her sweetly. "Thank you for the ring."

Suddenly they were shy with each other. They'd taken the room to make love and Gat was eager to start. The arousal he'd felt on the beach was impatient to find its release. Petra took off her dress, but instead of feeling beautiful under his eyes, as she had at the beach, standing in her bra and half-slip she felt naked. She held the dress up before her. Gat had been watching her and smiled. She went to a chair well across the room from him and sat on it. She lowered her eyes.

He removed his shoes, put his wallet, handkerchief, and watch into one of them. When he started to take off his trousers, he sensed that she was not yet ready to have that done. This was a nuisance, he thought, but she was very young. If there was to be pleasure between them, he could not take it from her. She would have to give it. He rezipped his fly and fastened his belt.

"Come sit with me here," he suggested. He went to the bed and sat with his back against the headboard. She came to the opposite side of the bed, still holding the dress before her. She sat beside him and looked out the window at the sea. He took her hand and held it in both his hands. Neither of them spoke.

Finally she asked, "Why did you come to Africa?"

Gat glanced at her. He really did like her very much: her beauty, her courage, both her boldness and timidity, her desire to find out who she was and who he was. If he must, he could wait a few minutes to make love to her. He smiled a little embarrassedly.

She sensed his embarrassment and looked at him curiously. "Tell me."

"When I was a kid—I couldn't even have been ten—I heard about a remote area of the Congo. Some Belgians had visited it. Our cockeyed parish priest must have told me about it. And I was so young that I believed every word. This place was so removed from areas where men went that the animals—zebras, gazelles and giraffes, elephants and hippos, rhinos and warthogs—all lived there in peace. They had never seen man."

"I'd love to know that place," Petra said.

"When these Belgians found the place, the animals were not afraid of them. They could walk right up to them and touch them." Gat smiled ruefully, dismayed at his own gullibility. "I thought of it as some enormous petting zoo. Men could go up to grazing animals and pet their hides and put their arms around the necks of gazelles and wildebeests and waterbucks who were grazing. Somehow they could even reach up to giraffes with their heads stretched into clouds of leaves . . . That's how I imagined this place."

"How sweet," she said. She leaned against him, lay her head on his shoulder.

"You won't tell anyone, right?" he asked.

She shook her head. "Your secret is safe with me."

"I think I came to Africa to find that place." He smiled to himself. "Isn't that dumb?"

"No," she said. "I like you for it." She turned to him, took his head in her hands, and kissed him. Then she left the bed and finished undressing, enjoying the feel of his eyes on her.

As THEY lay side by side, listening to the pounding of the distant waves, Petra said, "My father would be horrified at what I'm doing."

"Let's not talk about your father."

"He'll be furious when he finds out. He has very black moods."

Gat said nothing. One problem with seducing a girl who had not yet left home was that she was likely to talk about her parents.

"Sometimes he doesn't talk to us for several days," Petra said. "He'll be at home, moving around in a black cloud, and he won't say a word to me or my mother."

He stroked her blonde hair. "What brings on these moods?" he asked. It was important that they talk. If this was her subject, they would pursue it.

"His work. He claims that he never brings his work home." She imitated her father, replicating his Afrikaans accent. "'A policeman should never take his work home.' He means the mental part. That's what he always says. But, of course, he does exactly that when he's in one of his blacks."

"He never tells you anything about his work?"

"Nothing. Ever," she said. Gat thought that he could tell her a few things about it. "I think he sees things . . . Or reads things . . . That turn his stomach."

"What sort of things?"

"The kaffirs take knives to each other," she said. "And to their women." Gat thought of someone knifing Michels and of things he himself had seen in the *cités* of Congo towns. "I guess there are sexual crimes that are pretty terrible to think about."

"Like me taking you to places like this."

"It's the sort of thing he might get pretty exercised about."

"Should I have asked his permission?" Petra smiled. Gat asked, "What about torture? Do you think that causes black moods?"

The girl was quiet. "He doesn't torture anyone. Please."

"Didn't I hear you talking about people being thrown out of windows?"

"Kaffir police do that to other kaffirs. It's never supposed to happen, but sometimes . . . Do you think he . . . ?"

"You know him better than I do. I'm sure he doesn't."

"You met him on one of his better days. He's always in good spirits when Kobus is around. Kobus admires him the way a dog admires its master."

"Yes, I thought Kobus had some canine features."

The girl snuggled closer. "Kobus is like a second son to him."

"You have a brother?"

"JC. Jan-Christiaan. Like Smuts. He and Kobus were great friends before he left."

"He left?"

"He and Father disagreed over just about everything. He thought kaffirs should have more rights."

"You don't think so?"

"Of course. But it's very complicated. We do have different ways of living. Father feels—"

Lying in bed with the man's daughter Gat did not care what her father thought. He kissed her mouth to stop her talking. The look of longing on her face told him that she was still thinking of her brother. Finally she said, "JC's the one who played the piano in the parlor."

"Where is he now?"

"In the UK. London. He hasn't spoken to Father in two years. Father never mentions him. We never talk about him at home."

Gat wondered what Rousseau would do to him if he ever caught up with him. "Is your mother in touch with him?"

"Now and then. But Father mustn't know."

"Your father must love him very much if he won't talk about him."

"It hurt him very much that he left South Africa."

"Would he be hurt if you left?"

"Not as much as with JC," she acknowledged. "Father has a strong sense of family. He wants us around. Wants to know the people we do things with." After a moment Petra said, "I love him very much."

"That must please him. Your going off with me won't."

"I love it that he has something he believes in." She paused, then explained. "The *volk*. His people. It's like a religion with him."

"Not 'our people'? You said 'his people.'"

"Funny, isn't it? I don't feel like an Afrikaner. Mother wouldn't let us speak Afrikaans at home. It's a big disappointment for Father."

THEY DECIDED to spend the night in the little hotel. At sunset they walked barefoot along the water line of the beach where they'd swum, their arms about each other's waists. Petra breathed deeply of the salt air and watched the sky redden in the west. Was this, she wondered, what it was like to be newly married? On a honeymoon you could drift wherever you liked and make love whenever you wanted. She was a newlywed. She did not feel naughty, felt hardly a trace of guilt.

How could she? Gat was so sweet. So able to make both her body and her soul feel as she had never dreamt of them feeling. And still as naive and idealistic as a child! Yet admittedly an executioner. How strange!

"Do you have brothers and sisters?" Petra asked.

"An older sister. We were great friends. I haven't seen her in years."

"Why not?"

"She married an American, lives there. They met traveling as students. We write now and then. And I have two younger brothers. I hardly know them."

Petra was glad that Gat and his sister were friends just as she and JC were.

"Why did you join the army?"

"You're full of questions."

"I want to know you."

Gat continued to march along the beach, holding the girl tightly against him, nuzzling her blonde head. "When I finished secondary school," he said, "my parents sent me to Britain. My mum is English. I was there for a year. I lived with relatives of my mother's."

"Did you have girlfriends?"

"Five or six." She glanced up at him. He was grinning and she did not know whether or not to believe him. "Let's see . . . Brenda and Deirdre and Eleanor." Were these girls real? She did not know. "Shopkeepers' daughters."

"Did you sleep with them?"

"Whenever they let me!"

He halted, laughing. He kissed her and hoisted her into his arms. "Put me down!" she ordered. "I must weigh a ton."

He continued the march at the water line, Petra in his arms. "In fact, in England I was very lonely. I spoke bad English with a Flemish accent and all the girls laughed at me." Petra flung her arms about his neck, making it easier for him to carry her. "At the end of that year I didn't want to stay in Britain. Or go back to Belgium."

"You wanted a place big enough for your dreams."

"You're the corny one!" he said. He took her to dry sand and dropped her onto it. She threw sand at him. He skipped toward the surf. She came after him, stooped to splash water at him, then ran off. He chased her, homed in on her as a predator might on a prey, grabbed her, and devoured her. He once again swept her up into his arms and marched along the beach.

"The choices of where to go were America or Africa," Gat said. "I took passage on a boat to the Congo because, being

Belgian, I figured there'd be jobs in our national colony for a young man like me."

"Were there?"

"I tried different things. They didn't work out. The Force Publique needed officers. So I joined up."

"Did you look for that remote place where the animals had never seen man?"

He shook his head. He put her down and they walked without speaking.

After a while Petra said, "You don't seem like an army officer to me."

"Oh?" Gat cocked his head. "How should I seem?" Petra did not reply. She feared that if she mentioned what she saw as his idealism, he might take offense. Certainly her father was scornful of idealists. "As officers of the Force Publique, we were really there to maintain public order," Gat said. "We saw to it that people played by the rules. At least the blacks and the lower-class whites."

"Were your Force Publique mates ruthless? I don't think you are."

"You've found my failing." Gat smiled. "Promise to work on that, sir!"

"My father is," Petra said. "He can be very charming. In fact, most of the time he is. But he can also be very demanding."

Interesting, Gat thought, that Petra recognized her father's ruthlessness, but seemed not to understand how that trait expressed itself in the work he never brought home. "It's command quality," he said. "Most top officers in the Force Publique have it." They reversed direction and as the light faded from the sky walked back toward the hotel. Gat asked, "You don't see command quality in me?"

"Yes, I do," Petra said. "But you're not ruthless. If you were, they wouldn't have had to send you here after whatever it was that happened in Katanga."

Gat watched the breakers. The foam, pink-orange at sunset, was now a muted gray. "These men in Katanga . . ." he said. "They were very special men."

"Ordinary people: you don't mind killing them?" Petra teased. Gat did not reply. "These official murders. They've been eating at you," she said. Gat shrugged. He did not want to acknowledge this fact; it seemed womanish to let sentiment complicate duty. "That sort of thing doesn't eat at my father," Petra said. "Of course, he doesn't— He just supervises. So long as he's convinced that what he does furthers the interests of whites in South Africa, especially Afrikaners, he'll do it."

"And what do you think about that?" Gat asked.

"I'm not supposed to think about it. He tries to keep me a child so I won't." They walked in silence.

Finally Petra asked, "What about your parents? Do you love them?"

"We've lost track of each other."

"Really?" After a moment she wondered aloud, "You have no one?"

"I have you."

Petra could not tell if he was teasing. But his needing some stranger like her, a woman to sleep with, to save his life now seemed to make more sense.

BACK IN the hotel Gat made a reservation for dinner in an hour. While he used the public men's room off the bar, Petra went to their room. She used the bathroom, appreciative of Gat's delicacy in offering her privacy. She went to the window and stood facing toward the waves she heard, but could hardly make out in the gathering darkness. She wondered what they would do in the hour before dinner. What did people do in hotels anyway? Should they again? Wouldn't too much sate their appetite for it? If Gat made no moves toward it when he came in, would she be disappointed?

When Gat returned, he lighted a bedside lamp. He went to her, placed his hands gently on her shoulders, and stood close behind her. He kissed the back of her head. He went to his luggage, opened it, fished around, and pulled out a book. He kicked off his shoes and went to the bed to read with his back against the headboard, the book in the yellow spill of light.

Petra stood at the window, looking from it, but seeing nothing, feeling hurt, feeling angry. Did he no longer want her?

Gat opened his book, found his place, read a few words. He looked up. Why did he feel tension in the room? "Come sit beside me," he suggested. "You can see out the window from here."

"There's nothing to see," she said. He looked back at the book. She turned toward him. "What are you reading?"

He had to look at the cover to tell her the title of the book. "Something called *The Stranger*," he said. "French. By a fellow named Camus."

"You like it?"

"Hard to get into." He patted the bed beside him. "Come sit here." Petra did not move. "It's about Algeria. I asked for something about Africa at a place on upper Kloof Street. I had time to kill before the coffeehouse and this is what they had." He closed the book and laid it in his lap. He once again patted the bed beside him. She felt strangely self-conscious, uncertain what to do.

Gat watched her, masking his amusement, understanding that she was stuck in that region where she was neither woman nor child and that she could not move until she sorted out which one at the moment she was. Gat rose, went to her, took her hand, and pulled her to the bed. He seated her on one side of it. She folded her hands in her lap. He bounced across the bed to resume his seat beside the lamp. Finally she was able to place her back against the headboard next to his. He took her hand in his.

"Why was that so hard?" he asked.

"I don't know," she said. "It just was."

He kissed her hand, turned to glance at her. "You're silly," he said, "but rather likable." He turned off the lamp. He put his arm around her shoulders. They held each other in the darkness until it was time to go to dinner. The only sound was that of their breathing and the far-off murmur of the waves.

Locals gave them the once-over as they passed through the bar. Feeling the weight of their stares, Petra glanced at Gat with an apprehensive expression. Obviously the hotelier had told the locals that he had newlyweds as guests. In fact, they looked newly married, shy with each other, but each still enjoying—and sustained by—the touch of the other. Entering the dining room, Gat drew Petra close to him and whispered, "Head up. Who cares what they think?" Petra smiled at him gratefully and forced herself to stand erect. The hotelier led them outside. He seated them at a secluded table at the far end of the dining porch. With an amused smile playing at the edges of his mouth, he lighted candles, offered them a choice of two entrees, and left them alone.

Gat whispered, "You don't like getting credit for what we haven't been doing?"

"I hardly know you and they all think I'm married to you."

"I wouldn't say hardly," Gat objected. "I've had my hands all over you."

Petra blushed. Watching her redden in the candlelight, he chuckled. He leaned close to her, slipped his hand under her dress and slip, and patted her knee. "What would you like for dinner?"

"What I would like is that you take your hand out from under my dress." Amused, Gat complied. "Thank you," she said, a little primly.

They both had the fish. While waiting for it to arrive Gat gazed at Petra. It made her very self-conscious. "Please don't keep watching me."

"You feeling that you've been on a rather long date?"

"I've never been alone with a man for a full night and day." He took her hand. "Is this what marriage is like? I mean: it just goes on?" He nodded. "Have you ever been married?"

"No." He smiled indulgently. "I like being with you. You're my friend. So I don't mind that it just goes on."

"I keep thinking I have to make conversation."

"Your parents have brought you up to be a good little— What?"

"A good little something I don't want to be."

"Let's not worry about talking. Let's just be friends."

It distressed Gat that they had been so comfortable in their room, holding one another, he drawing survival from her, as darkness enclosed them in its quietude. And now, as if that interlude never happened, she needed reassurance that they were linked by golden threads of conversation. But if she needed those connections, he would try to supply them.

When their dinners were served, he told her about his first years in the Congo: how he had arrived there with a harebrained notion that because he was young and willing to work, he could become a planter. How he had taken it for granted that because he was white, rubber trees would grow out of the soil of the colony's Equateur province for him, that their latex would flow and provide him a livelihood. How he had assumed that the failure of the plantation from which he rented his hectares was caused by the laziness and drunkenness of the planter, his sexual indulgence with black concubines, not by bad soil and unreliable rains. "I was such a fool!" he told her with a laugh. "I had bought an old pickup and was living out of the cargo bed. I disapproved of the dissolute planter and would not turn to him for help. I probably would have starved if it had not been for the Africans in a village nearby. They took pity on me. I was grateful to eat the scraps they threw away."

Petra stopped eating. She stared at him with astonishment as if he filed his teeth and had a bone through his nose. "You ate what Africans did not want?"

"And was glad to have it." They stared at one another. "I couldn't subsist on the fruit of rubber trees." She put her fork down and folded her hands into her lap. "Shall I take you back to Cape Town? You could telephone Kobus to meet us somewhere." Petra stared at her plate. Gat went on eating.

After a moment she shook her head. "I was attracted to you because I'd never met anyone like you." She glanced at him. "You really are different."

"'*Was* attracted.' Has the feeling flown?"

She pushed fish onto her fork with her knife. "Did you ever find that place where the animals had never seen man?"

She had already asked him that. But he would answer again the question in order to keep them conversing. "Now that I think of it," Gat said, "I'm sure that story must have been told me by the priest, a man who'd never been anywhere."

Petra glanced at him, grateful they were talking. "Seems that as the Belgians went farther into that peaceable kingdom, they came across what appeared to them to be monkey creatures."

"Monkey creatures?" Petra asked. She gazed at Gat with an amused and disdainful expression, no doubt often bestowed on her father.

"Except they had no tails," he persevered.

"You believed this as a child?" she asked.

"As the Belgians investigated this unexpected discovery, the monkey creatures became aware of them. They scrutinized each other. And they all realized at the very same moment . . ."

"That they were men," said Petra.

"Yes! And recognizing each other, they rushed together and embraced. And the monkey creatures said, 'We are men like you!' And the Belgians said: 'We will show you how to live more fully! We will make art together and do science and you will be more fulfilled than you ever have been!' And so they all embraced and danced together."

Petra smiled at Gat indulgently. She took his hand.

"Do you know this story?" he asked her.

She shrugged. "Go on."

"That's it," Gat said. "That's what I learned at the priest's knee."

"Did you also believe in Father Christmas? I did—for a time."

"I believed this because the priest told me. Seminary was the most he'd seen of the world. They told him fanciful stories there too. I'm sure he believed them."

AFTER DINNER they walked again on the beach. Petra told Gat about her schooling and friends and family vacations, about the arguments she'd had to endure before her father would permit her to apply to Wits. Gat asked about the studies she hoped to pursue and she told him about how those pursuits had raised the ire of her father. Anthropology? No! Sociology? No! Political Science? No! She would take a variety of courses her first year to survey possibilities.

Petra asked Gat about joining the army. He told her about running out of options, about wanting to make a success of himself after failing as a planter. "So I joined the Force Publique. The surest way to succeed there was to take on the attitudes of the Belgians who were my comrades. They all thought Africans were savages—*macaques,* we called them, monkeys."

Petra glanced up at him. They were walking in step, their arms about each other's waists, and in the darkness she could make out only the outline of his face.

"For the first few years I accepted that Africans were savages, at least the ones we were dealing with in the Force. After all, we were the civilizers. But I knew that they weren't all 'savage'—whatever that's supposed to mean—because when I was trying to be a planter, the people in the village had come to my rescue."

"They saved your life. Right? Just the way I'm saving it."

He drew her against him and kissed the side of her head as they walked. "What I've come to understand is that there's raw savagery. I've seen plenty of that: people running around all but naked, living in grass huts, and hunting with nets and knives. There's also civilized savagery; lately I've seen plenty of that. Civilized people should know better; they make the rules."

Petra stopped walking. When Gat turned toward her, she put her arms around him and held him close. "You're angry," she said. He did not move, but she felt him drawing away. He started walking again. She followed beside him. "Why?" He said nothing. She stopped walking and watched him disappear into the darkness. She wondered if he would leave her. At last he returned and put his arm around her shoulders. They began walking again.

"When I was playing at being a planter," Gat finally began, "I was near to starving and the villagers helped me. They were the ones who showed me what was civilized." It angered him, Gat said, that virtually all Belgians in the Congo knew Africans were men, but treated them if not precisely like monkeys, then like a lesser species of humanity.

"At first we made them carry loads," he said. "If that worked them to death, no matter; there were plenty of others to take their places. Then we made them gather wild rubber for us. Each man had his quota. When he didn't fill it, we chopped off his hand. That didn't matter either, we figured, because there were plenty more. The collector of hands—there was such a person—began to suspect that he was being sent the hands of women and children. So when a man did not fulfill his quota, they began to cut off his penis."

Petra recoiled. She had never heard a man use that word in conversation. She stopped walking and turned away from Gat. He came to her slowly, touched her. She brushed his hand away. "Why are you telling me these things?"

"You asked why I was angry."

"Do you even know if they're true?"

"They're true."

"Who told you?"

"The people in the village. I had a friend whose great-grandfather lost a hand."

"I'm going back," Petra said. She started walking toward the distant lights of the hotel. Gat trudged along behind her. When they reached the hotel, she went toward the small library. "I'll join you in a bit," Gat called. He headed to the bar.

In the bar Gat wanted to order a whiskey. He needed one. He knew he had said too much. The girl might be trying to escape too much protection, but she did not know how to deal with what he told her. If she smelled liquor on him, he thought, she might not let him kiss her. He looked about to see if there was someone from whom he could bum a cigarette. But if he smoked, the girl would smell its odor. She would taste it on his lips if she allowed him to kiss her. She might pull away. So he ordered coffee and drank it in a corner by himself.

In the library as Petra thumbed through magazines, her mother's voice chattered in her head, repeating advice she had often provided about strange men luring trusting, inexperienced girls into trouble. Petra glanced about the room. Could she spend the night here? Certainly she could not spend the night in the room with Gat. She paged through magazine after magazine, hearing her mother's voice, seeing her father's face.

After a time Gat entered. Petra glanced at him, then looked away. He took a chair across from her, picked up a magazine, and feigned reading. At last he looked up at her and said, "I'm sorry I've frightened you."

Petra said nothing. She felt him watching her. She focused on the article before her. She forced her lips silently to form the words of the article in order not to feel self-conscious about being watched. At last Gat said, "I asked about another room. There's one available." He had inquired of the bartender.

"Is that what you want?" She was relieved. But suddenly it seemed unfair that he should have to pay for two rooms. "I could sleep here. Or on the beach."

"It's not that expensive."

"I'm sorry I'm so—" She searched for the word.

"You're lovely. Don't apologize for anything."

His compliment made her want to trust him. She glanced at him, felt she should explain herself. "When you said you needed me to save your life . . . I thought you were tossing out some enormous whopper to intrigue me . . ." Her voice trailed off. She looked across the room at him. "That is sort of what you need, isn't it?"

"I seemed merely a liar. Is that why you took me home?" She looked down. The question embarrassed her. "I'm a bit more complicated than Kobus Terreblanche, I'm afraid." She glanced at him. "Have there been other men in your life besides Kobus? And me?"

"My father. You are definitely more complicated than him!"

Gat had a very strong impulse to cross the room and sit beside her, but he did not move.

"Why are you so angry?" she asked again. "Can't you tell me?"

"I thought I was telling you."

They gazed at each other a long moment without speaking.

"The villagers who rescued you when you were starving. Who were they?"

"At first there were three or four boys, maybe ten years old, who sometimes watched me work. They must have told people how hungry I was because late one afternoon they appeared at my truck with a girl. She had some food for me wrapped in a banana leaf."

"Who was she?"

Gat shrugged. "A village girl. Sixteen. Maybe younger."

"Pretty?"

"I saw her through my starving stomach. She brought me food. Of course, she was pretty!" Petra watched him, wanting more than an evasion. "By local standards she was too skinny. But then so was I."

"Did you fall in love with her?"

"I'd have fallen in love with a witch if she'd brought me food!" They were silent for a moment. Gat added, "The truth is, we could hardly communicate. But after I'd eaten her food, I rubbed my stomach and kicked my legs in glee. She understood that I was thanking her."

"Did she come often?" Petra asked.

Gat nodded. He knew what she was asking and he told her. "It wasn't long before she was spending the night." He watched to see how she would react to learning that he had slept regularly with an African girl. It did not seem to surprise her. "I'd erected a frame over the back of my pickup. There was a tarpaulin on top for when it rained. Underneath that was a mosquito net. And a mattress."

"Was she the person whose great-grandfather had his hand cut off?" Gat nodded. "You loved her."

"You're thinking like a schoolgirl. We could hardly communicate."

Gat stared off across the room. He thought of nights in the back of the pickup: rain drumming on the tarpaulin, pounding the roof of the cab, streams of it splattering the ground, while mosquitoes buzzed seeking holes in the net, the smell of wet canvas dense in the nostrils and the thick wet air as he and she snuggled, dry in a sheet and light blanket and warm in the darkness.

"You loved her," Petra repeated.

"I loved being nineteen . . ." Gat shrugged, hearing in his mind the rain falling on the tarpaulin.

"I'll be nineteen next year," Petra said.

"I was out on my own. I savored doomed love and having a girl in my bed every night for a couple of weeks, a forbidden girl who fed my mouth and my body and was warm in the darkness. All this at a time when I had nothing and was sometimes aching with hunger." He looked at the ceiling, remembering the odor of wood-smoke the girl sometimes carried on her skin when she came from her mother's hut. "I thought about marrying her. At nineteen you can think of marrying anyone."

Not Kobus, Petra thought to herself.

"I loved the thought of marrying her because I knew it could never happen. I'd 've had to give goats to get her and we couldn't even talk to each other." Gat stared at the ceiling without speaking. Petra watched him, feeling strangely jealous of the uneducated village girl who evoked such nostalgia in him. "It wasn't all that idyllic," Gat said finally. "She wanted a child. African women want children. I didn't want that. I'd seen the truth of that: half-caste was outcast. I didn't want any kid of mine to face ridicule from playmates because of the skin color I'd given him." After a moment he added, "Her father didn't like her coming to me. He wanted nothing to do with white men. He was the one who told me about hands being cut off. And the other mutilations."

"How did it end?"

"She stopped coming. After three or four days I went to the village, afraid she was sick. It turned out she was married." Petra sat forward as if uncertain she had heard correctly. "Her father had taken goats from a man in a nearby village who wanted a third wife, a young wife. She had not even been able to say good-bye." Gat pulled his gaze down from the ceiling and looked at Petra. She realized that once again he was in the room with her. "I was devastated," he said. "I looked around at what I'd accomplished. Which was nothing. So I packed up the pickup and drove out of there."

As they looked at one another, Petra realized that it would not be necessary, after all, for them to sleep separately. But how could she let Gat know this? She could tell him, but the words would not come.

Gat understood what she was thinking. He knew he must go to her, but how—without scaring her? Finally he made himself traverse the four paces to the couch and sat beside her. He did not look at her. He took her arm and placed her hand in his. They sat without speaking. Finally she looked at him. He leaned toward her. They kissed tentatively at first, their lips hardly touching. Then with more passion. Finally Gat said, "I think we better go upstairs."

In their room holding one another in the darkness, they chatted and kidded each other. They lay slumbering, caressing, kissing.

"I definitely like you," Gat said. It was a promotion from "rather." "So let me give you some advice."

"No advice! All the other men who like or say they love me—my father and Kobus—always give me advice. I don't want advice."

"Get out of South Africa," he said.

She was quiet for a moment. "They don't give me that advice."

"Forget varsity, as you people call it. Go someplace. Now."

"You're serious, aren't you?"

"You want to be a woman. Be a free one."

"Don't I need an education?"

"Of course, you need one." He stroked her hair. "But you're a bright girl. Go someplace where you can get into university. The UK. Where your brother is."

They lay in the quiet of the night. "Going someplace: it would mean starting my life all over."

"It'd be hard for a few years," Gat admitted. "Eventually you'd make friends. Get an education, find a job, find a husband, have children. You'd be glad you did."

She made no reply and turned her back to him. He moved against her, his chest against her back. He slid one arm under her neck and the other across her body and under her. Gat held her close, knowing that this advice made her feel very alone. She moved her hand to her face and brushed tears from her eyes.

"Are you crying?"

"This is my homeland."

He held her even closer and whispered to her. "If you go to university here, you'll marry a South African."

"Is that so bad?"

"I'm sure he'll be a very good chap. Quite overcome by your beauty, your goodness. Eager to care and provide for you."

"Someone like Kobus."

"Yes. And if you wanted to be with him, you wouldn't be here with me."

"He's really quite a nice person."

"Yes. And he'll make sure you have a privileged life."

"Isn't that what we're supposed to want?"

"You think that privilege is going to last forever?" She made no reply. Gat said, "I've just come from a place where white people are trying to make their privilege last. And let me tell you: there's a cost involved in that. It's a cost I don't want you to have to pay."

At last she said, "There weren't enough of you. There are enough of us."

Gat held her close and thought, No, there aren't.

As GAT held Petra, taking from her the warmth and comfort that he regarded, a little dramatically, as saving his life, Kobus Terreblanche was downstairs in his father's den in his parents' home in Cape Town, calling yet again to the Rousseaus' hotel in Pretoria. This time the various operators put him through. "Colonel Rousseau," he said, "it's Kobus. I'm sorry to call so late. But the hotel kept saying you were out."

"How are you, Kobus?" Rousseau had stopped reviewing papers for his next day's meeting. Margaret was in bed, reading a magazine. "Everything all right?"

"Well, I'm not sure."

"Where are you, son? Stellenbosch?"

"I'm still in Cape Town, sir."

Rousseau glanced at his watch. "And Petra's with you? Is she all right?"

"She's not with me." Kobus closed his eyes against the dim light of his father's desk lamp. He sat in his underwear and was cold. "I think she's with the Belgian officer, Captain Gautier. The man we had lunch with Sunday."

"What?" Rousseau looked over at his wife. She put her magazine aside and sat straight up in bed.

"She told me she was sick yesterday," Kobus explained. "I went over to see her and she did look ill. I went by again this morning. She looked fine. The captain was there cooking them breakfast and he hadn't shaved."

Rousseau stood. Margaret left the bed, pulled on a robe, and came beside him to listen. Rousseau tilted the phone away from his ear so that she could hear what Kobus said. "Is this some kind of joke, Kobus? Because if it is—"

"It's not a joke, sir. I've been struggling with it all day—" Kobus stood as well. "Because I thought she loved me. But she spent last night with that bloke—"

"Spent the night with him? You mean—"

"I'm afraid so, sir." Margaret drew her robe closer about her. "She told me he was driving her to Wits and when I went by this afternoon, your Ford was gone." Rousseau and Margaret looked at one another, their mouths open in perplexity. "I thought you'd want to know, sir," Kobus said. "Anything you want me to do?"

"No, I don't think so. Thank you, son. We're glad you called. Good night."

Rousseau replaced the receiver in the cradle. He looked at his wife with an expression of complete bafflement. "Why would she have done such a thing?"

"Do we even know it's true?"

"Kobus certainly thinks it's true."

"Kobus is a nice boy," Margaret said. "But he tends to act as if he owns her. Petra may simply have wanted to give him a jolt."

"That Belgian? Was he attractive, did you think?"

"Attractive enough," Margaret said because her husband did not like her to find other men interesting. "He looked at her in a way Kobus never had."

"And she would have—" Rousseau could hardly speak the words. "Have spent the night with him because of that?"

"It's only sex, Piet. She had to try it out with someone."

"But she's so young!"

"You'd tried it out at her age." She smiled at her husband. "Yes, I know you think it's different for a man. But, after all, she's on her way to varsity."

Rousseau turned away from his wife. He did not want to listen to her. She saw one of his black moods coming on and knew to say nothing more. She hoped he would have himself under control the next day for his meetings.

Rousseau felt a quiet fury settle over him. He wondered what connection existed between Gautier and the man who'd been killed in District Six. The two men were connected; he was certain of that. They had come to do mischief in South Africa or flee mischief done elsewhere. He did not want this Gautier with his daughter. He called the hotel operator and had him put a call through to their home in Cape Town. Very shortly the operator called back to say there was no answer.

CHAPTER SIX

NEAR HERMANUS

WEDNESDAY, FEBRUARY 8, 1961

Petra lay absolutely still. Gat's arms were about her. They had been sleeping when suddenly he trembled, cried out, and sat up in bed. He had spoken to the darkness, words she could not understand. She had touched his back, felt the tension in it, and reassured him, "It's all right. You're here with me." She had felt him listening to the night, peering into the darkness. She had stroked his back. He had turned toward her, wrapped his arms about her, and finally relaxed. The strength of his grasp lessened. He lay back and began to snore.

Now she stared into the night, heard the far-off sound of waves breaking. She wondered: Did he know that she was Petra and that he was holding her in a hotel room not far outside Cape Town? Or was she just Woman, any woman. Was he back in Katanga? Or wherever else it might be?

She thought: I've got to let someone know I'm all right. She wondered: Am I all right? Why was Gat crying out in the night? What had happened that made him turn with such need to her?

He mumbled again. The trembling started. She put her lips against the ridges of his ear, kissed them. He struggled. His knee came hard against her. She bit her lip so that she would not cry out. He sat up. He thrust his arm out before him and spoke very sharply to the darkness. Then he looked about as if suddenly realizing that his body was not in the place where his dream was.

Gat slid to the edge of the bed. He placed his feet on the floor. He rested his head in his hands. His breathing calmed. This is not Katanga, he told himself. I'm in South Africa. A girl's with me. Petra. He reached toward her.

When he touched her thigh, Petra tensed. Let him want me! Please! She had just been wondering about him. Now she wanted him making her body hot and hungry, her head dizzy, her soul nervous. Yes! Was she dissolute? Yes! She felt shameless! Wanton!

"You okay?" she asked. The darkness grunted an assent. "Bad dream?"

He plodded to the bathroom and closed the door.

She wished his hand had slid to the top of her thigh. Vile thought! It seemed all they were doing was feasting on one another. She must stop thinking about his body. She rose quickly, tiptoed to her suitcase, found her nightgown and donned it.

When Gat returned to the room, he put a condom where he could reach it on the bedside table. Petra slipped into the bathroom. Washing herself she wondered if she were pregnant. She dried off, telling herself she could not possibly be. Gat was quite careful about that. But why the nightmares? Who was he anyway? She knew if she returned to the bedroom they would make love. She must not let that happen. She took a towel and spread it into the bathtub.

Lying in the tub, thinking about the last two days, she felt a physical aching for the lostness of her soul. She was wicked. She constantly wanted sex. When she and Gat drove through Afrikaner dorps on their way to Joeys, puritanical *tannies,* "aunties" who protected public decency, would recognize her wickedness and pull her from the car. They would beat her bloody for being immoral with Gat. Curled into the bathtub she wondered, this that she was feeling: was it love? She had never felt this way before. Dizzy like this. Did her parents feel this way about each other?

Her thoughts turned to her mother. On the afternoon of her eighteenth birthday Margaret had driven her down to Cape Point. Because she was now a woman, her mother said, because Kobus Terreblanche seemed to have decided he would marry her, Margaret would tell her about the first man in her life. He was a farmer's son from Rhodesia. They had fallen in love her first year at varsity at Grahamstown. He lived in a room over a garage behind a house near the campus. For a long time she did not go there with him. He did not want her there because they felt such love for one another that neither was sure, if she went to his room, what would happen.

But she went there eventually and, to use the phrase that Margaret used, that was where she "became a woman." She added, "a pregnant woman." The "lad"—that was the term her mother used—was stunned by the pregnancy. Because they had been taking what they thought were precautions. Careful precautions were not always enough. That thought made Petra shiver in the bathtub.

Still, her mother had related, once the lad became accustomed to the idea, he was delighted. He wanted them to marry. He would have to leave varsity. Margaret meant more to him than his education. They could farm together in Southern Rhodesia. But she would not allow that sacrifice for her. In fact, Margaret told Petra, she'd had no desire to be a poor farmer's wife. Living on a farm: that would kill their love.

So she left varsity. She went north to Rhodesia and told her parents she had found a job in Salisbury. In fact, she had lived on a farm managed by the husband of the lad's older sister who was barren. She'd had the baby there. Somehow the midwife had gotten the baby registered as the offspring of the lad's sister. The young family soon moved to a new farm where the baby, a boy, was accepted as their own. He was now twenty-four. He had heard of Margaret only as a Cape Town acquaintance with whom his mother exchanged cards at Christmas, often sending a photo of him.

After the baby was born, Margaret did go to Salisbury. She found a job there. When the lad came to visit, they were shy with each other. Their lovemaking, when they finally managed it, made them cry it was so lacking in the old passion. It turned out that the lad had progressed so well at varsity that he'd won a scholarship to England. Subsequently he emigrated.

For her part Margaret eventually went to Cape Town. There she met Piet Rousseau. It pleased him to be seeing a woman who was not an Afrikaner. "In those days your father was as feisty as you are," Margaret told the now eighteen-year-old Petra. "When he asked me to marry him," she confided, "I told him about the child. He was devastated. He thought about it for a week and decided it didn't matter. But, of course, it does. It's something we never discuss." As Petra knew, there were a number of things that the family never discussed. "Sometimes he'll make an oblique reference to it," her mother continued, "when he wants to score points off me. He doesn't know that I get Christmas notes from the family in Rhodesia. He would be horrified if he knew I was telling you."

Petra asked if Margaret sometimes thought about the lad. Her mother admitted that she did. She said there was a movie, a story about young lovers at varsity. The couple had married and, despite having very little money, seemed likely to make a success of it. The movie upset Margaret for an entire week. She found herself suddenly weeping. She got over it. She had a good life, a good family. She loved her husband and her children. She would not cry over spilt milk.

Lying in the bathtub, Petra wondered if a quarter century down the road she would find herself crying over a song or a ride in a car that reminded her of Gat. Would she still wonder who he was? Wonder what had happened before they met that caused his need?

A knock sounded at the door. It opened. Although she could not see him, Petra felt Gat's presence in the bathroom. "You in here?"

"In the tub."

He crouched beside her, touched her shoulder, and felt the nightgown. "Why're you here?"

"I sometimes do this at home." They both knew it was a lie. "I'm thinking."

"Come back to bed," Gat suggested. Then: "What about?"

"My mother. She got into some trouble when she was young."

"We're being very careful," he said. "There won't be any trouble." When she said nothing, Gat returned to the bedroom, found underwear, and put it on. He returned to the bathroom. "Look," he said, "I'm in my nightgown too." She examined him. "Come to bed. I won't touch you."

"But I'll want you to," she confessed. "I'm kind of afraid of wanting you all the time." He smiled and slid his hand onto her breast. She pulled it away. "I'll be okay here."

He took her head in his hands and kissed her. He left the bathroom. The kiss made her dizzy. She wanted to be back in bed with him. Then she thought again of her mother and the lad. Maybe she should flee. Desert her luggage. Rush back to Cape Town. Beg her parents to forgive her. Make it up with Kobus. Yes, that would be best—even though she knew that she really wanted to be back in bed with Gat.

GAT SLEPT fitfully, still bothered by dreams. An early morning breeze woke him, raising gooseflesh on his arms and chest. He patted the bed for Petra. Ah, yes, the bathtub. Seeking refuge from sex because it was so good. Gat tiptoed from bed, hoping that abstinence now would make her more ardent later on. He put on his swimsuit and a sweatshirt. He tiptoed into the bathroom, grabbed a towel, and left Petra in her enamel cocoon, lightly snoring.

Memories had disturbed Gat's sleep, not nightmares. Memories of huts set afire. Of thatch crackling. Of villagers fleeing flames. Of a wailing child racing out of a hut. Of bullets spattering after the child. Reaching him. Knocking him off his feet. Before the child hit the ground, blood gushed from his stomach with a whooshing sound. The red of blood, the orange-yellow of the flames, their roar and stench and crackle. And worst of all, the excited, joyful yelling of his soldiers massacring innocents.

Even now on the beach, memories assailed Gat. Alone in the darkness, he fell to his knees. He held his hands in a gesture of supplication. "Please forgive me," he cried. "I lost control of them. Forgive me for— Everything." But to whom was he shouting? The breaking waves? The dawn?

He rose and ran wind sprints to get his blood circulating. He jogged along the surf and plunged through darkness into the white foam of a breaking wave. The water shocked his groin. He swam swiftly away from shore. Looking behind him, he could not be sure where land was. Panicking, treading water, he thought, What the fuck have I done? He listened for the sound of waves breaking, swam in their direction, and rode one onto the beach. He located the towel. He was much farther down the beach than he had reckoned. He buffed himself dry. He put on the sweatshirt and, feeling vigorous, ran in the direction of the dawn until the sun rose over the eastern horizon.

PETRA HEARD Gat enter the bathroom to get a towel. She breathed heavily, hoping he would think her asleep. When she heard him leave, she listened to be sure he was gone, then scrambled out of the tub and returned to bed. She napped, rose, showered, dressed, and went alone to a breakfast of fruit and rolls. Wanting to reclaim the safety of childhood, she drank milk. Afterward she walked along the road before the hotel, trying to sort out her options. With the sun warming her and fortified by food, she was less certain that Gat had brought her to the brink of depravity. Still, she must keep him at arm's length. And do something about contacting her family.

When she returned to the room, Gat had just finished dressing. "Have you eaten?" he asked. She nodded that she had. He scrutinized her. She avoided his eyes. "Breakfast is included," Gat said. "So I better have some. Come talk to me?"

"Will you tell me why you're having nightmares?"

"My nightmares were about your leaving my bed for a bathtub."

"Don't patronize me." She gave him a challenging and hostile look.

"It's too nice a day to discuss nightmares." She shook her head; he could breakfast alone. Gat kissed her forehead as if she were a child and left the room.

It infuriated her that he was treating her the way Kobus and her father did. Then she thought, Well, what else could he do? He had started off on the trip with a woman who had turned into a child, sleeping in a bathtub. Suddenly it infuriated her that she was infantilizing herself.

She stared across the room at the telephone. It was out of the question to call her parents. She decided on Hazel. Just to chat. The call must seem motivated simply by a desire for girl talk. It had only been about thirty-six hours since they were together at the San Francisco Coffeehouse. Hazel answered on the second ring. "You still in bed?" Petra asked. She heard Hazel's radio playing in the background.

"Where in God's name are you?" Hazel shrieked. She lowered her voice. "Are you really with him? Are you— You know! Is it— Are you—"

"Kobus didn't call you," Petra said. "Who'd he call?"

Hazel gave her the whole story: after Kobus's call Piet Rousseau telephoned his brother, Hazel's father. Was Petra spending the night with them? No, she was not. Well, then, even though it was midnight, would he mind going around to the house to see why Petra was not answering his calls? He had received a curious phone call from Kobus. He claimed that Petra had run off with a man she hardly knew. Hazel's father investigated. He found the house empty, the Ford gone from the garage.

"Oh, god!" cried Petra. "I called because I was afraid this might happen."

"The police are going to be looking for you," Hazel said. "Your father's in a blackie. You know, roadblocks, all Fords searched. Are you with Gautier? He might be deported. Where are you anyway?"

"You promise not to tell anyone? *Anyone!*" Hazel gave a sacred pledge that Petra knew she would violate. "Touwsrivier," Petra said. It was the only town she could think of on the highway to Johannesburg.

"Touwsrivier!" screeched Hazel. "You're playing house with a man in Touwsrivier?"

"I'm not playing house with anyone, Haze. Gat's being a perfect gentleman." Petra crossed her fingers because that is what she had seen ingenues do in American movies when they lied. "He hasn't even kissed me."

"Liar!" squawked Hazel. "He practically ate you alive at the coffeehouse."

"He sleeps in the car and uses the gent's. Tell your father I'm still a virgin."

A long silence. Then Hazel said, "That must be distressing!" She cackled. After a moment she said, "You're lying, Pet. I can always tell. How is sex?"

"Stay away from it, Haze. It enslaves you. Really."

"Have you had a— You know."

"Well, if I haven't, I hate to think what that'll do to me. It's gotten so I can't think of anything else."

Suddenly Hazel asked, "Are you crying?" And to Petra's surprise she was. She sobbed into the phone. "Are you all right?" Hazel kept asking. "Has he hurt you? What's wrong?"

Petra let it all spill out. She admitted to having real doubts about the wisdom of what she'd done. Sex was wonderful. Really. Too wonderful. Gat was caring, gentle, funny sometimes, a fabulous lover. But he'd done terrible things. You got a charge hearing a man tell you he needed you to rescue him from a black void because you knew he was feeding you a line, trying to win a smile. Then to discover that he really did need rescuing, that was scary.

"Are you saying: Get me out of this?" Hazel asked. "Because we can call your father and he can have police there in—"

"Oh, god!" Petra shuddered. "Don't do that!" She thought of her father, furious with her, in a blackie, mobilizing the entire police force to hunt them down. "It's just that— He scares me. He's done— And he's so needful. He wants to make love all the time. And I want him to. I'm sure it must be wrong."

Hazel began to hoot. "Are you in love?"

"Oh, god! I don't think so. I spent part of the night in a bathtub to get away from him."

"Does he rape you?" Hazel asked. Her voice sounded deeply shocked. Petra said, of course he didn't. Had he kidnapped her? No! Was he holding her against her will? No! No! Suddenly she realized that on the table beside the phone were the keys to the Ford. Gat had left them, probably intentionally, to let her flee if she wanted. Gat was wonderful, she told Hazel. Maybe she did sort of love him.

"Then stop crying," Hazel replied firmly. "If your father catches Gat, he'll do something awful to him, especially if he hears you've been blubbering." Petra denied that her father would hurt Gat. Hazel reminded her that her father was a colonel in the Special Branch. He knew how to hurt people; that was his job. Petra defended her father. Hazel made an impolite noise into the phone. She said, "Don't get scared. You're tasting passion. I wish it were me."

Petra did not answer. She listened. Hazel said, "You may never taste it again. You'll end up with somebody like Kobus. You'll have a safe, comfortable life. You may even love him—when you're not bored—and you'll have this to look back on. Drink some coffee and think carefully. Then call me back if you want to be rescued. I'll get in touch with your father."

"I won't call you back," Petra said. "I just needed to talk to somebody."

"Do something for me," Hazel said. "Get absolutely destroyed by passion."

Feeling better now that she had examined her uncertainties by articulating them to her cousin, Petra went to the breakfast room to join Gat. He stood when she came to the table, held her chair, and asked the waiter to bring her a cup for coffee. "Would you like some rolls?" Gat asked. Petra shook her head.

She had trouble looking at him. After the coffee arrived and she could hold the cup and gaze into it, she told him, "I'm sorry I'm so young."

He smiled at her. "May I kiss you good morning?" She nodded. He leaned across the table and kissed her. "We can go back to Cape Town," he said. "It's not very far."

She shook her head. She took his hand and kissed it.

As HAZEL hung up the phone, she wondered if anything Petra had told her was not a lie. She assumed that Petra was all right, despite being somewhat knocked about by passion or whatever it should be called. But Gat? A perfect gentleman? Fat chance. Hazel put on a robe and caught her father drinking his coffee. She reported that Petra claimed to be at a hotel in Touwsrivier—she hadn't gotten the name—that the Belgian officer was sleeping in the car and using the gent's and that

Petra was apparently fine. Before leaving for the day her father relayed the information to his brother in Pretoria.

Margaret Rousseau watched her husband receive the news. After he hung up, she said, "Before you make a lot of calls, let's talk a minute." Piet gave her a hard look. "Let's let her be."

"This is the way kaffir wenches arrange their lives," Piet declared. "A strange man gives them a smile and they give him their bodies." Then he added, "There can't be many hotels in Touwsrivier."

"She's not there," Margaret informed him. "A girl like Petra does not have an adventure with a man in a place like Touwsrivier."

"I'll put officers watching traffic heading east on every road out of the Cape."

"Let her be!" Margaret said more forcefully. "She's chosen to learn about love from this Belgian. I hope she's enjoying her lessons."

"Our African wench-daughter takes after you," Piet Rousseau said.

"Do not say things that I can hardly forgive," his wife replied. "Haven't you seen this coming?"

To avoid answering, Rousseau began to pace. Margaret watched him. "And why shouldn't it come?" she asked. "Petra is now an adult. She should have a healthy curiosity about being with a man." Piet Rousseau clenched his teeth. "Young men certainly possess that curiosity," Margaret reminded him. "I expected this would happen with Kobus. He didn't want to let her go to Wits until he put his mark on her. That's what the week together in Stellenbosch was all about."

Rousseau replied, "She's too young for that. Kobus knows that."

"Does he? He sees her as the mother of his children. Of course, he wants his mark on her." She watched him pace.

"The afternoon of her eighteenth birthday I took her down to Cape Point. We had one of our little talks about life, men, sex." Rousseau stopped pacing. He regarded his wife. As a police official he dealt with the seamy side of these matters every day. But the intrusion of these topics into his family unnerved him. "We drove down Chapman's Peak Road. The cliffs plunging into that clear blue water: they were beautiful. I told her sex was like that: beautiful, exhilarating. But it was a cliff one could fall off and sometimes boulders from above smashed one's car."

"She knows about not getting pregnant?"

"We talked about contraceptive devices," Margaret said.

"So why has she done this?"

"Because you keep her on too tight a leash," his wife replied. "A little adventure: it's not such a terrible thing."

"Look who's talking."

"Be careful," Margaret warned. She watched him. "Why is it so hard for fathers to let their daughters have sex? Mothers worry if their sons go without it."

Piet paced up and down, ignoring her. When he had made up his mind to put patrols on the highways, he said, "We're going to find them."

"Let them be. The Belgian will see that she's safe."

"If I get my hands on him, he'll be out of this country in two hours."

"Just don't throw him out a window at police headquarters." Margaret said this because she knew it irritated him. "Don't tell your colleagues at today's meetings that your daughter's gone missing. They'll titter behind their agendas."

LEAVING HERMANUS, they went inland, away from salt smell and the sound of waves. Gat drove. Petra sat against the passenger door, watching him, her arm along the back of the seat. He stared at the road, conscious of her scrutiny, feeling that even though they had kissed good morning in the break-fast room whatever was bothering her was still not resolved.

He glanced over, saw her watching him. "Why are you sitting way over there?" he asked. "Is that where you sit with Kobus?" Although she did not feel flirtatious, she stuck out her tongue. "Come sit beside me," he suggested. "I like feeling you beside me."

She only shifted her position, lifting her knees onto the seat. He reached under the hem of her skirt and rested his hand on her calf.

"What were you dreaming about last night?" she asked. He withdrew his hand from her calf and watched the road. He slowed as they approached a dorp. They moved past its few houses, its Dutch Reformed church, pub, petrol station with general store attached. Whites entered the store directly from the pumps. Blacks went round to the side, where Africans were laughing, idling, and transacting their business through a window. Petra asked again about the dream. "You were trem-bling," she said. "You called out. What was that about?"

"It was a soldier's dream."

"What do soldiers dream about?" she asked. "Women?" Gat shook his head. "Killing people?" He shrugged. "Or don't real soldiers have nightmares about that?"

"They do."

"You said you'd killed three people," she said. "Was this dream about that?"

He looked back at the road. "What do you dream about?" he asked.

Petra shifted her position and stretched her legs out before her. She stuck her elbow out the window and did not look at Gat. They drove that way for some time, passing farm fields.

Finally Gat looked over at her, reached for her arm. Despite herself, she felt hot flashes at his touch. He tugged lightly. She scooched across the seat. The atmosphere between them softened.

Holding Petra's knee, Gat thought how careful a chap had to be with a virgin newly born as a woman. She was fragile and feisty at the same time.

For months the atmosphere of Katanga had suffocated him. He had witnessed only deceit and greed from the mining conglomerates' bland-faced, well-fleshed minions. He had grown tired to death of drinking and black girls brought in from whorehouses or the *cités,* tired of using their bodies, giving them francs, then tossing them out. He had taken up with Liliane, a conglomerate secretary, even called her his fiancée to make things easier with her. But he had no intention of marrying her. What romantics called love—a person feeling expanded by his devotion to someone else—could not possibly blossom in Katanga.

Could it blossom here? If that were to happen, he would have to tell Petra more about himself.

As THEY drove along, vineyards stretched away from the road on either side, their vines heavy with grapes and large leaves, deeply green in the sun. They watched blacks bent over crops in fields, saw squatter camps, collections of shacks, where migrant black farmworkers took shelter till they moved on to the next job.

Gat said, "You know what would make sense? To educate these people. We should have educated ours in the Congo. You should educate yours."

"There isn't the money to educate them," Petra replied.

"Cheaper to educate them than to keep the lid on their aspirations."

She did not look at him, her arms folded across her chest. "Would your Congolese girlfriend have been happier if she'd known how to read?"

The question surprised Gat. Was she picking a fight? He and Petra had not talked politics. But her defiance of her father, her provocations, her running off with him: these had all suggested that she had liberal ideas. Perhaps she did not. He finally said, "I think anyone who can't read would be happier if he could. Reading opens up—"

Petra interrupted, "Would you have married her then?"

Her father's daughter, Gat thought. He replied, "Literacy opens new worlds for people. Think of the potential that South Africa keeps locked up inside its Africans."

"You sound like a missionary."

"Do I? Why do you say that?"

"You don't like being told that Africans are savages."

"Some of them are. Some of us are."

"Then why get touchy about it? When we were talking about Lumumba—"

Gat said, "I don't want to talk about Lumumba."

"Why not?" She seized on the question as if hoping it would lead them to a confrontation. "What's wrong with talking about Lumumba?"

Gat glanced at her. She regarded him as innocently as she had her father when talking about the police throwing people out of windows. "Seriously," she said. "What do you know about him?"

"I read parts of a book he wrote," he said. "Somehow the Force got hold of the manuscript, passed it around. Something to jeer at. Reading it you can't help feeling sorry for the poor chap."

"What?" She laughed, astonished. "Sorry for him? He's a Communist."

"Reading his manuscript you realize he wants desperately to be recognized as capable of contributing more than a monkey creature's allowed to contribute. He laid out a plan for Belgians and Congolese to work together to create the Congo of the future. And all we did to people like him was to piss on them."

"You gave them the country," Petra pointed out.

"We're small-minded," Gat said. "We got frightened by the way the world was changing."

"Lumumba's a Communist. He was ready to turn the Congo over to the Russians."

"An African Communist is someone who got pissed on by colonials."

"Are you a Communist?" Petra asked.

"You smell the piss on me? Is that why you ask?"

They rode along without speaking. Petra studied Gat's face; he studied the road. He turned on the radio. "How about finding us some music?" he suggested.

Petra stopped dialing at a station playing a kwela. She wondered what he was thinking. Finally she asked, "Why did you say those things last night?" Gat glanced at her, puzzled. African children were playing in the road. He slowed the car. Radio music drifted from it, arousing the children. They began to dance, flailing their arms, throwing their hips in exaggerated poses. Gat waved and watched the children in the rearview mirror. "Last night you told me to get out of South Africa," Petra reminded him. "If I did, where would I go?"

"Australia," Gat replied.

"Not America?"

"You have to have money there. And it's hard to get in. Go to Australia."

"Would you come with me?"

Gat glanced at her, wondering if she were serious.

"I haven't the courage to go alone. I'd need courage, wouldn't I?"

He nodded.

After a time Petra asked again, "Why were you having nightmares last night?"

She was like a child, Gat realized. She would pester you with a question until it got answered. "Not everyone in Katanga supports the secession," he said. "The Baluba of northern Katanga do not support it. After secession, I was sent up there to—" He shrugged. "'Restore order.' I believe that's what they told the press."

"The men you took up there: who were they?"

"Black infantry, black officers, white advisors." Gat told her briefly what happened. "Soldiers don't kill civilians," he said at last. "Murderers do. When we got back to the Copper Belt, everybody called us heroes. It made me sick to my stomach."

Petra had moved back against the passenger door. She drew her legs up against her body, her chin resting on a knee. She thought: How could I let him touch me? He's killed children.

At the roadside Gat spotted a man in glasses and a fedora, young, possibly a student. He wore shined shoes, now well dusted by passing traffic, and his clothes included a vest and suit coat, emblems of status. The man stood erect, innately dignified, and moved with grace as he reached out in supplication toward passing cars to solicit a ride. A plastic valise, tied by a rope, rested at his feet. Gat pulled off the road. "What are you doing?" Petra asked, alarmed.

"This fellow needs a lift."

"Not in this car!" Petra said.

Gat ignored her, leaned his head out the window, and asked the man, "Where you headed?"

The man picked up his valise and ran toward the car, studying Gat to assess what kind of ride this might be. "To George, baas," he replied. Then he bent down to witness the panic evident on Petra's face and revised his destination. "Or to Mossel Bay, baas. Mossel Bay, if you please."

"We're not giving anyone a lift," Petra declared.

"Why not?"

"He's a kaffir." Gat's disapproving expression made her change the designation. "An African."

"There's plenty of room on the backseat."

"My things are there!"

"Can't we move them? The chap needs a ride."

"We don't give rides to— This is South Africa!"

"Mossel Bay is only thirty miles."

"I'll ride in back with my things." She left the front seat of the car, slamming the door, and moved to the rear seat where she shifted her boxes and his bags and sat with her arms folded across her chest. Petra wondered if Gat had stopped for the hitchhiker to test her.

"Get in front with me," Gat invited.

"Thank you, baas. Very kind of you, baas." He smiled at Petra. "Madam. Thank you, madam."

The man got into the car, sitting where Petra had been, holding his valise on his lap. He brought inside with him the smell of the dusty road and of sweat raised by long standing in the sun. Gat moved back onto the highway.

As he drove on, Gat asked the young man about himself. He said he was a student, returning to the University College of Fort Hare, the university for blacks at Alice. He had been visiting in Cape Town and would now see his mother and younger siblings before starting his third year of training. "And you, baas?" asked the student. "Just having a nice motor trip in the summer sun?"

"I'm visiting from Europe," Gat said. "From England. The Midlands. I'm loving this sun. It can be very cold in England in February."

"Snow," the student said. "You have snow, do you, baas?" Gat waved his hand to indicate that there was not much snow in the Midlands. "I would like one day to see snow," the student went on. He glanced over his shoulder at Petra but would not risk addressing her directly. "And the madam? Also from Europe?"

"Yes," Petra replied. "But I've been living a while in Cape Town."

"I hear Cape Town in the way you speak, madam," said the student.

"We are on our way to Johannesburg to—" In the rear-view mirror Gat saw Petra's chin tighten, the blood rush from her face. He knew he must be careful what he said. "To visit the University of the Witswatersrand."

"That is a fine place to study," offered the student. "Will the madam—"

"In a couple of months I'm going to America," Petra said. "Starting in September I'll be studying at the University of—" Suddenly she could not think of a single American university, she who had set her heart on attending one.

"Of New York," Gat interjected to help her.

"Yes," Petra continued, recovering. "New York University. NYU."

"Ah, New York!" said the student. "Empire State Building!"

"Yes," said Petra, feeling more comfortable.

"Snow. America. New York," said the student. "How I would like to see them!"

Gat and the student chatted on, the silence growing between topics. Petra rarely added a word. After a time Gat asked, "What's this treason trial about in Johannesburg?" The student said nothing. The tension inside the car was palpable. "I keep reading about it in the papers."

"I know nothing about it, baas," claimed the student. "Very bad business, these blacks who make all this trouble."

"But aren't they working for change?" Gat asked.

"Blacks are making good progress, baas," the student said. "Am I not studying at University College? Forcing change. Not a good idea."

GAT DROPPED the man off in the center of Mossel Bay. He bowed repeatedly, expressing his thanks. Petra made no move to switch from the rear seat. "Drive on," she said. When they had left the town behind, she told him to pull over. "What if I drove for a while? I need more experience behind the wheel."

"With you driving, am I safe?" Gat joked, trying to play it light.

"If I feel safe with you"—and she was not at all sure she did—"I guess you should feel safe with me."

"You feel safe with me? What a disappointment!"

Petra was not amused. While he got out of the car, she took a cloth and wiped the seat where the African sat. When Gat looked at her, disapproving, she glared at him.

When it was clear that Petra was comfortable behind the wheel, Gat asked, "What was that back there?"

"Why don't you tell me?" she replied with an edge in her voice. "Haven't you figured out anything about South Africa?"

"That you should get out."

"White people never pick up blacks on the roads. You put him in the backseat and drive off. He takes out a gun and holds it to your head and—"

"He didn't have a gun."

"How do you know? Or he fishes a knife out of his pocket and holds it to your throat."

"Come on."

"At the very least—if he's in the backseat—he filches some of my things."

"Your bras and panties?"

"There are kaffir girls who'd offer him a lot of favors for my unmentionables." She added, "He could have had explosives in that case."

"You are your father's daughter."

"Very bad business, baas, baas, baas," Petra said, mocking the African's accent. "Very bad, these blacks who make all this trouble." She gazed at Gat disdainfully. "So . . . You think he told you what he really thinks?"

"No. And I don't think you're going to be studying anytime soon at the University of Help-Me-Out-Here."

"University of New York?" she mocked. "Doesn't exist. Of course, how would a bloke from the Mids know that?"

"How could I know? I never went to university."

"You got your university training in the back of a pickup with a kaffir girl who couldn't even talk to you."

Gat answered. "Get out of this fucking country."

Petra said, "It wasn't 'fucking' till I met you."

Gat guffawed. "You weren't fucking till you met me."

Petra regarded him with distaste. "What are you trying to put right by picking up Africans on our roads? You're killing them in the Congo?"

THEY DROVE for miles without speaking. Both watched the road, Gat scolding himself for pushing the girl beyond what she could bear. Petra kept her hands at ten and two as she'd been taught. At last she said, "Once we get to George, maybe we should drive north and hit the main highway to Joeys." Her father would have police watching that road for their car. That would show Gat how things were done in South Africa. He could deal with her father and then get sent back to Katanga where he belonged. "We'd pass through Bloemfontein," she added.

"Whatever you want," he said. "I'm just along for the ride."

"Let's do that," she said, pleased that there was now a plan.

"Whatever you want," he repeated.

What she wanted, Petra knew, was that they had made love that morning. She wished right now that his hand were under her skirt, on her knee, or even caressing her thigh. I'm terrible, she thought, but it was true. She knew he desired her. She wondered: Why am I being such a bitch? Maybe they could make love wherever it was they stopped tonight.

Finally she said, "You talked last night as if my marrying a South African would be a fate worse than death." She did not look at him. "It's probably what I'll do, you know."

"The fate worse than death," he replied, "is a young woman of good family bestowing her virginity on a passing soldier. That lucky sod." He lightly poked her ribs. "That means nothing can be worse than what you've already survived." When she did not reply, he added, "I expect you'll be very happy. For a few years anyway."

"And then?"

"Can't you guess?"

"You mean I'll start screaming in the middle of the night and sit up in bed."

"Your husband will put his arms about you, but you'll—"

"No, my husband will be downstairs. He'll be checking the locks with a pistol in his hand. That's what you mean, isn't it? And I'll rush to see that the children are all right."

They said nothing for a moment. "And they will be," she said, "because people like my father will make the country safe for us."

Gat repeated his advice. "Get out of South Africa."

"And go someplace where I won't know anyone?"

Gat did not reply. He watched Africans at the roadside, the women walking with stately slowness, parcels carried on their heads, toddlers hanging on to their hands.

"If you came with me, I'd know someone," Petra said.

Gat realized that he should not have gone swimming at dawn. He should have been patient, kidded her out of the bathtub and the nightgown, and made things right between them. He wondered what it would be like to go—say, to Australia—with her. She would expect him to marry her, of course, and maybe he would. Petra would be the one eventually to leave. One day after she had made a place for herself in her adopted country, she would look at him and see him for what he was and she would leave, dragging their children behind her as the African women were dragging their children behind them.

"If I should leave South Africa, then you should leave Katanga, right?" Gat said nothing, knowing she was right. "So why don't we both go to Australia?"

WHEN THEY reached the small city of George, they bought rolls at a bakery—Gat also bought a paper there—fruit at a greengrocer's, and cheese at a specialty shop. Gat read his paper in the car while Petra went into a hotel, so she told Gat, to hunt for a loo. But she was looking less for a ladies' room than for a public telephone. Knowing her father, she feared that he really might set constables and police officers

scouring the east-west highways of the eastern Cape for what
he might report as a stolen Ford. There was only one way to
foil such searches: travel north. Petra had a friend, a prefect
two years ahead of her at school, who had married an Afrikaner farming outside of Vryburg, almost due north, close to
the Bechuanaland border. Like Petra, Gillian was the product
of a marriage between an Afrikaner father, even more authori-
tarian than Piet Rousseau, and a more relaxed English-speaker
mother. Each young woman understood the other's family
problems. The difference between them was that, instead of
defying her father as Petra did, Gillian escaped hers by marrying a man very much like him. Petra was uncertain how
Dannie would react to her turning up with Gat. That they
were mere acquaintances traveling the same road was not a
story that Dannie would swallow. She would have the drive
north the next day to think of something to tell them.

"Gillian!" Petra cried when she got through on the phone.
"It's Petra! A strange thing has happened. I'm driving up to
Wits. I've got a bit of time to spare."

Gillian was delighted with the thought of a visit, especially since Dannie had gone to Rhodesia where his mother
was ill. "But you aren't driving alone," said the friend. "Your
father would never allow that."

Petra crossed her fingers again. "That's the strange thing
that's happened," she said. "A friend of my father's, down
from the Belgian Congo, is driving up to Joeys. I hitched a
ride with him. He's older, treats me like a child. But at least
my parents aren't taking me to varsity."

The house was tiny, Gillian said, but somehow they'd
arrange things. Perhaps Petra and Gillian could share the
double bed and the Belgian officer could sleep on the couch
in the parlor. "I can't wait to see you!" Gillian enthused.

During their picnic in a farmer's field Petra explained what she had arranged. "Why doesn't your friend sleep on the couch?" Gat suggested. "I much rather sleep with you." Petra blushed in a way that caused a stirring in his groin.

"I said you were a friend of my father's," she explained. Gat shook his head at this improbable idea. "Anything in your paper about Katanga? Is that why you bought it?"

"If I go back, I'll need to know what's gone on."

"Are you going back?"

"I thought there might be something about Lumumba."

Petra cocked her head and studied Gat. "What's so special to you about Lumumba? We keep talking about him."

Gat cut himself another slice of cheese.

"I'm serious," said Petra. "What's so special?"

"He was an original," Gat said. "He had a national vision for the Congo. Which was what everyone said was needed: we Belgians, the Brits, the Americans, the UN. He launched a cohesive movement to build that vision. Created a political party. Sold that party to voters who were also being offered regional tribal parties. Won the election. Took office only to discover that what the West really wanted was what it had always wanted: to be able to play the tribes off against each other. The Belgians wanted a weak government so that it could continue to extract the country's riches and bank them in Brussels. The Americans wanted a supine government that would follow its lead on the Cold War. The UN, which the Americans controlled, wanted to run things. Lumumba, determined to build a strong, unified Congo, was a nuisance. So they killed him."

Gat spoke with such conviction that Petra could not watch him. She said, "I thought he was in jail somewhere."

"He's dead. In a day or two a Katanga spokesman will announce that he escaped from jail. A couple of days later he'll announce that Lumumba was found in some remote place by villagers who discovered his identity and killed him."

Petra stared at Gat, suddenly understanding. She said, "You killed him."

He nodded.

CHAPTER SEVEN

AT BEAUFORT WEST

WEDNESDAY, FEBRUARY 8, 1961

All afternoon they drove north toward Beaufort West, a small city on the main highway linking Cape Town to Johannesburg. After nightfall they found a small hotel, rather rundown, on the southern outskirts of the town. They registered as Dannie and Gillian Prinsloo of Vryburg. The reception clerk looked carefully from one to the other. He spoke to Gat in Afrikaans. When Petra quickly answered for him in her English-speaker-accented Afrikaans, the clerk knew that while she might be Gillian, he was not Dannie and neither was Prinsloo. He handed over a single key.

"We didn't fool him," Petra said as they climbed the stairs to their room.

"He's seen plenty of couples like us," Gat replied.

They ate a farm wife's cooking at a restaurant they had passed and returned to their room. Once inside it, before turning on the light, Gat took Petra by the arm, brought her to him to embrace her. "Let's talk about why you need me to save your life," she said. Escaping his embrace, she flicked on the overhead light and moved across the room.

"What's there to say?"

"You tell me." She went to a corner of the room, pushed out of the way the chair that sat there and settled onto the floor, her legs sticking out before her, her back wedged into the corner. Her arms across her chest, she waited.

Gat sat on the side of the bed, braced his elbows against his knees, and stared at the floor. "Once this trip started," he began, "I knew you'd want to know."

"Tell me."

"That first night with you brought me a peace I hadn't felt for a long time, well before the Lumumba business."

Petra watched, wondering if she should believe anything he said.

"There's a woman in Elisabethville." He shrugged. "She called herself my fiancée. But I felt shriveled inside with her. Dead even. You made me feel alive again."

"Did you intend to marry her?"

"There's a poison in her. It's inside most of the whites up there." He wondered how much he should tell. But why not tell it all? "My first night in Cape Town I spent with a woman I met on the plane."

"You don't have to tell me this," Petra said.

"You might as well know."

Petra nodded, offering him permission to continue. He gazed at the floor. "Was she glamorous?" she asked.

"Experienced. Knew how to pick up a man on a plane." He stared at the memory of— He had forgotten her name. "She told me she was an actress. Maybe she was. She performed in bed for me. I performed for her. That's what you do on such occasions. I felt afterward that she had sucked what was left of my soul right out of me." He watched the floor, finally glancing up. "My first night with you, I felt filled up with— I'm not sure what."

Now Petra felt filled up too, proud that, despite her lack of experience, she had pleased an experienced man.

"It was the honor of being your first. That's a woman's greatest compliment to a man. It was your purity and innocence. They're an antidote for what was just the opposite in me."

"There's a purity in you," Petra said. "Even an innocence. If there weren't," she said, "none of this would bother you. I've been watching it bother you."

"I haven't wanted this time to end," Gat said. "I guess I hoped you'd never have to know about— Who I am. The things I've done."

No man had ever opened himself to Petra like this. She wondered if she could fall in love with Gat. Maybe she already had. He might be the most honest man she'd known. But being her father's daughter she knew that some men are virtuosos in the confessional mode.

"Being with you makes me feel young and very sexy," Gat told her. "Also very old. Older than your father."

"Older than my father?"

"The worst is ahead for him." He added, "You really did sort of save my life."

They fell silent. She said, "Lumumba."

He rose, flicked off the ceiling light, came around to the foot of the bed, and lowered himself to the floor. He stretched out his legs, lodging his feet and ankles against the outside of her calf, finding solace in her warmth. A security light over the hotel's car park and a neon sign over its dining room gave a faint illumination to his face.

"It was a Tuesday. January 17. I won't forget that date anytime soon. They flew him into Elisabethville late in the afternoon." Gat stared into the darkness as if seeing the events on a screen in his mind. "He'd been held for a month at an army camp south of Leo. In a kind of limbo. That was because the men who'd taken over his government—Congolese with European advisors in the background—kept arguing about what to do with him.

"Then a mutiny broke out at the army camp. A lot of soldiers there wanted to set him free. The mutiny was put down, but it was clear that Lumumba couldn't remain there. So they sent him to Katanga, knowing what was likely to happen. That was with the connivance of the Belgian ex-colonial administrators. The American CIA and the palace in Brussels gave their approval."

Gat glanced to see how Petra reacted to this detail. She stared at him, perhaps a little bored, but ready to hear it all.

"At around four that afternoon I received a telephone call—I was at the military camp, Camp Massart—from Major Perrad. He's the gendarmerie's chief of staff. He ordered me to take a squad of military police to the airport. While I was assembling the men, I was called to the Interior Ministry. There the Security Service biggies, both Katangese and Belgian, were meeting. Lumumba was arriving at the airport, I was informed. Victor Tignée, officially—"

Petra said, "These names mean nothing to me."

"I have to speak them!" Gat looked at her imploringly. "I was getting orders. From real people who outranked me."

Petra nodded to assure him that she understood although she did not.

"I was saying . . . Minister Munongo's private secretary, Victor Tignée, who made most of the decisions, he instructed me to take charge of Lumumba and the other prisoners."

"Who were the prisoners?"

"Lumumba associates." Petra watched him carefully enunciate the names. "Maurice Mpolo, top commander of the army. Joseph Okito, deputy president of the Senate. They'd been caught with Lumumba trying to reach Stanleyville. Congolese officials—and the Belgians, the Americans—were afraid Lumumba might stage a comeback from there."

Petra nodded.

"I went back to Massart," Gat continued, "to assemble the men and round up every Belgian officer I could find."

"There was no African in charge?" Petra asked.

"Technically my superior was an African, Major Norbert Muke. He commanded the battalion and the camp. He palavered with the men; I made sure things got done. That was my job. To do that there was a direct phone line between the Interior Ministry and me." Gat looked at her to make sure she understood, "Tignée was giving me the orders.

"At the airport everything had to be controlled. So there'd be no problems with UN troops. Blue Berets—UN— were milling around the regular terminal. And we didn't want Baluba troops—or townspeople—suddenly rallying to Lumumba. Control, control. Protect Lumumba. That was my job."

Petra nodded to encourage him.

"It was late afternoon, about five, an hour or so before sunset. The heat of the day was receding, but out on the tarmac you still saw muggy shimmers rising off the pavement. It was quite a crowd: seventy or eighty Katangese ministers and their Belgian advisors, top police and military, even civilians, these last all Belgians. We waited in a kind of hush."

Petra saw that in his mind Gat was out on the tarmac again, waiting for Lumumba.

"People whispered together, waiting for things to begin. I'd been sweating and my mouth was dry, with a bitter taste.

I had no idea what would happen. Lumumba was coming to us as a prisoner. I knew that."

Gat closed his eyes and gestured with his hands.

"I expected Lumumba to come off the plane in a suit. Subdued, not waving or smiling, but still moving with the dignity of his office. After all, he was the prime minister of a sovereign country. And surely it served the interests of Katanga to observe protocol. There were cameras everywhere. Photos of Lumumba's arrival would appear throughout the world. Katanga showing respect seemed the obvious course."

Gat shook his head. "But I've seen African troops rampage like hyenas on a kill," he said. "So it was always possible that an animal wildness would sweep across the crowd when they saw him. They might want to tear him to bits."

Gat seemed to get stuck. For a moment he said nothing.

"And then," Petra urged.

"We heard the DC-4. Then we saw it, a mere speck. It landed and taxied across the tarmac to a section reserved for the military.

"To make sure we kept the prisoners safe, I formed a double rank of soldiers from the plane to the vehicle that would take them away." Gat shook his head as if resisting the memory. "I set the men up as a bulwark against whatever might happen if emotion swept the crowd. The door of the plane opened. Out came a Congolese soldier, Zuzu, a huge man, given to outbursts of violence. Oh, my God! I knew the man. I'd commanded him before independence. The sight of him scared me. Maybe Lumumba had not been treated with dignity.

"The three prisoners came out." Gat shook his head at the memory. "I clenched my teeth when I saw them. So I would not gasp before my men. Tall. I recognized Lumumba immediately. Even battered and bloody he had dignity."

"He was bloody?" Petra asked.

Gat nodded. "Seeing him took my breath away. He was dazed, beaten half-dead on the plane. Like a common criminal chased through the streets, caught and pummeled. His face was swollen. He was pushed onto the stairway in a torn shirt, tied to the other prisoners. Blood oozed from his mouth and nose. They'd even pulled hair out of his goatee. Soldiers shoved him and the others down the stairway onto the tarmac."

As he spoke, Gat glanced at Petra to read her reaction. She nodded to assure him she was following his narrative. She wondered if she should have sat on the bed, holding Gat's hand. No. The floor was hard, like the story. The hardness forced her attention.

"My double rank of soldiers turned into a gauntlet. As the prisoners stumbled to the jeep, beatings continued. Soldiers pounded them with rifle butts, blacks and whites both. I kept shouting, 'That's enough now! Enough!' But restraining blood lust, that's like stopping a rainstorm. When we got him into the jeep, he lay on the floor. Soldiers stamped on him even there."

Gat looked through the darkness at Petra, reluctant to continue. She watched his face, dimly illuminated by the security light and the neon sign. She gestured to him to go on.

"The police commissioner—Frans Verscheure was his name—had requisitioned a small house outside town. We took the prisoners there. It was still light. We got them into the sitting room. I did a walk-around the outside of the house. I set up guards outside and had men watching the roads."

"Did you know what was going to happen?" Petra asked.

"It was worse than I expected. I knew it might get even worse."

She persisted, "Couldn't you say, 'I won't be a party to this? Count me out?'"

A smile briefly crossed his lips. He shook his head. "Soldiers do as they're told." Gat watched her through the darkness. "Fine to say they shouldn't, but they do."

Petra said no more.

"I expected a trial of some sort," Gat continued. "Maybe not a fair trial. After all, Lumumba was in the camp of his enemies. But I assumed charges would be set forth. That Lumumba would have a chance to answer them—even if that was futile."

"Why a trial?" Petra asked.

"To show the world that Katanga respected the rule of law," Gat explained. "That it observed the forms of civil society. I knew he'd be declared guilty and jailed or put under house arrest. Then, I assumed, negotiations would begin. Lumumba would be used as a pawn in talks to settle Katanga's secession."

Gat shrugged. "It would show that Belgium had given its colony workable mechanisms of government and that in Katanga they worked."

Gat thought of the chill in the air outside the small house that night, the smell of fear and blood lust inside it.

"I went back inside the house and transferred the prisoners to the bathroom."

"Why the bathroom?" Petra asked.

"I wanted to stop the beatings. When I returned to the house, they were continuing. I locked the prisoners into the bathroom and kept the key. That way I controlled access to them."

Gat thought of the long minutes passing, of the cigarette smoke gathering at the ceiling and fouling the air, of the solace of warm beer in his throat. That night important visitors, both

Belgian and Katangese, came to the house. The Katangese big-gies reeked of liquor. At the home of Moise Tshombe, Gat later heard, Katangese ministers celebrated Lumumba's capture by feasting and drinking. President Tshombe was said to have consumed an entire bottle of whiskey himself.

When he and his Interior Minister Godefroid Munongo came to see Lumumba, Gat saw their liquored-up eyes gleam-ing with menace. He remembered—after he unlocked the bathroom to let the visitors see the prisoners—the screams that issued from it. Two soldiers brought the prisoners into the living room for the ministers' inspection. Gat remembered the ministers' thudding blows onto the prisoners. He tried not to watch. He recalled the prisoners' groans and the blood that spilled onto Tshombe's suit. He recollected Gabriel Michels raining blows down on Lumumba.

"Throughout the evening," he told Petra, "everyone asked to see the prisoners. The bigwigs demanded it, and I had to accede. The beatings went on.

"In the end Belgians turned out to be as savage—in our civilized way—and as bloodthirsty as the Katangese. The Katangese were like soldiers I've led into combat: gripped at first by anger and fear, then rampaging against an enemy over whom they had complete domination. It was unnerving to see the president and the interior minister of Katanga beating the prime minister of the Congo, especially when his hands were tied and he was already half dead."

Gat stopped for a time as if exhausted. Then he continued.

"I began to understand that the Belgians would not stop the excesses. Our Belgian biggies weren't sure what to do with Lumumba. They had wanted to get him in their possession. He seemed the source of all their problems. Now that they had him, they weren't sure what to do."

Gat rose from the floor and walked from one side of the bed to the other. Petra did not stir. She watched Gat moving in a kind of trance.

"About ten, ten thirty," he finally said, "a convoy of vehicles formed outside the house: black American cars for the biggies and two jeeps. I knew what that meant: word had come from the palace in Brussels, giving the go-ahead for Lumumba's execution. But the Katangese must be seen as doing the mischief. Belgium wanted the world to know it had clean hands. That was fine with the Katangese as long as Belgian officers did the dirty. The execution."

Gat stopped moving and sat tiredly in a chair. He looked down at Petra. "I had contradictory feelings," he admitted. "I felt it was wrong to execute Lumumba. Foolish as well. But I understood why they wanted it done. His understanding of the world was as undeveloped as his country. He'd frightened allies that he needed. He seemed to be a problem that could only be solved by killing."

Gat stared at the wall.

"Going to the convoy of cars, I felt: it has to be done. I rode in the fourth car with the police commissioner and the prisoners. They were handcuffed in the back. We drove maybe forty-five minutes toward Jadotville. There's a lake up there formed by the Francqui dam, a fine place to view birds. In the darkness, as we passed, it looked like ghosts gathered there. We arrived at a clearing with a large tree. We left the vehicles. Policemen began digging graves in the sandy soil. Some of us were nervous, chain-smoking. Others made jokes."

"And you?"

"I felt like I was moving in a dream. Everything was dark. I was shivering. It's cold in Katanga in January. That's the rainy season. Part of me was trying to be military. I had a job to do and . . ." His voice trailed off. "But I also felt depressed. What we were doing was historic, but we were doing it like criminals. I was to be in charge of the firing squad even though among the men of the convoy I ranked just above a common soldier. History would record that the others, the ones who took decisions, only watched. I was the one who commanded the deed to be done. My superiors were using me. But that was the job. I did not want to be there. So I just did it."

"Did it take long?"

"Not long. We took the prisoners, one by one, and stood them in front of the tree. I gave the orders. The firing squads did their work."

"And Lumumba?"

"He went last. All three of them were resigned to their fate. After all, it was a fate they'd known all their lives: white men telling black men to kill other black men. Lumumba had a dignity about him. Even at the end the beatings and humiliations had not stripped him of that."

Gat and Petra sat without speaking.

Finally Gat said, "When we got back to Elisabethville it wasn't much after midnight. The news quickly spread through town. Tshombe and Munongo and their pals went to the president's house to empty more bottles of whiskey. Whites celebrated in bars and homes. Belgian advisors who had not been at the execution boasted to others that they had. And those of us who were there kept our mouths shut."

"Did you celebrate?"

"I had a small apartment. Liliane was staying with me there: the secretary I told you about. When I got there, she'd put on a party dress. People were celebrating in the streets. She could hardly contain her joy. She wanted to go dancing and drinking and demanded that I come with her. I didn't want to be with anyone. Or see anyone. Or touch anyone. While I was in the shower, she ran out."

Gat paused as if deciding what more to tell. "I took three showers that night. And more the next day. Lumumba looked at me just before we— I was trying to wash that look off me.

"When I left the bathroom, I poured myself a beer and sat in the darkness. I had presided at the murder of a man I admired. I wanted to be somewhere else. To be someone else. I kept hearing the sounds of revelry in the streets, the music, the firecrackers. I tried to shut it all out. Finally I gathered up Liliane's belongings and threw them into the hall."

Gat said nothing for a long time. "That's not the end of the story," he finally acknowledged. "The biggies decided the bodies must disappear. They didn't want Lumumba supporters making pilgrimages to his burial site. Or claiming that witchcraft had resurrected him. So the next night two Belgian police commissioners took a dozen Katangese policemen back to the graves. They dug up the bodies, took them to the Bayeke heartland where Munongo's brother is the paramount chief, and buried them there.

"A couple of days later one of the police commissioners— Gerald Soete is his name—and his brother dug up the bodies again. They cut them up with meat knives and hacksaws and threw the remains into a barrel of sulphuric acid provided by Union Minière.

"At the same time the biggies started having second thoughts. They realized Western countries would never recognize Katanga if it came out that Katangese officials had murdered Lumumba. So under orders a week or so later a squad I led took three policemen, impersonating the prisoners in civilian clothes, and drove them to a village called Kasaji, almost at the border with Angola. My men told people in Jadotville and Kolwezi—those are mining towns—that we had the prisoners in the vehicles. People saw three men. They were supposed to assume that one was Lumumba and he was still alive. Later the prisoners would 'escape.' Villagers would kill them."

"That's what you said would happen this noon," Petra said.

Gat nodded. "Our photographer took photos of the supposed jailhouse. A mud hut. He also took shots of a car disabled in a ditch. Those photos are probably being circulated right now."

Gat fell silent. "I've done a lot of thinking since all this happened," he said finally. "I don't pretend I was not a willing participant. At one moment I may have even been proud of myself for having a role in the affair. But no more. I was just an instrument in the hands of rich men, a tool to serve their purposes."

He added, "Life is a process of using and being used. This time I got used and I may be used again. Get blamed for what happened. I received death threats in E'ville."

Darkness and silence filled the room. Finally Petra said, "You take the bed. I'll stay here."

Gat nodded. If that's what she wanted, it did not matter to him. He was spent from telling and remembering his story. For a long time neither one of them moved. Finally Gat rose. He pulled off his shoes and lay down on the bed. He wondered if Petra would leave. Why not? What were they to each other anyway?

PETRA SAT wedged against the corner of the room. She wondered if her father did the kinds of things Gat had talked about. Her father who never brought his work home, who never talked about that work, who was never keen—from modesty, she had always supposed—to offer the information

that he was with Special Branch and a colonel. Special Branch
was, in fact, a phrase never spoken in his home. So what
about his work? She knew only that he was a good man who
loved his family and sought to preserve "the South African
way of life." Because of his goodness she had never inquired
too closely about what exactly that preservation involved.
She had sensed that at times it meant bearing down hard on
Bantus, especially those who did not accept their place. But if
Belgian officers and Katangese bigwigs beat a country's prime
minister . . . If they tortured him, for surely it had been torture . . . If they cold-bloodedly ordered his execution . . .
Well, what would her father do—or order done—to Africans
who were not prime ministers, but counted for nothing except
as possible enemies?

No! She could not believe it! Her father would not do
that. She recalled the family taunt, used sparingly by her
mother, more frequently by her, about kaffirs being thrown
out the windows of police headquarters. She had assumed it
was a joke. Or if not, that it was kaffirs mistreating kaffirs.
Now she realized that behind the taunt was— Tears filled her
eyes. No! It could not be!

Gat's breathing grew regular on the bed. She listened to
the soft inhalings and exhalings, knowing that she could not
spend the night in this room with him. Probably the hotel
had another room. But what if she just left? Took her suitcase and the car keys and drove off? Quietly she rose, took
her purse and the car keys. Reaching for her suitcase, she
sensed that the rhythm of Gat's breathing had altered. She
stood stock-still. The regular rhythm returned. She got the
suitcase, tiptoed toward the doorway. As she passed the bed,
Gat's hand touched her arm. It closed around her wrist. She
gave an involuntary intake of breath, frightened by his touch.

"Thank you, Petra, for being with me during this time."

She said nothing. The grip of his hand tightened. She waited. He released her wrist. They listened for each other in the silence. He was letting her go. Did he know she was leaving? Was he saying good-bye?

"No other woman has—"

"I'm just going out for some air."

"I'll stay here."

"Sleep well. See you later."

She moved quietly, quickly, along the hall and down the stairway into the lobby. As she crossed it, the reception clerk watched her. She tried to smile. He greeted her, "Mevrou Prinsloo."

She responded, *"Dankie,"* and pushed her way outside into the night. She got into the car, settled herself, telling herself to calm down. Driving at night, it was not that much more difficult than during the day. She shoved the key into the ignition, turned it. The motor started. But where was the switch for the headlights? She fiddled with knobs on the dashboard. She started the windshield wipers, depressed the cigarette lighter. Finally the lights went on. She shifted into reverse, searched the rearview mirror from every angle, seeing only darkness behind her tinted with the red glow from her brake lights. She backed out of the parking space and moved out onto the road.

She drove into town so slowly that she knew she could have walked there faster. That idea made her laugh. Her confidence about driving at night increased. She reached a filling station and had her tank filled with petrol. She asked directions for the highway going north. Continue straight on. She left Beaufort West behind her and began to relax. There was no traffic. All she had to do was stay awake and alert and drive slowly enough to avoid trouble.

At first she thought of nothing. She seemed to be moving through a huge bowl, the lower half of which was deeply black, the upper half speckled with stars. She could feel that the country was dry and monotonous. She rolled down her window. Warm air swooshed into the car, whirled around her, and helped her stay alert. As she began to feel more confident, she wondered what she was doing driving alone at night through this sparsely peopled country. She thought about Gat. He would be with her all her life. Twenty years up the road there would be times—afternoons having tea alone or at night when she lay awake beside her husband—when he would come to visit. Would she remember having left him stranded in a small hotel in the Great Karoo?

Driving through the night, she thought of Jan-Christiaan, her brother. She understood now why he stayed in England. JC treated her much the same way Kobus and her father did, as if she were a decorative child to be humored with patience and understanding and protected from things that children and women need not know.

The siblings corresponded two or three times a year. The intiative always came from Petra. She would get to worrying about JC. Was he surviving? Did he have friends? Father sent him no money; Mum could send only what would not be missed if Father carefully reviewed her checkbook. JC must have a job to meet his everyday needs. Petra would write, asking about these matters. He would answer, always cheerful, asking about their mother, but never mentioning their father.

JC and Kobus traveled to England together on the trip from which JC never returned. Petra more than once asked Kobus to explain exactly what happened in England. One evening they were at Kobus's parents' home, ostensibly listening to music in the library while actually necking. Petra crossed her legs and pushed him away, saying Kobus could not touch her until he revealed what happened in England. Finally he told her that while touring the Cotswolds, passing themselves off as Americans, he and JC traveled with other students on tour. Among them were young Caribbeans. JC fell hard for a girl from Jamaica. They began the kind of summer romance forbidden JC in South Africa.

"From Jamaica?" Petra asked. "She was black then."

"But *lekker,*" Kobus assured her. "Truly. Not your stumpy Zulu maiden with balaclava and blankets. Slim and sexy. Quite intelligent."

"You liked the looks of her too."

Kobus smiled. "Why not? We were in England. The girl knew JC was not American even when he insisted that he was. Finally it came to their negotiating sex."

"JC wanted that with her?" Petra asked, amazed. The girl was black.

"He was very attracted to her." Petra tried to hide her surprise. "She refused him because he lied about being American. So he admitted to being South African. She immediately threw him over."

"Why?"

"She assumed she'd be just an 'experience' for him. Something he'd boast about back home." Petra assumed that any girl would count herself lucky if JC wanted an involvement with her. That the Jamaican girl could send him packing meant that she had a sense of herself. Kobus continued, "She told JC things about South Africa that he'd never heard before from someone he respected. That it was a police state, that secret police tortured and killed people."

The Jamaican girl planted bad seeds. Kobus insisted to JC that she was angry because she was forbidden fruit. She was pulling his chain, parroting the insults the liberal Western press threw at South Africans about their homeland. "I told him:" Kobus said, "Look at the advances Africans have made under our tutelage, advances in health care, education, employment opportunities."

JC could not be convinced. He began to do research. He read books and talked to people. He decided there was something to what the Jamaican girl claimed. He said he learned things that could not be denied.

"What things?" Petra asked.

"Things about your father."

"What?" Petra felt astonished.

"I told him it was ridiculous," Kobus insisted. He shrugged, putting his arm around her shoulders. But before she let him kiss her he told her, "I said, 'Look, man, well-intentioned people sometimes have to do these things. Take what the Brits—we're visiting Britain right now, man!—did to us in the Boer War. Put us in concentration camps. Fed our women and children crushed glass. And now we're here. Terrible things can happen to gain necessary ends.' But JC only shook his head. He turned his back on his father and on his people."

Because Kobus suddenly became passionate, Petra did not pay much attention then to what he said. She was preoccupied with controlling him. But now, driving through the night, she thought about JC. He saw the Jamaican girl as beautiful; their father would have seen her only as black. She thought of the African hitchhiker Gat had picked up. Riding with him had alarmed her but, despite what she'd told Gat, she did not seriously suppose he might be a terrorist. She hated his obsequiousness, the baas-baas-baas, the calling her Madam. Now she understood that servility was a protective mechanism. It warded off the possibility of— She could hardly think of the word. "Forcing change. Not a good idea, baas-baas-baas."

Now she wondered what he really thought. What did all of them think?

JC had concluded that their father was a torturer. If he did not inflict torture, he certainly authorized it. That was why JC had not come home. Their father understood this; that was why JC's name was never spoken. She thought they were a happy family. Now she realized how many things were never mentioned in their home: neither of her mother's sons, the nature of her father's work.

Tears began to fill her eyes. She slowed the car. She bit her lips and brushed the tears away. Was it torture that gave her father his black moods? She wondered if her mother knew. She must at least suspect. Her parents had married a dozen years before the Afrikaners took control of the government. Her mother had had two young children before her father began to get promotions. So what could she do?

Petra suddenly made out a white form on the highway before her. Some kind of boulder. She panicked, screamed, swerved off the pavement, bumped over the roadside shoulder, and hit a veld fence post. The car died. She sobbed, finally calmed down. She realized that the boulder she had swerved to miss was a sheep. Stupid beast! It was still standing on the road, watching her. She got out of the car, reached into the dust for a dirt clod, and hurled it at the sheep. It did not move. Petra circled the car. It seemed all right. She got back inside, nervously pumped the accelerator, and turned the ignition. The car would not start. She tried repeatedly. The motor would whine and grind with complaint as she held the ignition on, but it would not start.

Petra left the car and walked down the highway toward the sheep. It still had not moved. She ran at it, yelled at the top of her lungs, "Get off the road!" The sheep baaaed and trotted off. Petra turned back. She got into the car and tried to start it one last time. On this try the motor immediately fired into action.

Petra sat with the motor idling, wondering: Why am I here all alone in the middle of nowhere? What am I fleeing from? The horror of Gat killing Lumumba? Wasn't that also what Gat was fleeing from?

She got the car back onto the highway and headed south toward Beaufort West. When she neared the city, she wondered if she could find the hotel.

The entrance to the hotel was locked. She had to ring the bell several times. When the night clerk appeared, wiping sleep from his eyes, he regarded her through the windows of the door, then opened it for her. "Mevrou Prinsloo," he said.

"Dankie," Petra said again. "I'm sorry to wake you."

The man stared at her a long moment, then let her pass. "Your husband came down looking for you," he said.

"I'm sure he'll understand when I explain things." She tried to smile. "I'm afraid I'll need a key to the room."

"Maybe there is something I should show you," the night clerk said. He disappeared behind the reception counter, got a second room key, and returned holding a folder. "The police brought this by awhile ago." He opened the folder and showed her what was inside it: a photo of her, identified as a missing person. The clerk watched her stare at the photo. "Shall I call the police?"

"That won't be necessary," she said.

"Are you with Mr. Prinsloo of your own volition?"

"Yes," said Petra. "He's my fiancé. My father, who's a government official, thinks I'm too young to marry."

"You don't need to explain," the night clerk assured her. "This government spends too much time regulating our lives.

I myself live with a Bantu woman. We pretend she's my servant." He handed Petra the photo and the room key.

"Thank you," she said as she tiptoed toward the stairway.

SHE ENTERED the room as quietly as she could. She looked
at Gat asleep on the bed in his safari suit and tiptoed across
the room to set her purse and the photo and the keys on
the bureau. She went to the bed, sat on it slowly so that
the changed pressure on the mattress would not waken Gat,
reached down to remove her shoes, and lay down beside him.
She felt his hand fumbling for hers. He took it, brought it
to his mouth, and kissed it. She understood that the kiss was
a gesture of thanks. "I don't blame you for leaving," he said.
"I'm glad you came back."

"Your story frightened me."

"This is a beautiful little community, but I didn't want to
get stuck here."

Petra smiled.

"If you aren't sure you like me, knowing what you do
about me now . . . Well, I'm not sure I like myself."

They lay side by side, his hand enclosing hers. Gat had
pulled the shade down before the window overlooking the
car park. The red neon light outside the hotel bar had been
turned off. Now the ceiling loomed dark above them. Petra
felt gooseflesh rise on her arms. She wondered about getting
into the bed, about pulling away from Gat's hand, and standing and taking off her dress and sliding between the sheets.
Finally she said, "I have something." She rose from the bed,
got the photo from the bureau, and returned with it. Gat sat
up and turned on the bedside lamp. He looked at the photo
a long moment. "I was wishing I had one of you."

"The night clerk won't turn us in."

Gat pulled her down beside him and put his arm around her. "We could leave right now, but neither of us has had any sleep."

"What if we left when the man brings us tea? I could get a couple of hours."

Gat nodded and turned off the light. She returned the photo to the dresser, removed her dress, and came to the bed wearing her slip. She pulled back the spread and got in between the sheets. Gat rose and stripped to his shorts. He did not get into the bed, only pulled the spread over him.

They lay silently for a long time, each feeling a tension that held sleep at bay. Finally Gat whispered, "It's very hard for me to lie next to you and not want to make love to you."

"Maybe we should get married."

"You mean as a way to stop?"

They laughed and lay back, holding hands and staring at the darkness overhead. The pull toward lovemaking was strong, but Petra had been awake all night. Nor had Gat slept once she left. As they contemplated the possibility, sleep crept over them.

They did not waken until Gat heard the man knock with the tea. It was still dark outside. He gently wakened Petra and went to the bathroom. She joined him in the shower and finished up while he shaved. They drank tea quickly and got on the road.

CHAPTER EIGHT

EN ROUTE TO VRYBERG

Thursday, February 9, 1961

Gat drove the Ford north through the darkness. Petra slept on the backseat, her belongings piled on the seat beside Gat or on the floor. The air had an invigorating crispness. The sun would soon cook the entire landscape, turning the air to heat, burning skin, sucking juices out of animals and plants. But right now Gat felt a tingle of pleasure at being alive, moving through star-scattered darkness, the girl asleep behind him, a scent of her rising now and then from the belongings beside him, an occasional gasp in her breathing breaking the quietude, the hum of the motor a kind of lullaby. It occurred to Gat that if he had the power, he would command that his life go on forever like this.

Soon stars disappeared from the sky. As the sun rose, the air was so clear Gat could see for miles. Eventually—the sun was high now, the air heating up—he felt Petra's hands on his shoulders. He glanced in the rearview mirror to see her smiling, strands of hair glued to her face by sweat, saliva bright at the edges of her mouth. Her eyes were not yet fully open, sleep dust in their corners. "Meneer Prinsloo," she said, "are you hungry?"

"Mevrou Prinsloo," he replied, "shall we stop somewhere for breakfast?"

They got eggs, sausage and coffee, bread and cheese at a general store and pub in a tiny dorp. They drove on, Gat at the wheel, one hand steering, the other arm wrapped about Petra who sat with her back against him, her feet bare, watching the road.

Finally she asked, "Do you think we should get married?"

"What!" Gat burst out laughing.

"Why not?" He did not reply. "Wouldn't you like to keep driving like this forever?"

Gat would not admit that he had contemplated this very thought while she slept. "Why would we marry? You know nothing about me."

"But I do! Unless you've been lying."

"I'm a practiced liar, inveterate fibber."

Miffed, she slid across the seat and put her back against the door. She watched him. She was being provocative and he was damned if he would look at her. Petra swung her body toward him, stretched out her legs, and plopped her bare feet in Gat's lap. She ground her heels back and forth, hoping to excite a reaction in Gat's groin. When she succeeded, she crowed, "I know a great deal about you."

He grabbed her feet with his hands, steering with his knees, and began to tickle them. She screamed. She kicked her feet. Her kicks veered the car across the road. She screamed again, giggled. Gat grabbed the steering wheel and righted the car's direction.

After a time she asked, "Why not? We could go to Australia together." He drove on for a time. At last she repeated, "Why not?"

"Because I'm not eighteen."

"You're not going back to Katanga, are you?"

"Must you keep asking questions?"

"You say I don't know you. How am I going to if I don't ask questions?"

They drove in silence, past miserable farms: a house with pepper trees or scrawny acacias, a wind pump, and pond. Some distance away would be brick houses, painted white at a time beyond memory with roofs of corrugated tin weighted down by boulders, the huts of the laborers stuck, generation after generation, in servitude to the farm.

Seeing these dwellings, Gat felt almost as much a prisoner of his situation as the farmworkers were of theirs. If he did not go back to Katanga, he wondered, what would he do? If he returned, was there a future for him in the Belgian forces?

Petra said, "I think you've had too many women."

"My share, I guess. Maybe more than my share."

"I hate you for that!"

Gat reached over, picked up her foot, and kissed it. "Pity me," he said. "I need a longtime partner. Where there's love."

"We could love each other," Petra said. "When you hold me, I know that."

Gat kept driving.

"If you haven't been married—"

"You keep on, don't you?" he asked. "Like a little three-year-old!"

"Then how do you know you wouldn't like it?"

He placed an affectionate hand on her foot. "I could love you," he said. "And maybe I do—although I'm not sure what the hell that is. I'd still be the wrong man for you. You know that, don't you?"

Petra watched him, feeling off-balance, hearing at the same time what seemed to be both yes and no. "At least I got your attention."

Gat smiled. "You're young," he said, quite gently. "About to start university—where I've never been. You have your whole life ahead of you. You really have done something like save my life. I cannot repay you by nipping yours in the bud."

Petra said, "Stop the car! Stop it!"

Gat sped onto the shoulder and braked to a stop. Petra hurried from the car, leaving her door open. She leaned over, opened her mouth, and made retching sounds. Gat leaped from the car and hurried to her. "Are you sick?"

"Sick of your nobility!" She took a swing at him. He caught her arm, grabbed her, and embraced her. He pushed her back into the car.

They drove on, passing wretched homesteads. Gat caught sight of their inhabitants: farm laborers bound to peonage, wind-bitten, sun-burnt Afrikaner farmers, their wrinkled faces set grimly against all that opposed them in this land that desired to be desert.

Petra had been watching him. "Let's both start fresh," she suggested. "We'll disappear and become new people."

"I need to do that."

"If we were married, we could go to Australia together."

"How?" Gat asked. "Do you have a passport with you?" Petra nodded. "Oops!" Gat laughed. "I shouldn't have asked." He was quiet for a time. "I thought Mozambique," he said. "Or even Madagascar."

"I'd prefer Australia. They speak English."

Gat watched the road, realizing that it was indeed possible for them to get on a plane together for Sydney or Melbourne or Perth. Who could stop them? After a time he said, "You know, we don't have to be married to go to Australia together."

"I'm not going with you to Australia, unmarried, and have you leave me two weeks after we get there." She considered a moment. "We'd have to agree to stay together for a year."

"Six months," said Gat. He realized with a kind of horror that they were bargaining the way one did in an African market. That by saying "six months" he had accepted the basic framework of the arrangement she proposed. Now he was merely negotiating the details. "In two weeks you might find that you couldn't stand being with me."

"You'd still need to take care of me for a year. Until I got on my feet." As soon as she made the statement, Petra knew she must revise it. "We'd take care of each other."

As they moved past a stand of trees, their view suddenly opened onto a farmhouse edging a field. In their speed Gat saw a flash of a white man standing over a laborer. Was he beating him with a cane? He and Petra both heard the piteous cry—"Nie, baas! Nie, baas!"—and the whack of the cane. Gat took in the scarlet of blood running down the man's yellow face. By then the scene was gone. He and Petra looked at one another.

He glanced in the rearview mirror, suddenly pulled on the steering wheel, and swung the Ford across the road and in a half-circle. Thrown against the door, Petra gasped, "What're you doing?" The scene flashed past again. Once again Gat pulled on the wheel. Petra slid toward him, grabbing the dashboard. By then the Ford was heading onto the farmhouse lawn, directly toward the white man whose arm was raised and his mouth open as the Ford bore down on him. Gat held down the car horn. Three other laborers stood nearby—Gat had not noticed them—uncertain what to do. Gat skidded the car up to the white man, the horn still sounding, and shouted, "Stop that!"

The white man was well into middle age. Enraged by this impudence, he brought the cane down onto the hood of the Ford. Gat shot out of the car. The white man started away. Gat overtook him. He grabbed the cane and wrenched it from his grasp. The man stopped to confront Gat. Gat raised the cane. The man turned to hurry away. Gat brought the cane across his buttocks. The man looked back, his eyes fiery with anger. He screamed toward the house. Gat turned toward the fallen laborer. Petra shouted to him, "Get to the car! He's called for a gun!" The other laborers had lifted the wounded man. They were running, carrying him away. One of them shouted, *"Dankie, baas!"* Petra took Gat's arm, propelled him toward the car. A shot rang out. They ran for the car. The white man brandished a rifle. He took aim at Gat. Gat and Petra dove for the car. Gat slithered behind the wheel. Petra hunkered below the dashboard. Gat floored the accelerator. The car fishtailed across the yard. The white man aimed his rifle. He fired another shot. And another. And Gat and Petra were off down the highway.

As soon as it was clear they were safe, Gat burst out laughing. Petra watched him, astonished. She began to laugh. "What in God's name were you doing?"

"I was going to ask for directions," Gat replied mildly.

Petra shook her head. "You only made it worse for that kaffir, you know."

"Maybe," Gat said. "But they'll be talking about that moment for years." Pleased with himself, he reached over to tousle her hair.

"You're right," she told him. "I really know nothing about you."

THEY PICNICKED in a field on food left over from the previous day. When they got to Kimberley where the diamond rush had occurred in 1871, they stopped at a bar. Gat had a beer while Petra went to a telephone booth to report their progress to Gillian Prinsloo and get directions to the farm outside

Vryburg. After calling her friend, Petra telephoned her mother who had now flown back to Cape Town. "How was Father's meeting?" she asked when her mother came on the line.

"Darling, where are you?" Margaret exclaimed. "How are you?"

"I'm wonderful, Mum!" she said. "I think I'm in love." As they drove north, saying little after escaping bullets, Petra pondered the best way to advise her mother not to worry. This seemed the best approach; she would call when her father was still at his office.

"Oh, Pet!" her mother reacted.

"Aren't you happy for me?"

"Of course, darling. Is it anybody we know?"

"Don't tease me, Mum! I know Kobus called you. He must've been terribly upset."

"He talked to your father."

"He tried to seduce me. I wouldn't let him."

"Really? I don't think he told your father that." The two women chuckled together across the miles. "Where are you?"

"I can't tell you because I know Father has the police out looking for us."

"I told him that was not a good idea."

"I'm safe and happy. I just wanted you to know." She added, "And in love."

"Do you and Captain Gautier— Make love?"

"Whenever we can," Petra said. Then she giggled. "We're very restrained," she insisted. "Only when we go to bed and when we wake up. Isn't it fun?"

"Be careful, Pet. You don't want to get— You know, preggers."

"We may get married," Petra said, just to keep her parents off balance.

"Oh, darling, please be careful. Where are you?"

"I can't tell you, Mum! Tell Father that I love him. We expect we'll get to Joeys tomorrow."

While Petra phoned, Gat nursed his beer, thumbing through a month-old South African newsmagazine. The advertisements seemed pale copies of those displayed in *Paris Match* or the European edition of *Life*. One of them showed a woman of means, trim and very pretty, late thirties, standing beside a locally manufactured Ford convertible. A balloon rising out of her head shared her secret thought: that the vehicle would be the perfect getaway car for a romantic weekend with her husband. "Hello there, chum." Gat heard the voice; he knew it was in his head. "How are you these days?" The woman in the advert was the actress he'd spent the night with in Cape Town. She looked good.

"I called my Mum," Petra said as she rejoined him. "I told her we might get married." Gat said nothing. "She asked if we made love. I said, 'Whenever we could.'"

"We missed yesterday."

"I couldn't bear to tell her," Petra said.

As THEY approached Vryburg, they encountered a roadside market and a crowd of people, standing in the highway. Petra, who was driving, slowed the car and pulled onto the shoulder. Bystanders surrounded the car, jabbering in a language Gat could not understand. "There's been an accident," Petra told him. "A woman's been hit by a car." Gat got out and pushed through the crowd.

In a small open space, fetid with the heat and stench of bodies, a young, pregnant woman lay in the road. Littered around her were the vegetables she had been carrying in an enamel pan. It rested nearby. Gat crouched beside her. She looked up at him, imploring him with her eyes for help. Gat rose erect, still on his knees, and gestured for the onlookers to give the woman air. Petra came beside him, holding a thermos. She knelt beside the woman, put an arm under her shoulders and, holding up her head, poured water into her mouth. Gat stood and urged, "Stand back! Please, stand back!" Flailing his arms, he opened a pathway out of the crowd.

A white woman suddenly appeared. "Thank God you're here!" she said. "I was afraid there might be an incident." The woman was perhaps thirty-five. A boy of about ten stood at her side.

"Let's go, Mum," the boy said. "Let's get out of here."

"I don't know how this happened," the woman told Gat.

"It was your car that hit her?" he asked.

"She came out of nowhere. I was driving along very carefully. Suddenly she was there. Under my wheels. I couldn't stop!"

"Have you sent for an ambulance?" Gat asked. It was obvious she hadn't.

"I don't think we should move her," the woman said.

"You just want to leave her in the sun? It could take hours." The woman seemed not to know what to say. "Can we put her in your car?" Gat asked.

A look of confusion swept across the woman's face. "In my car?"

"Do you know the area?" Gat asked. "We're strangers here."

"I can't have her in my car," the woman said. "I've got my son here."

Gat gave her a friendly, reasonable smile. "But you hit her."

The woman looked as if more was being asked of her than she could manage.

"Let's get out of here!" the child said again.

"If we put her into my car," Gat asked, "can you lead us into town?"

"But I have no idea where the Bantu hospital is," the woman said. "I suppose I could ask, couldn't I?"

"Mum, let's go!"

"You find out where the hospital is," Gat said, taking command. "We'll get her into my car. Then we'll follow you."

"Good idea." The woman grabbed her son's hand decisively and started through the crowd.

Gat again pushed through the bystanders to kneel beside Petra. "I guess it's up to us to get her to hospital," he said. "The woman who hit her can't cope."

"I'll go fix the car," Petra said, starting off. "Can you carry her?"

Gat knelt close beside the woman to lift her into his arms. When he reached his arms toward her, she looked terrified. Tears filled her eyes. A wail escaped from her lips and with it a rush of breath that carried the odor of her fear. "It's going to be all right," Gat reassured her.

As he crouched, he could feel the crunch of vegetables beneath his knees. "I'm just going to lift you," he said quietly. As he moved an arm around her shoulders, the woman grabbed his shirt with one hand and his neck with the other. "We'll get you to the car." She whimpered as he slid an arm beneath her legs. As he lifted her, she swooned. As he stood, she sobbed. She jabbered frightened words, gesticulating for the enamel pan. Someone handed it to her. As Gat moved her toward the Ford, he saw the white woman and her son speed off toward town and disappear.

HE AND Petra got the injured woman onto the backseat. Gat felt a pride in Petra that in an emergency, a peasant woman injured, she did not think about her belongings. She found an adolescent who said he knew the way to the hospital for non-whites. Gat and he and Petra, who held the woman's hand, got into the front seat. Gat started off. The boy proved not to know where the hospital was; he merely seized an opportunity to ride in a car. But by stopping passersby and asking directions they found the facility at last. It was a bungalow in need of a new roof, more a clinic-dispensary than a real hospital.

Even at midafternoon lines of people waited in its courtyard for attention from the doctor: ancients hobbling about on makeshift crutches, a blind woman led by a child, men with knife wounds received in fights over women or with them, bawling babies with open sores. Some of these patients stood tiredly, half-asleep, worn out beyond emotion, all vigor drained from their faces. Others yakked and laughed, even in their misery. The relatives of patients were camped before cook fires in the yard.

When Gat and Petra emerged from the car, the courtyard fell silent. All eyes turned toward the whites who had suddenly appeared in this realm of blacks. Children began to howl. Those who could scurried or limped behind their mothers' legs, then peeked out. Petra glanced at Gat, a look of puzzlement on her face. Just then a nurse hurried toward them across the courtyard. Her speed and the officiousness reserved for whites embarrassed Gat. When the nurse saw the woman he and Petra helped from the car, she shouted commands at an orderly. He brought a stretcher. He and Gat moved the injured woman onto it and carried her inside the bungalow past people who seemed to have waited since the dawn of time. The doctor, an Indian, came at a run. When he saw the patient was black, he relaxed and assured Gat he would attend to her as soon as she was admitted.

Admitting the woman proved more complicated than Gat expected. While Petra waited in the car, he filled out papers.

He agreed to pay the woman's medical fees, stressing that it was not he who hit her. A second batch of papers demanded Gat's attention; he must explain what he knew of the accident.

The Indian doctor reappeared. With a smile he said, "The nurse tells me you are not South African. Is that correct?"

"I'm a Belgian. Just driving through."

"Come to my office," the doctor urged. "It's more comfortable there."

"This is fine," Gat told him.

"Please come." The doctor spoke with a tone so importunate that Gat examined him. "I insist that you be comfortable at my clinic."

Gat followed the doctor to a small office in an adjoining building. Its desk overflowed with medical files, patient charts, and requisitions for supplies. The doctor cleared space for Gat to work at the desk, stacking the medical files on one of the wooden chairs facing it, leaving a second chair empty. Nodding toward the empty chair the doctor commented, "You never know when a patient will enter."

"This really is unnecessary," Gat assured the man. "I had plenty of space in the waiting room."

The doctor closed the door. He said quietly, "Two Africans were killed this morning." He looked at Gat with such intensity that Gat heard no other sounds. The doctor repeated his query, "You are not South African?"

"No."

The doctor lowered his voice to a whisper. "They were killed by the police." Gat nodded. "Special Branch officers brought them here, hoping to extract information from them. But they both died." The doctor smiled apologetically. "Things are a little tense right now. I thought it might be easier for you here."

"The young woman with me is out in the car," Gat said. "Should she—"

"No, no." The doctor gestured assurance. "She is perfectly safe. In fact, I will go talk to her until you are finished. Excuse me."

The doctor left the office. Gat returned to work on his short narrative of the accident. As he wrote, he heard footsteps on the porch outside. The door opened. A man entered the office without knocking. Gat glanced at him and said, "The doctor's in the clinic." The man nodded, shut the office door, and lowered himself into the chair that the doctor had emptied. He studied Gat in silence, his body bent forward, elbows resting on the chair arms, hands folded together. Gat returned to his narrative. Without looking at the man, Gat scrutinized him. He was an African, middle-aged, but he did not belong among the impoverished supplicants outside. Dressed in a coat and tie, wearing glasses and boots made for walking, he carried himself with the self-respect and quiet confidence of a white man. Finally he said, "I see that you are a friend to Africans." The man spoke in a voice so low that Gat could hardly hear it.

"Not everyone would say so."

"I can see that it's true."

Gat glanced at the man and continued with his work.

The man said quietly, "I need to get to Lobatse. Could you take me there?"

The man did not seem like any African Gat had ever encountered. "I don't know Lobatse," he said. "Where is that?" He returned to his work.

"Due north. Not far. In Bechuanaland. Just across the border."

Gat did not look up from his work. He replied, "We are headed to Joburg."

"It's a matter of great urgency," the man said. "Even life or death."

"Are you from South Africa?" Gat asked without looking up.

"I'm a Xhosa. From the Transkei. I've been in America for fifteen years. Sometimes I'm taken for an American."

"And you've come back here. Why is that?"

"To help my people. But there are dangers here just now." Gat scrutinized the man. Through his glasses he met Gat's gaze. Gat judged that he was perhaps forty and educated and possessed a certain presence. "I thought I might make a small difference in South Africa now," the man continued. "Things are happening here. But to do my bit, I must get to Bechuanaland."

Gat asked, "What makes you think you can trust me?"

"One develops a sense about such things." The men stared at one another. Finally the African added, "Also I've run out of options."

Gat returned to his writing and said nothing until he finished. "I'll be here tomorrow morning. To check on a woman's progress. If you're here, I may be able to help you."

"Thank you, my friend," the man said. He offered his hand. Gat shook it. "Till tomorrow." The African left the office quietly. Gat heard his footsteps moving off along the porch.

NEITHER GAT nor Petra spoke as he drove through Vryburg. Once he had turned onto the unpaved road leading to the Prinsloo farm, Petra said, "The children shrieked when they saw us. Why was that? Because we're white?" Gat nodded. "Those dear people," Petra said. "They'd been waiting all day in the sun and no one to help them. We got helped immediately." Gat grunted, thinking that her noticing this was good for her.

After a moment he informed her that an educated African had asked for a lift into Bechuanaland and that he was inclined to take him there. "Do you mind if I use the car?" he asked.

"Not at all. I'll go with you." She assumed an imperious air, challenging him.

"No, no. Stay with your friend. Have the day with her. I'll drive up there and come back."

Petra, who had told Gat what good friends she and Gillian were, now said that they really were not that close. "We've really come here so that I can show you off." Gat gave her a skeptical look. "All the girls thought I was goody-goody because I was the policeman's daughter. Gill was the ringleader. I want to show her I've grown up."

"Will you tell her what you told your mother?"

"Of course not! I'll make her ask." Petra smiled exultantly.

"And what do you say when she does?"

"I'll tell her to ask you."

"And I'll say I've made a vow of chastity," Gat said.

"Yes, do that. Chastity looks like being your middle name."

A pickup drew up behind them, coming fast. It gave them a warning blast from its horn and hurried past, filling the Ford with dust. Once it cleared, Petra and Gat made out sheep grazing in a pasture with a herd boy keeping watch. "That's probably the farm up ahead," said Petra.

"I'll run the fellow up there and be back by midafternoon."

Petra's expression showed that she was determined to go along.

"He probably belongs to the ANC," Gat said.

"Of course he does. That's why I want to go."

"I might be arrested. Police might confiscate the car—not that your father will have any trouble getting it back. If you're not with us, you won't be involved."

"I want to be involved!" Petra exclaimed. "I couldn't arrive at varsity a virgin and I can't arrive saying I've never helped a terrorist escape from this police state."

They saw a bungalow sited on the top of a knoll and came abreast of a sign saying "Prinsloo." They followed the tire tracks leading up to the house and found before it the pickup that had passed them. The driver's door was open and the motor still running. In the doorway they spied a couple engaged in a passionate greeting, the young man bending the woman backward as he kissed her, one hand under her skirt grasping her buttock and the top of her leg. When Gat stopped the car, Petra leaned over and sounded the horn.

"Halloo there!" called the young woman, disentangling herself from the embrace. "Guess who just got home!"

"Been away for a week," Dannie Prinsloo said. "I missed home."

Petra left the car, ran to Gillian, and embraced her. She shook hands with Dannie and introduced Gat.

"Where did you find him?" Gillian asked.

"Floating on a pond in a reed basket," Petra said. "Just like Baby Moses."

The Prinsloos laughed, but the comment, suggesting a jocular and intimate relationship, took Gat by surprise. He stood erect, hands behind his back, and explained, "I'm a friend of Petra's father. He and I met on an earlier trip I made from the Congo where I'm serving." Gat managed to seem stiff and boring, and Petra's comments suggested a ridiculing of that stiffness. The Prinsloos hardly greeted him, thinking about getting Dannie properly welcomed home.

"The captain wanted to see some of South Africa," Petra improvised, "and Father suggested he drive me up to Wits as a chaperone. And here we are."

Gillian gave Petra a skeptical look, but it was only fleeting for Prinsloo took her by the waist. With a grin he suggested, "You wouldn't want to look at sheep for half an hour, would you? I'm just home and that would give me time to clean up."

"We're passionately interested in sheep!" Petra declared. She and Gat headed back toward the Ford, Gat walking stiffly, seemingly a rigid presence who regarded Petra as he might a child.

"Make it forty-five minutes," Prinsloo shouted, "and I might even be able to shower!"

As they drove into the pasture, they each thought that, despite the heat, they might occupy themselves in the same way the Prinsloos were doing if only they could find the shade of a tree under which to park. But there were no trees. And as soon as the Ford crept onto the other side of the knoll half a dozen boys ran toward them out of the shanties that were the farmworkers' houses. The boys stared at the car as if they had never before seen such a thing.

AT SUNSET Piet Rousseau joined his wife in the garden where she was reading an American novel called *The Invisible Man.* Her sister in England had sent it to her. Piet carried drinks for both of them, gin tonics, and wore shorts, sandals, and a faded madras cloth shirt. He gazed out across the roofs of Cape Town and broke the news to his wife that there was nothing to report on the disappearance or kidnapping of their daughter.

"I heard from her," Margaret said. "She said to say she loves you."

"But she made sure to call when I'd be gone," he grumbled. "How is she?"

Margaret told him that she sounded happy enough. She neglected to mention the lilt and merriness in Petra's voice, her assurance that she was in love, or her pleasure in the new adventure she had discovered, namely lovemaking. "She wouldn't tell me where she was. It's ever so much more delightful an enterprise if we don't know." Rousseau grunted. "She also claimed that Kobus tried to seduce her."

"She must have looked ready for it, the way she's been acting."

"You really are annoyed with her, aren't you?"

Rousseau took a long swallow of his gin tonic, nurturing his anger. "Is she with that Belgian?"

"Apparently."

"Does she give him what she withheld from Kobus?"

"I don't ask questions when I don't want to know the answers."

Rousseau swore under his breath in Afrikaans. "He better be taking her to Joburg, not Katanga."

"She said they'll be there tomorrow." Then Margaret added, "She's not happy about your trying to hunt her down."

Rousseau swore again in Afrikaans. It infuriated him that Petra had run off, just the way a kaffir would, with a man she did not know. He was sure that she had given herself to that man with the same casual abandon that had caused her mother problems at the same time of her life. It was his conviction that if women were introduced to sex too early, it came to dominate their lives. They hungered for it, became wanton. Wisely he had never expressed this thought to Margaret. Still, he considered her an example that proved the rule. Once he began to take her places, she had offered very little resistance to his importuning for sex.

As a young man he had supposed their lovemaking confirmed his personal magnetism. By the time he learned of her child, he had fallen too much under her spell to break off the relationship. During the early disagreements of their married life, he brooded over her association with the child's father. He pestered her with questions about other lovers and would not believe her contentions that there had been none. Once the marriage became solid, he stopped worrying about other men she had known. Instead he congratulated himself on saving her from a dissolute life. Now he felt affronted that his wife's blood had passed her profligacy to his daughter. While Petra's action reminded him of his own defiance of his father, he resented her defiance of him. And he hated the fact that men, both Kobus and this Belgian, sought to dally with his well-brought-up girl.

He himself had dallied with African girls; that was where young white men should work off their lusts. He vowed to himself that he would punish Captain Gautier. In doing so, he would right the wrong that a college student had done Margaret so many years ago. He sat nursing his resentments in the same way he nursed his drink. "We should fly up to Joburg to see that she's all right," Rousseau told his wife. "We can find her at varsity."

"Darling," Margaret said with as much patience as she could muster, "she's not your little girl anymore. We trained her for eighteen years. Now she wants to be on her own. I feel certain this business with the Belgian is not 'an adventure.'" Although she knew that Petra was truly having an adventure, she said the word in a way that mocked it, mocked him. "She's just guaranteeing that she does not arrive at varsity looking like a child starting school. We have to stay here."

Rousseau swore again under his breath, determined that Captain Gautier would be called to account. And interrogated about his connection to the man murdered in District Six. He thought of the various tortures he might inflict on the man whenever he caught up with him. He was certain that he would catch up with him.

AFTER DINNER while the day's last light faded from the sky Dannie Prinsloo walked Gat around the farm. Petra remained inside to help Gillian clean up. She asked if Gillian thought she had done the right thing in choosing the hard life of farming with twenty-four-year-old Dannie in preference to pursuing her education. Gillian gazed out the open kitchen window. "If you love the man, why not be with him?" she asked, speaking as much to herself as to Petra. "You saw how eager he was for me this afternoon. That makes me feel good."

A breeze lifted the hair hanging over Petra's forehead and cooled her face. Her friend tiredly returned to her chores. "If I'm here in ten years with more tots underfoot than I can count, I may wish I'd gone to varsity."

Petra smiled. She wondered where she would be in ten years. And what would have happened to Gat?

Walking around the farm together, Prinsloo told Gat, "I apologize for being so ardent with my wife when you arrived this afternoon."

"I doubt she minds being missed."

"I needed to be sure everything was all right with her," Prinsloo explained. "The best way to find that out was to—Well, you saw what we were up to." The men walked on. "I stopped in town on the way out here. Heard some news. Got out here as fast as I could. Wanted to be sure she was safe. That she felt safe."

"What news? Mind if I ask?"

"Two kaffirs were murdered outside of town. Terrorists, probably. Late last night, early this morning. In a place they had no business being."

Gat said nothing. They walked on.

"Police found them. Tried to get them to their own hospital to save them. But it was too late." Prinsloo spat into the dust. "Bloody kaffirs have no regard for life. Kill each other every weekend in knife fights over women. There are warrior gangs in every hostel. Terrorists come through here, demanding food and lodging. Terrorize our people. Rape girls. No wonder some of them end up dead. I know you've seen this very thing in the Congo."

"The men killed in Vryburg were terrorists?"

Prinsloo nodded. "Up by Zeerust near the border the ANC has stirred things up. The kaffirs refuse to pay taxes. A chief was assassinated not long ago for being a government lackey. Anybody tries to accomplish something: he's a government lackey. A kaffir dies violently: it was the police killed him. No one's hurt around here but the kaffirs mutter we caused it. Why would we kill kaffirs? For God sake they're our work force!" Prinsloo shook his head with frustration. "Why would we kill the people who do the work that makes it possible to farm here?"

Gat gave a noncommittal grunt.

"My wife doesn't know about the murders," Prinsloo confided. "Don't say anything. I'll tell her after you're gone." He swore in Afrikaans. "I love living on this land. But one day we'll have to move into town. Before any babies come."

Back in the kitchen Gillian was apologizing to Petra about the smallness of the house. It served for now, she said, but if she and Dannie were to have children, they would need to add bedrooms. "I'm sorry there's no bed for the captain."

"He's been sleeping in the car anyway," Petra said. "I guess after places he's slept in the Congo that Ford is pretty luxurious."

Gillian examined her face. Because two years had passed since they'd seen one another, the examination offered no clues as to whether Petra was telling the truth. "Do you still see Kobus Terreblanche?" Gillian asked.

Petra nodded. "He tried to get with me the other morning in my bedroom."

"What was he doing there?"

"Trying to get into my bed!" The women laughed.

"You might have enjoyed it. I do."

"I'm going to Wits to meet other men."

"What's wrong with Captain Gautier?"

"He's years and years older than Dannie."

"What's wrong with that?" Gillian teased. "He knows the drill."

Petra turned up her nose. "He seems a little stiff, don't you think?"

"Stiff is just the thing in bed, you know."

LYING ON the sitting room couch, waiting for sleep, Petra heard snickerings and shushings from the bedroom. Next came the steady rhythms of poundings and thrustings followed by gasps and sighs. Petra gritted her teeth, wishing it were hers and Gat's bodies making those noises. They had not made love in what seemed an eternity. She wondered if she dared go outside to the car.

Outside in the Ford Gat could not sleep. The front seat was not long enough for his body. His head kept jabbing the handle that raised and lowered the window. Now and then his legs bumped the steering wheel. He had rubbed his body with sticky insect repellent. Even so, he had closed up the car against mosquitoes and wore socks to cover their favorite places of visitation. He sweated in his shorts and tee shirt.

The smell of Petra's perfumed belongings annoyed him; it reminded him that with better planning they could have been together in a hotel.

Then out of nowhere he heard faintly the distant throbbing of drums. The Africans in the workers' camp of the farm must be dancing. He wondered about the African who said he needed to get to Lobatse. Who was he? What dangers were involved in taking him there?

When it seemed he had lain on the front seat forever, Gat stuffed his feet into shoes and left the car. Standing outside it, he put on the shorts of his safari suit and trudged off in the direction of the drumming. He moved across the knoll and down toward the workers' shacks. In a circle before a fire men and women danced, clapping their hands, chanting to the beat of the drums played by men at the edge of the firelight, a leader designating steps from the center of the circle.

Gat began to move to the rhythms. The drumming, the clapping, the raised voices, the motion of the dance: these all set up a physical longing for Petra. And a deep sense of pleasure in Africa. If he and Petra went to Australia together, would he miss Africa? Some people claimed that its hold—despite all that you complained of it—never released you. Would he feel that way? But he knew he would never go to Australia. He had a job in Katanga. He was owed pay there. Had an apartment and belongings. He could not leave them behind.

As PETRA waited for sleep, Dannie's deep-throated snoring assailed the nocturnal quietude. Petra slipped off the couch. She tiptoed to the front door, pulled it open, and ran barefoot to the car, wearing only her nightie. As soon as Gat wakened, she would—

Where was he? His shoes were gone. So were the shorts of his safari suit. Had he gone? She dared not call for him. Had he left her? She peered into the darkness, heard the drumming. Had he gone there?

She stood, wondering what to do: get inside the car and wait for him? Or go back inside? Infernal man! He was supposed to be in the car!!

Coming back across the knoll, his eyes now well adjusted to the darkness, Gat saw Petra, and her light pink nightgown, standing beside the car. He had a strong impulse to run to her. Instead he stopped stock-still. He made out her arms, waving off mosquitoes. He wanted to be with her, to hold her. They could spend the rest of the night together in the car. He watched her figure turn this way and that, searching for him in the starlight. He might whisper her name. But he did nothing.

He watched Petra return inside the house. He waited for a time, wondering if she would come out again. If she did, he would go to her. Why, he asked himself, had he done nothing? Because she was beginning to mean too much to him. He must keep some distance.

CHAPTER NINE

VRYBURG

Friday, February 10, 1961

At dawn Petra, already dressed, marched out to the Ford, carrying a tall mug of tea, and peered through the windshield. Gat lay stretched out on the front seat, his knees bent under the steering wheel, his spine against the seat backs, his right arm folded beneath his head as a pillow. He looked like a package stuffed into a box too small for it. Petra grinned at the sight and rapped sharply on the hood. At the tinny sound of banging, Gat looked at her sleepily. Through the windshield she showed him the mug of tea. He sat upright. She opened the door and offered him the tea.

He got out of the car, barefoot and in underwear, stretched, and touched his toes. He took the tea, drank deeply of it, and set it on the roof of the car.

"Did you miss me last night?" Petra asked.

Rotating his torso, he shook his head dismissively and beamed. She felt pleased.

"I came out here in the middle of the night," she confessed.

"You did?" Across the roof of the car Gat noticed Gillian Prinsloo watching them out the kitchen window.

She leaned close to him and whispered, "I wanted you to make love with me on the front seat of a car. So that I can tell everyone at varsity that I've done it there."

"I don't suppose I should kiss you," he said. "Your friend Mevrou—what's her name?—is watching us. I'm not good at names."

"Her name is Gillian Prinsloo," the girl said. Gat raised his cup of tea to the woman watching them. "My name is Petra."

"Petra," said Gat. "I must remember that."

"You might get dressed as well," Petra suggested. "Where were you last night?"

"I took a walk to think about today," he said. He reached inside the car for the shorts of his safari suit and his shoes.

"What about today?"

"Look toward the house," Gat instructed. He turned his back to the car and the house, adjusted himself inside his underwear, and stepped into the shorts of his safari suit. He sat down on the car seat, dusted off his feet, and withdrew socks from his shoes. "I don't want you to come with me today," he told her. "It's too dangerous." She said nothing while he put on his shoes and socks. Then he stood beside her, drinking tea.

"Thank you for abandoning me," Petra said, angry at his male instinct about protecting a female, his adult's instinct about protecting a child. "I really don't want to be here. And if it's too dangerous for me, why are you going?"

"I root for this chap trying to escape the police." Petra regarded him disdainfully. He took a mouthful of tea and gazed off across the veld, at the sun turning it a tawny color. "The police have all the power, all the weapons. Hard not to root for a man who's trying to beat those odds."

"You think taking him to Lobatse cancels it with Lumumba?"

"I'm not abandoning you," he told her. "Have a day with your friend. You haven't seen her in a long time. I'll come back this evening. We'll tell the Prinsloos I spent the day seeing about the woman at the hospital."

He did not tell her that he assumed it would go worse with him and the American if they were caught at the border and she were with them. Piet Rousseau would claim that they were kidnapping her, taking her out of her homeland against her will. If Gat had judged Rousseau correctly, Petra would not be permitted to give her own statement. Her father would give her statement for her.

Experience had taught Gat that preparation was key to the success of any operation and he regarded the border crossing as an operation. He was unsure how Petra would act at a border post. In a situation of danger it was not beyond possibility that her self-possession might falter, that she would lose her self-control.

"And what about tonight?" Petra asked. "You sleep out here again?" Gat shrugged. "And that's fine with you?"

"What else do you suggest?"

"What about Australia? If we're going to Australia, I'm coming with you to Lobatse."

"And if we're not going to Australia?"

"I want to know it right now."

Gat finished his tea and left the cup on the roof of the car. He reached inside the Ford for the safari suit tunic and his shaving kit. When he emerged, Petra was watching him, her expression as cold as ice. "I don't know what's happening to me," he told her, "but I know what's happening to you. You're going to university to get a decent start in life."

"Don't treat me like a child," she said. "When I'm in your bed—"

"Enough of that." Gat tightly shook his head. "This man is an African. Maybe dangerous. You were upset when I gave an African a lift the other day."

"I understand you better now."

Gat put an expression of annoyance on his face. He said, "I have to piss and I have to shave." He took the mug and started toward the house.

As THE women made them breakfast, Gat and Dannie stood at the back of the kitchen listening to the morning news, the Prinsloos' one connection to a world beyond the veld. The newscaster did not report the murder the previous day of two terrorists near Vryburg, but he announced that Patrice Lumumba, the deposed premier of the strife-torn Congo, had escaped from his jail in the western part of the breakaway province of Katanga. Petra stopped making toast and looked at Gat. He stared back at her. Lumumba had escaped with two colleagues, the newscaster went on. He was being hunted throughout Katanga.

"They've got that monkey on the run!" Dannie exclaimed. He stepped excitedly across the kitchen and slapped his wife's bottom. "I hope they catch him," he cried. "Chop him into little pieces and feed him to the crocs!"

The situation remained confused, the newscaster said. Reports from East Bloc sources suggested that Lumumba was heading toward Kivu province in the eastern Congo. However, a United Nations observer, a Ghanaian, claimed that the escape of so valuable a prisoner was improbable; in all likelihood it was a cover-up in-the-making to hide the fact that Lumumba had already been executed. Moise Tshombe, president of Katanga, denied reports that Lumumba had been killed.

Watching one another, neither Petra nor Gat moved during the report of this news.

"What will happen, Captain?" asked Gillian. Then she added, "Petra, you're falling behind with the toast."

"I expect we'll know in a day or two," Gat predicted.

"If they've killed him," Gillian asked, "what happens to the Congo?"

"Chaos and confusion!" Dannie shouted exultantly. "And nothing could be better for us! Let those kaffir terrorists who want to run this country see what a balls-up blacks make when they try to run something! Am I right, Captain?"

"My father's sentiments, I'm sure," declared Petra so that Gat did not have to answer.

GAT WAS quiet as they drove away from the Prinsloo farm. Petra ventured, "You won't be sorry you brought me along."

"You're a woman who has to have her own way."

"Am I?" Petra smiled enigmatically. "You know why you've never married? Because the only women you've ever known were dishrags. You sleep with them, but they don't interest you."

"What a miserable place to live," Gat declared. "How much longer do you suppose that marriage will last?" Petra did not reply. "The sex with him must be great. I can't imagine why else she'd stay."

"It is great," Petra informed him. "I heard them at it for hours last night." Then after a moment she added, "It made me miss you."

Gat watched the road for a long moment. Then he reached over to touch her shoulder.

EVEN BEFORE they entered the hospital compound, all Gat's senses were alert. He turned off the radio and glanced around them completely and into the rearview mirror. His tension put Petra on alert. "Police," he said. She started to speak, but he put an index finger to his lips. She realized that the hospital courtyard was virtually silent despite the Africans waiting in it.

"When we enter the *cités* in Elisabethville," Gat whispered, "a hush always greets us. They're usually noisy places, full of jabbering. But when we enter, looking for someone, even the radios grow hushed." He nodded to her. She followed the direction of his nod and saw two uniformed Africans standing near the entry to the surgery. "They're looking for our American," Gat said.

"Are we going in?" Petra asked. Gat nodded. He parked the car, got out, and started for the hospital office. Petra followed him. They spoke to an African receptionist about the woman they had brought to the hospital. Gat paid her medical fees. As an orderly took them across the courtyard, Petra felt the eyes of the Africans camped there shifting between them and the African policemen at the door of the surgery.

In the ward where the woman lay recuperating in a bed, her husband and sisters surrounded her. Upon seeing Gat, the husband stood and bowed humbly to the two whites. "*Dankie! Dankie, baas!*" he said, his hand ready to grasp Gat's as soon as Gat might offer his. Gat extended his hand. The African took it in both of his hands and, holding it, bowed again, addressing him in grateful Afrikaans.

"The man says you saved his wife. And his baby's life," Petra explained.

The injured woman reached up gratefully from the bed. Gat and Petra took her hands and spoke encouraging words to her. They shook hands with her sisters. As they returned across the courtyard, the receptionist intercepted them. He handed Gat an envelope and said, "Here is the receipt for your payment, baas. Thank you."

"I don't need a receipt," Gat said.

"Take it, baas. Take it!" The man quickly moved away and Gat understood that the envelope contained a message.

As they moved toward the car, a voice called out, "Excuse me! Just a minute, please!" A young police officer, white, hurried over to them. "Maybe you could give us some help," he said. "We're looking for a terrorist."

Gat and Petra stopped beside the car as the officer approached. He seemed not for some time to have beheld a young woman as pretty as Petra and hardly took his eyes off her. "How can we help?" Gat asked.

"Have you seen this man?" The officer held out a photo to Petra. She studied it, shook her head, and passed it to Gat. Examining it, he recognized the American as he might have appeared more than a decade earlier. Petra watched him for some evidence that this was the man who needed a ride to Lobatse.

Gat shook his head. "What's happening?" he asked, returning the photo.

"The treason trial's winding down in Joburg," the officer explained. "Once the death sentences are handed down—"

"There'll be executions?" Petra asked with surprise.

"We expect so," the officer said, smiling at her. "We're trying to protect you."

"Oh," Petra replied quietly.

"We assume these fellows will try to make some mischief once the verdicts come down. This is a big one. We know he's in this area, trying to get across the border." The officer smiled again at Petra. "Could you let authorities know if you see him?"

"Of course, Officer," she said, smiling shyly. "We'd be glad to help."

As they drove away from the hospital, Gat remarked, "I think our young officer was a lot more interested in winning a smile from you than in finding his terrorist."

Pleased at this observation, Petra slapped Gat's arm. "Was that your American?"

"An old photo. But the same fellow."

Once they left the town, Gat pulled onto the shoulder to open the envelope. He read the note and looked at Petra. "We could be in Joburg by nightfall," he said. "Get a room in a good hotel. Enjoy ourselves in a way we haven't for a while."

"Is that what you want?" He shrugged. "It's not, is it?"

"I don't want you getting hurt. Or scared. Or arrested."

She watched him for a moment, then turned toward the empty veld that stretched uninterrupted by buildings or trees or rock outcroppings as far as the horizon. "I didn't know they expected to execute these treason trial defendants." She listened to the wind. "I haven't paid much attention to the trial. Father says it's a foregone conclusion they're guilty. Do you think they are?"

Gat gestured uncertainly.

"I knew they'd convict them," Petra said. "But not execute them." She felt the sun growing hot on her skin and the dryness of the air. "If they catch this American, will they execute him?"

Gat watched her growing up before his eyes. He said nothing.

"What's the note say?" she asked.

"Three miles out of town on the left we'll find some farm laborers' dwellings," Gat said. "We stop there to check our tires. One of them will need changing and we unload the spare tire." They looked at one another. "That's apparently a signal that we're willing to take this man to Lobatse." Petra again stared out across the veld, beginning to understand, with the news of probable executions, how it was that the Lumumba business haunted Gat. "Or we can be in a good hotel tonight in Joburg," Gat said, "enjoying ourselves."

"Let's go to Lobatse," Petra said. "So we'll enjoy ourselves even more tomorrow night."

Once they were moving again, Gat said, "You understand there are risks involved in doing this." Petra nodded. "I can't imagine that it serves any useful purpose for him to know that I'm a Belgian Army officer. I assume that would only make him nervous. Let's say I'm a furniture manufacturer from Belgium looking at the possibility of siting a factory in South Africa."

"Who shall I be?" Petra wondered. She thought a moment while Gat scanned the roadside for the workers' encampment. "I'll be the Chamber of Commerce guide taking you around." She paused for a moment. "Do I seem old enough for that?"

THEY FOUND the farmworkers' shacks standing off behind the growth of weeds beside the road and pulled off the pavement. A boy, perhaps seven, raced off to the shacks. Gat pretended not to notice his flight through the weeds. Under Petra's supervision, Gat unloaded her belongings from the trunk of the car, placing them carefully on a blanket spread over the dust. He extracted the jack, tire iron, and spare tire and began work on the left rear wheel. Petra kept an eye on the road. As

Gat was loosening lug bolts, he heard the rustle of vegetation. Someone approached behind him. Before Gat could look up, the person had set down two ancient suitcases and asked in American-accented English, "Who's the young lady?"

"A friend of mine," Gat said. "You can trust her." He looked carefully at the man whose endangered life might endanger their own lives. "I guess this tire isn't as bald as I thought." He started tightening the lug bolts he had just loosened.

The American asked, "Mind if I put these cases in the trunk? Way in back." Gat nodded his agreement and the man leaned into the trunk, stretching his body, to place the cases as far back as he could reach. He also returned the spare tire to its nest below the floor of the trunk. Gat placed the jack and tire iron beside them. "I'm grateful to you for doing this." The man extended his hand.

Gat shook it and began to replace Petra's belongings into the trunk. She put some of them on the rear seat and went back to watching the road. When Gat finished, he wiped his hands on a rag lying in the trunk and passed it to the other man. Gat called to Petra, "We're ready to go." As she returned to the car, she and the man examined one another. "Let's do this without names," Gat suggested.

"Good idea," said the American.

"This is Joan of Arc," Gat said, introducing Petra.

"Hello," Petra said, amused by this game. "Call me Joanie Dark."

"I'm Marcus Garvey," said the American. "Mister Garvey." He started to offer his hand to Petra, then controlled the urge. She noticed his hand start forward and wondered if she had ever in her life shaken an African's hand. "I guess it's not a good idea for us to shake hands out here in the open air," he said. He looked at Gat. "And you are?"

"We'd name him after a famous Belgian—if we could think of one," Petra teased. "Let's call him Voltaire, shall we? He was a great crusader against tyranny, bigotry, and cruelty. Do you mind a French name?" She grinned at Gat, challenging him the way she did her father.

"Hiya, Voltaire," said Mr. Marcus Garvey.

Gat suggested that Garvey sit in the rear seat. He agreed and, when they had all taken their places, said, "I'll try not to muss any of your belongings, ma'am."

"Call me Joanie," Petra said, turning toward him. She reached a hand back across the seat. "I guess we can shake hands now." And they did.

As THEY moved off, Petra watched the workers' shanties disappear. She turned to Garvey and asked, "Do people live in shacks like that in America?"

"I've seen worse places over there," said Garvey. "Though not many. Some whites in America live in shanties as bad as that."

"I thought everyone in America was rich," Petra replied.

"So did I when I went there," Garvey said. "That's why I went there!" He laughed deeply. "Americans had to be rich because they lived so close to God." Petra suppressed a smile and glanced at Gat. Garvey snickered from the backseat. "You must understand that missionaries taught me what I knew about America."

"They sent you there?" Petra asked.

"I was to train to become a minister of God for my people." He laughed heartily. "The trouble is: Like Columbus, I discovered America. Learned that Americans do not really worship the God of the missionaries."

Petra asked what Americans worshipped.

"A box," Gat stated. "With an enormous glass eye in it. That box is their altar."

Petra raised a mischievous eyebrow at him. "Myself, I would not mind having the option of worshipping at that altar," she said. "It shows that South Africa is still a Third World country that we do not have television." She turned to Garvey. "Did you watch it a lot?"

"Sometimes. After a long day. Its silliness makes you smile; its chatter rests your mind. You stretch out before it and quickly you are asleep."

Petra asked what else Americans worshipped.

There were many other idols, Garvey informed her. The main one was flat and green and hardly bigger than a man's hand. There were special temples where these idols were housed and they were held in such reverence that everyone wished to have as many of them as possible. Printed on each one were the words, "In God We Trust," but one did not have to be in America for long before he understood that it was these idols most of all in which people trusted.

Gat glanced at Petra laughing. What a beauty, he thought. The fact that Garvey seemed to be playing comedian at a time when, in fleeing, he might be silent, tense, all his senses alert, revealed how unusual it was for him to flirt with an attractive white girl. For it was flirtation although Petra did not realize that.

Petra watched Garvey's expressive face, her arm crooked over the back of the seat. Gat checked on him in the rear-view mirror, even adjusting its position the better to monitor the show. The performance piqued Gat's curiosity as to who exactly was this man for whom he and Petra were undertaking considerable risks. He became more aware that earlier prudence might have been a wiser course than simply driving off across the veld toward Bechuanaland and the uncertainties that awaited all of them at the border. Gat wondered how long Garvey had lived in the States and how long he had been back in South Africa.

Quite strangely, Garvey went on, Americans also worshipped books of rules: things to do, things not to do, how to hold a spoon, how to use a knife, how to influence people, how to get them to buy things they didn't want, and how to make a woman happy in bed.

The flirtation became very pronounced, Gat thought, when Garvey mentioned this last. Petra's smile faded. She turned to face forward, watching the road ahead of them.

Garvey went on, not realizing he had given offense. Americans, he said, also worshipped new cars and white teeth, the suppression of body odors, the chewing of gum, and baseball. Also apple pie, motherhood, and Old Glory. He did acknowledge that on Sundays, most Americans actually spent an hour worshipping the God of the missionaries. But you did not have to live long there to understand that "getting ahead"— which Americans also worshipped—did not happen if you spent most of your time with a Bible in your hand.

"You know America very well," Gat said, his voice seeming to offer an innocent conversational gambit. "You must have done well there. What made you return here?"

"All these African countries getting their freedom. I thought things in the Union might be changing too. Maybe I could lend a hand."

"Now that you're here, do you still think that?" Petra inquired. She looked back at him.

"The best way for me to lend a hand is to get across the border." Garvey laughed as if to reassure them.

As he drove, Gat continued to make conversation, posing questions about the man's background. The picture that emerged was this: Garvey had spent his first year of college training in America studying religion. In the succeeding years he'd added classes in business and finance. Once he'd finished his schooling, Garvey had moved to Washington, DC, a southern city where a black elite was wealthy and other blacks were expected to know their place. There he distanced himself from the church, partly because he had begun to wonder, so he said, what relevance Jesus had to his future.

Gat took this to mean what relevance Jesus had in black people's quest for better conditions in a world run by whites. This experience of the States struck Gat as credible.

Continuing his story, Garvey said he had gotten a job as a teller in a bank. The position was probationary. No Negro had ever held such a position. However, the bank president wanted to encourage racial harmony even though he worried that customers might close their accounts. There was the promise of a loan officer's position, if all went well.

But after a year, when Garvey was still being paid less as a teller than whites just hired, he realized that the bank had no call for a black loan officer. This was partly because it had few black borrowers, whom it considered bad loan risks, and partly because white borrowers in Washington were affronted by the idea of seeking money from—or giving personal financial information to—a Negro banker.

An associate at the bank had had a business on the side, chauffeuring clients in limousines. To cover the shortfall in his earnings, Garvey worked in his spare time as a limousine chauffeur. He soon began to wonder about moving full-time into the limo business. When he talked to his bank associate about it, the man advised him to drive a taxi for a year. That way he would learn the ins and outs of the business. So Garvey researched the best cab company in the area that would hire a black driver, got a job driving for it—it was in Maryland—and worked the job for a year.

He learned how to be courteous to passengers, how to engage the interests of black clients, and how to satisfy the desires of white clients who felt they were bettering race relations by allowing him to serve them and tipping him well. The cab drivers owned their own cars and paid for their own insurance. The company believed that if they owned the cars, the drivers were more careful with them.

With borrowings from friends and a small loan from his bank, Garvey made a down payment on his own cab. After a year with the cab company, Garvey went out on his own. He built up a regular clientele and augmented it by soliciting patronage from firms, embassies, and professionals he met. In the first year he made $7,000—he had hardly made $4,000 at the bank—and did better every subsequent year.

"Things are beginning to change in the States," Garvey explained. "Young blacks in the South are making small steps, sitting in at drugstore lunch counters mainly. Small steps meet big resistance, but the young people are determined and it's clear that change is coming. I thought change might be coming here too."

Considering this account, still assessing Garvey, Gat decided much of it was probably true. If it were, Garvey seemed to have talents that could prove useful to people across the border.

"Do you have a family in America?" Petra asked.

"I have a wife in Pondoland," Garvey said. "We have not lived together since I went to America. But even so I'm a Christian."

"But surely you had—" Gat said without finishing the thought. "A man with a successful business."

Garvey shrugged and gazed out the window at a shepherd boy tending sheep, wearing a hat and a cloth and leaning against a long, thin pole. "Please don't be offended, Miss

Joanie, at what I'm going to say. Things are different in America." He stopped talking for a moment, his eyes fixed beyond the window on some memory. "I became involved with a white woman."

Petra turned to watch Garvey speak. Gat glanced at her, her surprise evident. This would be the kind of tale she had never heard before.

"She was the wife of a member of Congress. Four or five nights every week they went to parties and embassy receptions. I would take her to the parties where she would meet her husband. If he had meetings or interviews, I would also take her home. He returned to his district two or three weekends a month to keep his face before the voters. His wife had a very lonely existence; sometimes she told me about it."

He paused for a moment. "I shouldn't talk about her because she is a wonderful person." He shrugged. "We came to have a kind of friendship. One night, returning with her after we had taken her husband to the airport, I carried some packages into the house. And spent the night with her."

Both Gat and Petra wondered if this were true. But neither spoke.

"That began to happen fairly regularly," Garvey continued, seemingly with regret rather than boastfulness. "Then the congressman began to suspect what was going on. I was afraid he would have me deported. Or have the green card that allowed me to stay in the States revoked. So it seemed like a good time to return to help my black brothers."

Garvey fell silent. Petra faced forward in the passenger seat and stared at the highway, hardly noticing the Africans who walked at the roadside. Inside her head she wrestled with conflicting feelings about the story she had just heard. She felt an uneasiness in her stomach at the thought that the wife of an American congressman, elected by voters, slept regularly with the unremarkable man—"this kaffir" was how she thought of him—sitting behind her. But she felt sympathy for the loneliness that drove the woman to such ends and a sadness for two people torn apart by circumstance. She glanced at Gat, wondering if circumstance would tear them apart.

For his part Gat doubted the account of the love affair. Garvey had related it, he suspected, to make himself more interesting, perhaps to titillate the attractive young white woman. Probably he had often repeated his account of being an American congressman's wife's lover. True or not, it would certainly credential him with young Africans.

Gat himself had been invited into women's homes when their husbands were away. But his experience was that they set high value on the prestige their husbands provided. They did not jeopardize it. What was more likely, he thought, was that Garvey had made a pass at the woman, had been rebuffed, and lost the clientele. If the clientele ever existed at all.

Gat wondered what role Garvey played in the African National Congress or in its MK, the military arm that he'd read about, the Umkhonto we Sizwe, The Spear of the Nation. He wondered what was in the suitcases Garvey had placed at the back of the trunk. He watched the road and he checked regularly in the rearview mirror.

As THEY approached Mafeking, Garvey informed his companions that getting him across the border might be somewhat more complicated than they realized. Because of the treason trial—yes, they had heard about that—an African traveling into Bechuanaland with two whites might be examined rather carefully. And not merely turned back, but arrested, and the whites with him. They would have a better chance, he thought, if they took one of the unmarked roads to cross the border. If they moved between midnight and dawn, there would be little chance of detection, especially if one of the brother members in Mafeking guided them.

Gat replied by suggesting that the obvious approach might be the surest. Why not simply drive through a border post? If explanations were necessary, he would simply lay out the truth: that he was a Belgian furniture manufacturer, considering relocating his operations to South Africa. He wanted to visit Bechuanaland to assess potential labor supply. The girl was acting as his translator and guide. Given his experience in the limousine business, Garvey might want to act as driver.

"But it's the driver they see at the border post," Garvey objected.

"Let me drive then," Petra suggested. "Perhaps we'll say you aren't feeling well."

Gat ultimately agreed to let Garvey off at a Bantu township outside Mafeking. There he would seek other arrangements for getting across the border or perhaps find someone to guide them at night. Meanwhile Gat and Petra would get something to eat. When they left him at the township, Garvey insisted on keeping the two suitcases in his possession. They agreed to meet again in two hours.

"What's in those suitcases?" Petra asked as she watched Garvey walk into the township. "Explosives?"

"Maybe. Or money," Gat said, driving quickly away. "It doesn't matter. We are not going to see him again."

"Why not?"

"Because I want to take you to a hotel for the afternoon."

"Why not?" Petra repeated.

"You don't want to go to a hotel with me?"

"Take me there for lunch. Why aren't we seeing him again?"

"Because it's too dangerous."

"For me? You going to leave me in the hotel and go with him?"

"It's too dangerous for both of us. He knows we're not who we say we are. If he has a guide take us across at night as soon as we're in Bechuanaland, they'll kill us and take the car."

"He'd kill us?"

"Without hesitation." Gat glanced at Petra as she began to understand how dangerous their enterprise might be. "Of course, he might take you along as his girlfriend."

They drove into the town of Mafeking and stopped for lunch at Dixon's Hotel in the center of town. Since they were in cattle country, Gat ordered steaks and salad for both of them.

As they waited for their food, Gat excused himself. He went to the reception desk and engaged a room. When he returned to the table, he took Petra's hand and said very firmly, "You are to stay here this afternoon."

"No. I'm coming with you."

"I've taken a room for you. You're to stay here." He placed the room key before her. She ignored it. They did not speak for several minutes.

Finally she asked, "Why should I stay here?"

"So you won't get hurt."

"Will you get hurt?" Gat shrugged. "Killed?"

He did not reply.

"If I were going to shut up and do as I'm told, I wouldn't be here with you." Gat could not keep himself from admiring her obstinacy. "You've had a good time with me this week because of the way I am."

"Even so, you're to stay here." Before she could ask why, he said, "Because I'm in command of this operation."

Again they sat in silence. Finally Petra spoke quietly, "If you leave me, don't expect to find me here when you come back. I'll go live my life."

The waiter brought their lunches. As they began to eat, not speaking, Gat wondered if Petra's habit of challenge would actually push her to take off on her own to Johannesburg. He glanced at her, stoking her anger while eating with the fine manners Margaret Rousseau had taught her. What he really wanted, he knew, was to take her up to the room for an hour before she went off to live her own life. In a day or two they would be living their separate lives.

They finished their lunches without speaking. When the waiter cleared the plates, Gat ordered coffee. Petra shook her head, still defiant. When the waiter withdrew, she said quietly, "You're acting like my father, giving instructions, treating me like a child. Why is that?"

"You're a woman whose safety is of interest to me. That's not treating you like a child."

"Then talk straight to me." She added, "Your safety is of interest to me."

The waiter arrived with the coffee and Gat drank, watching Petra without looking at her. Perhaps she was right. He wanted to take her to bed, but he did not have her around merely for the pleasure of that. Perhaps he should give her the respect he would give a friend. "Two Africans were killed outside Vryburg the day we arrived," he told her. "By police who were hunting them."

She challenged him immediately. "How do you know it was police?"

"The doctor at the hospital told me. Police brought the men there and tried to extract information from them before they died."

Loyalty to her father made Petra lift her head and thrust out her chin. Then she looked away and settled back in her chair, her challenge shifting through momentary anger to resignation. Gat moved beside her. "Let's go up to the room," he suggested. "What's Garvey to us? Let him take care of himself. We've brought him this far." He took her hand, but she would not look at him. "We can spend a couple of hours upstairs. We'll get into Joeys tonight."

"We've got to take him across," Petra said quietly. "As homage to Lumumba!"

"That's none of your affair. I'll drive him to Lobatse and come back for you."

"What if he tries to kill you? It's better if there are two of us."

"Please stay here."

"It's safer if we're together." She smiled as if the matter had been decided. "Once we get to Lobatse, we can find a hotel." Gat shook his head without looking at her. He drank more of his coffee. "If you leave me," Petra warned again, "don't expect to find me here when you come back." She rose and walked from the dining room. Gat watched her go.

WHEN GAT returned to the Ford after finishing his lunch, he found Petra standing beside it wearing a wide-brimmed sunhat. He unlocked the door for her and said, "Get in."

As they drove back toward the African township south of Mafeking, Petra asked, "Do you like my hat?"

"Very nice."

"How was the last of your coffee?"

Gat said, "I enjoyed the quiet."

They fetched Garvey outside a general store run by an Indian near the township gate. Leaving the Ford, Gat examined the documents that Garvey expected to present at the border. The South African identity papers he proposed to offer were authentic, but the photograph might arouse the suspicions of a zealous official, for close inspection revealed that the subject was not Garvey. "You think this will do the job?" Gat asked, looking from the photo to Garvey.

"It's the best I could come up with," the African said. "This is a Tswana name. That's important." Gat looked back at the photo. "I will be in this coat and cap I used to wear on the job." Garvey showed Gat a lightweight black coat and a black brimmed chauffeur's cap. "You will explain that I'm your driver. They will look at you and, if we're lucky, not at me. Often they don't really look at us." Gat was not persuaded. "If I'm stopped, you explain that you had no idea who I am. And you haven't."

Gat wished that Petra had stayed at the hotel. The girl was very headstrong; she had no idea of risks they were taking. If things went wrong, she would be considered a conspirator. Her father would get her released only at the sacrifice of his own career. So things must not go wrong. He asked Garvey, "Are you armed?"

"No," Garvey replied. The two men measured one another.

"I need to be sure," Gat said. "I won't endanger my life or my friend's."

Garvey regarded Gat with eyes that might be stone. "I am not armed."

"Turn around and put your hands on the top of the car. Spread your legs."

Garvey did not move. "You are humiliating me."

"Two men were killed outside Vryburg a couple of days ago. Terrorists."

After a moment Garvey corrected, "Freedom fighters."

"Were you with them? Or were you supposed to meet them?" Garvey said nothing. Gat told him, "We are trying to help you. But she and I are not going to get hurt doing it, either by the police or by you."

"By me?"

"I can pat you down or you can walk to Lobatse."

The men stared at one another. Garvey looked at Gat with such humiliation and hatred that it seemed to drive all sound from the air. The birdcalls and chatter of the township hushed. Noise from the nearby road abated.

"Not on the street. People are watching us. Come into the store."

Garvey handed his chauffeur's coat and hat to Petra and led Gat into the store. After the brilliance of the sunlight it was a place of darkness. In the airless heat its smells of spices and sundries clung to the flesh. As a realization spread through the store that a white man had entered, the chatter of shoppers hushed. Patrons and attendants stared at Gat. Even their breathing seemed to stop. In the sudden quiet the only sound to be heard was the whiney wailing of a radio playing Indian music. Garvey led Gat to the counter where the cash register stood. He leaned across it, whispered to the Indian standing there. The man nodded. Garvey signaled Gat to follow him.

They went down a hall, entered a small office. Garvey gestured Gat inside the room and closed the door. He turned his back to Gat, spread his legs, and put a hand and a foot against the door. Gat quickly ran his hands over the fabrics of the man's clothes, felt the sinews of his arms, the beginning flab of his torso, the warmth of his groin, the solid muscles of his legs. Someone tried to open the door. Garvey leaned against it. Above his right ankle Gat felt the hard shape of a knife in a holster. He said, "Take that off. Give it to me."

Garvey removed the knife and holster and presented them to Gat. He said, "You're not a manufacturer of furniture."

"No."

The person outside the door knocked urgently. "Let me in, please," called a woman's voice. She spoke in a singsong accent. "I must come in."

"Are you going to betray me?" Garvey whispered.

"No."

"Why are you helping me?"

"I have private reasons for that. Let's go."

Garvey opened the door. At the threshold stood an Indian woman in a sari. Her ear was pressed against the doorjamb. She stepped back. Seeing the knife in Gat's hand she registered an instant of panic, then watched the men with both affronted apprehension and a sense of violation. When she saw that she was not in danger, she reached out her palm. Gat took rands from his wallet and laid them across the palm. "Thank you," he said.

When they returned to the Ford, Gat opened the trunk. He tossed the knife and holster behind Garvey's suitcases. He closed the trunk and handed the car keys to Garvey. He said, "You drive."

THE FORD slowed as it approached the border post. Garvey drove, wearing his dark chauffeur's jacket and the brimmed hat. Beside him Gat silently appraised the post. At midafternoon the sun glared off it and the two or three vehicles in the car park. In the rear seat Petra refreshed her lipstick, fluffed out her hair, and released a button on her blouse so that it revealed a hint of the swell of her breasts. Neither man paid the slightest attention to her as Garvey pulled into a parking space and stopped the car. The men hesitated before moving.

Petra, however, left the car with a jaunty stride and hurried toward the post. Gat and Garvey looked after her, alarmed.

Opening the door of the building, Petra swung it so wide that the three officials behind the counter all looked up. She grinned at each of them and leaned on the counter in such a way as to push down the fabric of her blouse. She greeted the men in Afrikaans. "That car is so hot!" she said. "What a relief to get out of it!" The three officials nodded and grinned. They glanced at the open button of her bodice and the loveliness behind it and hurriedly finished with the documents they were putting in order.

"You wouldn't have something cold I could drink, would you? I'm sure I shouldn't ask," Petra acknowledged, flirtatiously, "but I am parched!" The two younger officials, both in their twenties, stumbled over each other en route to the water cooler to pour the poor traveler a drink. The older official approached her. "How do you manage to stay looking so cool and refreshed?" Petra asked admiringly. "I wish I knew your secret."

The younger men brought cups of water. Petra downed them with a ravenousness that tweaked the men's imaginations. She sighed, "My, but that's welcome." She smiled at the men. "How nice to see you blokes!" she enthused. "I'm guiding a European businessman who wants to locate a factory in the Union— Oops! I guess I mean the Republic, don't I?" The men laughed with her. As Afrikaners they had likely supported the referendum which would in a few months remove the country from the British Commonwealth and transform it into a republic. "He is so boring! You would not believe it." She looked toward the door to see Gat entering with Garvey trailing behind him, his face lowered.

Petra went toward the two men and said, "These gentlemen need your papers." She held out her hand for them to be delivered to her. Each man glanced at her with an expression of anxiety and handed over his papers. Petra took them to the officials at the counter, making faces to suggest that the European was the King of Boredom. The officials examined Gat, suppressing their smiles, and hardly glanced at Garvey. When Gat started toward her, Petra gestured out of sight of the officials that he should stay back. He retreated to the far wall, blocking the officials' view of Garvey. The African stood in a pose of obsequiousness, hoping to be invisible.

"I wonder if you could help me make a telephone call to Cape Town?" Petra asked. The officials looked uncertain about this. Allowing a traveler to use the official telephone was clearly against regulations. "I thought maybe you could dial the call for me," Petra said. "It's to Colonel Rousseau of the police there."

Gat glanced at Garvey and saw panic pass across his eyes.

"He's my father," Petra explained. "He wants me to call in every day or so." She gave the most senior official a flirtatious look of pleading and touched his arm.

"It's most irregular," he told her, fearing his younger colleagues' disapproval.

"It is to the police," one of them said.

Petra took a pencil and wrote the number on a piece of paper. "Well, since it is the police," said the senior man. "Come back here, Miss, if you like."

"You are so kind," Petra said, again touching the man's arm, while making a face that mocked his caution to his younger colleagues. The man led Petra to a phone and dialed the number. Waiting for the call to go through, Petra fluffed her hair and set her foot forward so that, as they arranged the papers of the three travelers, the younger men could admire her ankle.

"Colonel Rousseau, please," the senior official said to the telephone operator. When Rousseau's assistant answered the phone, the man explained, "I have the colonel's daughter here." He handed the phone to Petra.

"Colonel Rousseau." The voice came quietly into Petra's ear.

"Father," she said. "I thought I ought to check in."

"Where in God's name are you?" the voice demanded in a vicious whisper. "Are you all right? Are you still with that Belgian?"

"We're outside Mafeking and everything's going quite well."

"Mafeking!" The voice was now a frantic whisper. He did not want his office staff to overhear. "What the hell are you doing way up there?"

"The visitor asked to see Victoria Falls so we're headed up that way."

"Victoria Falls!" Her father still controlled his voice. "You're supposed to be at Wits!"

"We're trying to get to Francistown tonight. That's a bit of a stretch."

"Are you all right? Tell me that you're all right!"

"The driver you recommended is working out quite well. I'm fine. And since it's a long way to Francistown, I better ring off."

"Petra! Petra!" her father called as she hung up the phone. She smiled at the officials, all three of whom were watching her with a kind of bemused enchantment on their faces. She took the paper on which she had written her father's name and number, crumbled it, and stuck it demurely into her brassiere. The officials watched her.

"I guess we better hurry if we're to get to Francistown," she said, grinning at the men. One of the young officials handed her the documents. She touched his arm and thanked him. "Thank you all," she said to the trio of officials. "You've been so kind to me!"

She left the post and walked to the car, Gat and Garvey trailing behind her. She slid into the rear seat and closed the door behind her. Gat and Garvey got into the car without speaking. Garvey started the motor and drove it slowly out of South Africa. Once beyond the sight of the border post, he stepped on the accelerator.

No one spoke until they were five miles inside the protectorate. Then Gat started laughing. Garvey joined him, "Don't thank me, gents!" Petra declared triumphantly. "I was just certain I could do it better than either of you!" They laughed and laughed and Gat watched Petra with the knowledge that she was much more of a woman than he had realized.

LOBATSE PROVED to be a small, dusty place at the edge of the Kalahari Desert. The town's sun-bleached buildings hugged a gulch; it served as the bed for a trickle of water which after a long journey joining other tributaries would eventually swell into the Limpopo River. As the Ford moved along the town's main street, Gat and Garvey caught sight of a filling station adjoining a store. Beside it an acacia tree provided meager shade. Over the entrance a sign announced G. P. Patel, Proprietor. Garvey pulled into the station. Out of it came an attendant, a Motswana boy, not yet old enough to go work in the gold mines. Garvey told him to fill the car and, exhibiting a confidence he could not have displayed across the border, he moved into the store by the front entrance, hoping the place had a phone he could use.

Gat and Petra left the car to stretch their legs. Petra lifted her arms over her head and, raising herself to her tiptoes, grabbed for the sky. Gat watched her. "You were quite amazing," he said. "Garvey was rather shaken when your father turned out to be a colonel in the police."

"So was my father when he heard we were going to Victoria Falls." She strutted in a circle, then asked, "Where are we going?"

An intense longing for her swept over him. He did not try to mask it, knowing that was impossible. "To a hotel—as soon as we get rid of Mister Garvey."

She blushed, pleased that his desires were the same as her own. "I meant after that."

Her blushing excited him. "We need to talk about that."

His obvious admiration, his admission of desire, made her self-conscious. She remembered that she had unfastened the top button of her blouse and turned her back on him to fasten it again. When she turned back, she asked, "What is it about breasts that so fascinates men?"

"The fact that the peek is more interesting than the full view." With both hands Petra held the blouse closed at her neck. The power of his gaze made her blush more deeply.

"You're looking at me the way you first did in Cape Town."

"Oh, no!" Gat whispered. "That was wondering. This is *knowing*."

Garvey called from the station office. "You can drop me here. Someone will come for me."

They unloaded the African's suitcases. Gat said, "Nice sharing the road with you, Mr. Garvey." The two men shook hands.

Petra offered her hand as well. "I'm glad to have met an American from Pondoland, Mr. Garvey." The African wiped his hand on his trouser leg before taking the girl's hand.

Garvey thanked them and looked carefully at Petra. "Your father is truly a police colonel in Cape Town?" She nodded.

Garvey shook his head, disbelieving, and regarded Gat. "Just when you think the game is up," he said, "the most unexpected people help you."

"You might want to keep moving," Gat advised. "The colonel may have called the border post to check on us."

"Yes," Garvey said. "Someone will drive me to Gaborone tonight."

Gat paid the Motswana boy and drove Petra through Lobatse to see what it offered in terms of lodging. When they reached the northern edge of the town, Gat stopped the car. Petra fished the fake wedding rings out of her purse and the couple renewed their claim to respectability by putting them on.

Returning through town they stopped at an establishment calling itself a hotel and boasting air-conditioned rondavels. A porter took them to their cottage. It stood, surrounded by red and orange aloes in full bloom, beyond a dining terrace at the back of what was trying to be a garden. It was given sparse shade by thorn trees with gray-green leaves and thorns as big as clothespins and sharp as sharks' teeth. As soon as Gat tipped the porter and shut and bolted the door, he grabbed Petra's arm, pulled her to him, and kissed her with a ferocity she was happy to reciprocate.

"You were marvelous at the border post," he told her, "and you are marvelous now."

They made love in the shower with shampoo in their hair and soap in their eyes, their skins suds-sliding against each other. Each toweled off the other, each examining the other's body in detail. Feeling chilled in the air-cooled room, they sought refuge in the double bed, each curled about the other, kissing and caressing the other, their bodies becoming one. They grew hungry, but disregarded their hunger for food in preference for slaking their hunger for each other. They purred and slept and staggered to and from the toilet and washbasin and woke each other, making love in a state that was neither fully awake nor fully asleep, in a kind of dream of love.

IN ANOTHER city, in another country, another man and woman shared a different kind of union in the small parlor of their Cape Dutch home. Piet Rousseau paced the room, his jaw set, an icy anger chilling the air as his footsteps broke the silence, thudding across the carpet five paces in one direction, then turning to step off five paces in the opposite one. Occasionally Rousseau halted before Margaret. Hardly aware of her presence, he took the cup she had refilled yet again with after-dinner coffee. He emptied it and returned it to the low table, and paced on. Margaret sat on a sofa with apparent composure, holding the pitcher because it warmed her hands, taking refuge in the coffee's comforting aroma, and watching her husband's feet so that she did not have to meet his eyes.

At dinner Rousseau had reported to Margaret that, in their short, rather one-sided conversation, Petra had sounded well, even spirited. She was evidently about to cross into Bechuanaland, he had told his wife, and she claimed that she and the Belgian officer were heading to Victoria Falls. With Elsie moving in and out of the dining room serving, Margaret made no reply. But both women sensed the baas's fury. In the face of it, Margaret knew better than to express her opinion that it could not be such a bad thing before she started varsity for a young woman to see Victoria Falls—even if she were accompanied by a lover.

Now that Elsie was in the kitchen finishing up the dishes, and after that would disappear into her quarters, Rousseau explained that in crossing the border Petra and Gat were not alone. A Bantu had crossed with them. This fact seemed to deepen his anger. Margaret mildly replied, "There must be Bantus going across that border every day looking for rides."

"There are also terrorists trying to get across."

"You're sure a Bantu was with them?"

"She called me to help him get across," Rousseau said. "I telephoned the border post as soon as I got my wits about me. The officer I spoke with confirmed that it was Petra and the Belgian. A Bantu driver was with them."

"You think the Bantu was a terrorist? Where would Petra and the Belgian meet someone like that?"

"We really know nothing about the Belgian. He could be a Communist, a terrorist himself."

Margaret said nothing. Her husband tended to regard as a Communist anyone who disrupted his life. Any man who awakened his daughter to passion, who turned her from a decent, rather intelligent girl into a debauchee given over to lust, certainly fit that category. As far as Margaret was concerned, the important thing was that Petra was well. And if she were having a fling, Margaret was pleased that she was enjoying it. Why shouldn't she? What was a fling for?

Rousseau stopped pacing and turned to face his wife. "Do you think Pet might run off with this Belgian?" he asked.

"Pietie," Margaret replied carefully, "she has run off with him."

"If I catch her, I'll beat her backside so she won't want to be in bed with a man for a very long time. And if I catch him, he'll be minus some of his anatomy." Rousseau continued to pace, back and forth. Finally, almost gently, he said, "I've been hoping she's just cutting up a bit before varsity. Now I wonder: Is it possible he'll take her somewhere outside Africa?"

This was a new idea to Margaret. She did not know how to reply.

"If they plan to leave Africa," Rousseau declared, "they'll fly out of Johannesburg. I'm going there tomorrow to see that they don't!"

IN THE rondavel in Lobatse Gat lay holding Petra, his right leg stretched across both of hers, his left arm under her neck, his right hand lightly caressing her cheek. He told her, "I don't think I can send you off to university."

"I hope not!" She turned her head toward his.

"I don't want you to leave me."

"Me leave you! I thought we were going together to the far corners of the earth."

He murmured contentedly and bit the lobe of her ear. He held her close. Maybe, he thought, they should go take a look at Victoria Falls together.

CHAPTER TEN

LOBATSE, BECHUANALAND PROTECTORATE

Saturday, February 11, 1961

Gat woke in the night, wrapped a blanket over Petra and himself, and nestled beside her. A slight scent of night-blooming jasmine filled the air. Despite her warmth, he felt oddly alone. The night before he had resolved to demonstrate his regard for her by getting out of her life. Now he could hardly bear to think of leaving her.

Questions about Australia buzzed in his head. To risk emigrating wouldn't they need to love each other? Right now they were dancing through a golden buzz of infatuation, but headed where? Had he ever known love? Not really. It was undiscovered country. Could he find it with Petra?

Could he find a job out there? Petra would need to work too. Had she ever held a job? What skills could she offer? What skills could he? He could dig ditches if he had to, but he could not keep Petra happy for long on what a ditchdigger earned.

He stared into the night. Would Petra be happy in the kind of place he could afford? She might enjoy a tiny love nest. But for how long? He could survive alone. But could he do the surviving for both of them?

Did he love her? Whatever love was, this must be getting close. It was time he settled down. If he did love her, would he not insist she go to university? He had seen movies where lovers battled with such questions. Bullshit, he'd always thought. Now he was not so sure.

Far off he heard a radio playing a love song. He strained to listen, nestling against this warm and marvelous companion. He wondered where they would be at the end of the coming day. The love song faded into silence. He drifted back to sleep.

When he woke again, he was alone in the bed. Petra stood, naked, at the table in the middle of the room, pouring their tea. "You're very beautiful," he greeted her.

"Too skinny for local tastes," she informed him. "Bantu men like their women to carry some weight."

"Lucky I'm not local."

She set a plate of biscuits beside him on the bed and handed him his tea. Then she returned with her own and slithered under the sheet. "I'm famished," she declared. "When was the last time we ate?" After a moment she asked, "Last night— Did we decide anything?" She yawned. "To go—? Where exactly?"

"Wherever you fancy."

"Hmm." She set the tea aside and curled into a nap. Suddenly, with certainty, Gat knew that he loved this woman. Must he give her up? No! He could not relinquish her. He revisited the questions that had disturbed his sleep. Daylight filled the world with possibilities.

Petra woke. Gat assured her he would take her to Joeys or to the far corners of the earth. Her choice.

"What about America?" she asked. He grunted. "Some-day," she said, "I want to walk where Abraham Lincoln and George Washington walked."

"America's a strange combination of Puritanism and commercialism," Gat said. "Like a tree graft gone bad. It's too expensive."

"Millions of immigrants have gone there and flourished. Look at Garvey!"

Gat only grunted.

"Maybe Joeys is the likeliest possibility," Petra concluded. Gat could get an apartment and she would start university in a dormitory. That would make her parents happy. After a couple of weeks, she would move into Gat's apartment. She held her left hand in the air above them, looking at the fake and shiny wedding ring she wore. "We'll tell people I'm your younger sister."

Gat guffawed. "But I still look at you as if I'm going to eat you up."

"Australia then."

Gat reached up, removed the ring from her third finger, did some hocus-pocus over it with his other hand, and returned it to her finger. "With this ring I promise you Australia." They lay side by side, his commitment there between them. Gat said, "I agree to take care of you for a year."

More questions came. Would they find pals out there? They'd need help to arrive safely. To get established. Could they make it through a year together?

"After a year," he said, "you should have some idea of what you want from your life. Whether or not that includes me."

She asked, "Will we tell people that we're married?"

"They'll accept us more readily if they think we are."

A question hung unspoken in the air: Then why not get married?

WHILE STANDING in the shower, cool water washing over him, Gat realized that before he left Africa, he must cleanse himself inside as well. He must seek absolution for his offense against Africans, against Lumumba. Dressing while Petra watched him from the bed, he told her that he needed to run an errand. It might require an hour. When he returned they'd have breakfast in the garden.

With directions from the hotel receptionist Gat easily found Lobatse's Catholic compound. It was a dusty place with a school, priests' quarters, and refectory. Thorn trees and bougainvillea grew in the courtyard beside a church with its faintly Italianate façade. Gat wondered if he had come to the right place. The façade disconnected the church from the Tswana. It suggested yearnings beyond humble Lobatse. Moreover, although Catholicism offered absolution from the entire gamut of humanity's sins, its priests and bishops, so Gat felt, were part of the hierarchy of church actors who had conspired to finish off Lumumba. They had used him to do it. How, then, could the church absolve him of that offense? It couldn't. But he knew of no other channel to redemption. At least the priest to whom he confessed must be African.

Leaving the Ford, Gat thought of his parents. His British mother was a Catholic; his father an anticlerical Fleming, a Socialist. Whenever his father discovered that his mother had dragged Gat and his sister to confession, the house shook with shouting. His father would curse at the top of his voice. His mother would take refuge behind her locked bedroom door. At the top of his voice, raised so his wife could hear,

Gat's father would instruct his children not to believe that some pantywaist priest, who'd married the church because he had no inclination toward women, could presume to absolve guilt. Gat's father insisted that the children take responsibility themselves for whatever they did. As a result, whenever Gat's mother bundled the children off to confession, she made them swear not to tell their father.

Now, moving into the compound, he felt strangely as if his father reached out to take hold of his arm. His father's voice seemed to say, "What you're looking for, you can't get here. Don't go in." Gat stopped abruptly, turned from the church, and walked away.

As GAT left the rondavel, Petra sprang from the bed, dashed to the window, and peeked around the edge of the curtain to watch him walk away from her, his body erect, the shoulders rolling slightly. What, she wondered, was his errand? Would he buy her a present? She did not want presents from him. She wanted him to stay with her. As he moved across the hotel's dining terrace, she wondered when it was that he would walk away from her forever.

That thought made her cold. She pulled the light blanket from the bed and wrapped it about her. She was so hungry that her stomach growled for food. She poured herself another cup of tea and swallowed it down, feeling its heat warm her body. She set the cake tent aside and devoured the pound cake that remained on the plate. It was sweet to the nostrils but dry in the eating. She drank the last of the tea.

She ran herself a bath, filling the tub with hot water until it went cold. When she lay in the tub, the water mostly covering her body, she let her thoughts drift. She wondered: Did she love him? Or was she merely infatuated? Gat seemed to believe somehow that she had really saved his life. Would that feeling burn fast and bright and then be ashes?

If they really went to Australia, she wondered, would she bear Gat's child? Petra looked at her belly barely covered by water. She imagined a baby growing inside it.

Drying off, she knew that she did not want to bear a child out of wedlock. So they should marry. Ideas about marriage, instilled by her training, assumed that couples stayed together throughout their lives. If she married someone like Kobus, of course, she would assume that. Because they would be marrying their way of life. But with Gat? In a year they might hate one another. Petra knew she would feel lost if they parted. Would she feel lost if they stayed together? She wished she could talk to her mother. But her parents' knowing about this might ruin everything.

AT THAT moment her mother was sitting alone in the rear seat of a black, unmarked police car watching her husband in the seat before her grind his teeth. His driver was taking them to the airport for a plane to Johannesburg. Grinding his teeth was a habit Piet Rousseau indulged when he was deep in thought. Margaret knew that he was thinking of what he would say to Petra when he found her and to that seducer and scoundrel Gautier. She leaned forward. She patted her husband's shoulder and lightly touched the back of his jaw. He glanced at her sheepishly. "Relax," she advised with a smile. "Grinding your teeth only increases our dental bills."

LEAVING THE Catholic compound, Gat thought of Petra. He must get a present. But what could Lobatse offer? Looking up, he realized that he had driven beyond the edge of town. He was moving slowly through open country. He noticed three mopane trees up ahead. Without conscious thought he pulled off the road. He left the car and went to the trees. He looked beyond them at the flat plain receding endlessly before him to what might be a barely distinguishable line of mountains. He glanced up at the enormous blue dome of the sky and, suddenly self-conscious, glanced about to see if anyone were watching him. He moved behind the car where he could not be seen from the road. He fell to his knees.

Feeling foolish, he sat on his ankles. Then he rose again to his knees, closed his eyes, bowed his head. He raised his head, opened his eyes. Spreading wide his arms, hands outstretched, he spoke softly to the vastness before him. "Oh, Africa!" he whispered. "Forgive my sins." He looked out at the immense plain before him, at the trees, the sky, the land. He knew that he must shout. "Great Africa!" he called, crying out to the land that stretched before him. "Forgive my sins to your people, to Maurice Mpolo, Joseph Okito, and especially to Patrice Lumumba." He hesitated, then continued. "I acknowledge these transgressions. I want to be cleansed."

He began to weep, feeling complete obliviousness to anything except the sky-roofed confessional, the trees, the land.

Then he seemed to stand apart from himself, as if he were outside his body, looking at a white man absurdly weeping on his knees at the edge of the great Kalahari. You ridiculous penitent! he thought to himself. Then once again he was inside his body, feeling the hard ground on his knees, the strong heat of the sun, and the coolness where a stir of air was evaporating the tear trails on his face. Once again he said aloud, "Africa, please forgive me!"

Off to his left a bird began to cry, "Hoop-hoop-hoop!" He looked over to see a small creature with cinnamon plumage and black-and-white striped wings singing as if it were the voice of Africa, giving answer to his plea. Gat laughed, watching the hoopoe finish his singing and begin to walk about probing for food. New tears poured from him. He laughed at them, at the busy bird, at the absurdity of his asking the indifferent enormity of Africa for forgiveness and the even greater absurdity of Africa's granting it through the monotonous call of a cinnamon bird.

As he rose and turned toward the car, he saw two Tswana boys watching him. They seemed to have arisen out of dust swirls and peered at him with astonishment. He waved to them and seated himself on the fender of the car. He seared into his consciousness the look of this place where he had asked for forgiveness: the three mopane trees, the two Tswana boys, the hoopoe, and the immensity of the veld and the sky.

He suddenly realized that he had no idea how much time had passed as he knelt beside the trees. Feeling refreshed, he drove to the general store, G. P. Patel, Proprietor. Usually for a woman, he chose flowers, a gift that was beautiful, but also transitory, suggesting no thought of permanence. He selected an ostrich eggshell necklace, fashioned by a local craftswoman.

Driving to the hotel, he realized suddenly how truly marvelous a day it was, how healthy and magnificent he felt, how fantastic it was to be alive. When he caught sight of Petra, his heart exploded with joy. She was standing worriedly beneath a canopy of bougainvillea, obviously concerned about him. A warmth surged through him. For weeks he had felt himself lost, befuddled, betrayed, uncertain of what was ahead. He had charmed her because he knew about charm and needed a companion. Now he realized he loved her. Her concern at his absence expanded the joy he was feeling. He hid the gift behind his back and called to her, "Hello, Beauty! Don't worry! I haven't run off with your car."

"Where have you been?" she challenged. "And I'm hungry!" she complained with a smile. "Can we eat something?"

Gat said, "I have been off buying a present for the woman I love!"

Petra looked up sharply at him.

"I do love you."

Because they had never spoken seriously of love, these words popping out of his mouth surprised Gat. They also surprised Petra. But given the wondrousness of the day and the expansiveness possessing him, Gat felt he loved the entire world.

"Don't say that unless you mean it," Petra cautioned.

"I do mean it!" Gat handed her the present. "It's the best I could find in this quaint place you've brought me to."

"I've brought you, have I?" She opened the folded paper in which the present lay. "I love it!" she exclaimed, then laughed. "What is it?"

"A necklace. Ostrich eggshell. Let's put it on."

Gat fastened the object around her neck. Petra used the window glass as a mirror to admire it. "I do love it. You're very sweet." Gat put his head next to hers. They assessed and admired themselves. "My mother would say we're a handsome couple," she said. "'Handsome couple' is high praise from her." She asked, "Have you been out shopping for my present all this time?"

"All this time," Gat lied. "I am a meticulous buyer of presents!" As he pulled her away from the window toward the dining terrace, her stomach growled. "There must be a lion in there," he shouted. "How about some breakfast?"

A waiter brought them a Bechuanaland version of the English fry-up: eggs fried so hard their yokes looked like golden doughnuts, overcooked links of sausage, slices of fresh pineapple substituting for the baked tomato halves, and a rack of cold toast. Gat smiled at the sight of the repast, not out of criticism, but of affection. "At least they have the toast right," he said.

He told Petra about England and how during his time there he had breakfasted every morning on fare very like this. He was just her age then, learning the language of Shakespeare and Milton. She poured him tea, hardly listening as he talked, and ate hungrily. He wondered what he would have done if he'd met her then. She stole two links of sausage from his plate and giggled when he did not seem to notice. The silver sound of her snickering drew his attention back to her and he delighted in seeing her so carefree.

She wiped her mouth with her paper serviette and leaned against his arm. "Doesn't sex make you hungry?" she asked. "I've felt ravenous since daybreak."

"Me too. But for you."

"I'm craving food."

"I'm craving you."

"Why aren't you eating?"

"This is how I keep my weight down."

She speared another sausage link from his plate. "I like the shape of these. But they're awfully small." She bit the tip off the sausage.

"You're a very naughty girl," he said. "Should I spank you?" He took hold of her wrist. "Instead I'm going to ask you—." He paused, fell to his knee. "Would you like to get married?"

She set her fork with its half-eaten sausage onto her plate. "Don't say that unless you're serious."

"If we're going to Australia, it makes a lot of sense."

"That's romantic," she commented. "Do you love me?"

"Yes," he said. She pursed her mouth, peeved. "Shall I tell you why?"

"Please."

"I admire your independence. Your spirit of adventure. Your willingness to try things. Your curiosity about the world. I like talking to you. Watching you. Of course, it helps that you are beautiful."

"Thank you. But I'm not beautiful."

"Oh, yes! Not a wrinkle on you anywhere! I've made a careful inspection." She gave him a tolerant smirk. "I love it that you're responsive in bed. That you're eager for me. That you're a quick learner." Her face reddened. "Don't blush! That's important. I love it that you're not frightened when we consider Australia." He took her hand and whispered, "I love it that you saved my life."

She said, "I love it that you saved mine." She glanced at him, knowing that he had never taken his eyes off her. She sipped some tea and fiddled with the cup. "When most people get married, they expect to stay together forever and have children. Do you want children?"

"Maybe. If I can support them. Do you?"

"How do I know?" She looked up nervously. "A week ago I was going to varsity. One thing I was sure of then: I wanted never to get married." Then, after a pause. "How long would we stay married?"

"Forever." She seemed to flinch. "Or as long as you want. You're the one who'll walk out." As soon as he spoke the words, he realized this was not a gallant thing to say. He wished he had not said it.

"I won't walk out," she told him. "Do you want to know if I love you?"

"Why not?"

She confessed, "I don't know how to say it." Those words made her feel like a child—and she was not a child! Still, she could not look at him. "I guess I must—" The words "love you" would not leave her throat. She blurted on, "Because

I feel warm and comfortable with you. Sometimes tingly. Sometimes I get hot flashes." She glanced up at him. "Sometimes I'm afraid with you because of the things you say you've done. But I feel safe with you. All we've done together has seemed right. I wasn't even embarrassed the second time we were together to have you take off my clothes." She reddened. "With you it seemed perfectly logical to run away from my parents and the man who assumed he'd marry me."

He smiled at her. "So do we get married?"

She nodded.

"Today?"

She managed to blurt out, "I love you, Gat," and blushed such a crimson color that he laughed at her. She stuck out her tongue.

THEY RETURNED to their room and dressed in their finest clothes. Arriving at the office of the magistrate, they made an odd-looking couple for a small town on the edge of a great desert. Passersby stopped to watch them. Petra stepped from the car in a tea hat, white gloves, high heels, and a light frock. Gat wore his blue suit, a white shirt, tie, and highly polished Oxfords that were immediately coated with dust. As they moved toward the office, a sudden breeze welcomed them. It charmingly lifted Petra's skirt and almost sent her tea hat sailing. One of her hands flew to her head to anchor the hat while the other pushed her skirt over her knees. Gat moved beside her, with a steadying hand on her elbow.

The magistrate, a middle-aged Englishman, smiled involuntarily when they appeared in his office. On hearing that they wished him to marry them, he studied the couple for a moment. "Are you of age?" he asked. They presented documents and he glanced at them. "You do this of your own free will?" he queried. They assured him that they did.

He instructed an African assistant to fetch two whites from the gawkers outside the building—it did not occur to him that Africans could witness the marriage of whites—and when these entered the office in boots, bush hats, and work-spotted khakis, he performed the ceremony. Gat and Petra exchanged the fake—now genuine—wedding rings that they had worn to fool hotel receptionists and they kissed, sealing the union. The magistrate requested a kiss, which Petra placed on his ruddy cheek. Gat and Petra shook hands with the magistrate and with the witnesses. They all signed the documents that the African assistant had prepared. As the gawkers applauded, one of the witnesses took a photo of the pair with Petra's camera and they went to the car as husband and wife.

They returned to their hotel room, shed their finery, and made love—a little uncertainly for now they were not simply enjoying themselves but beginning a marriage. Somehow, being married, they felt safer in acknowledging their love for one another and somehow being married made the declarations seem likelier to be sincere. They slept, woke, talked about departing for Australia that very day. They believed Petra could enter that country without a visa because she held a passport from a country still—for the moment—a member of the British Commonwealth. They hoped Gat could enter as her husband.

"What a day!" Gat exclaimed. "And it's hardly more than noon! Early this morning I lay here wondering what would happen to us. And now we're married!" They rose, showered together, dressed in traveling clothes, checked out of their hotel after eating a light lunch, and got onto the road for Joeys.

THE NEWLYWEDS passed through the Ramatlabama border post outside Mafeking and reentered South Africa. As they drove toward Johannesburg through the warm summer day, the air made golden by brilliant sunlight, perfumed by flowers and crops, Petra sat close beside her husband. He held the steering wheel with his right hand and kept his left arm around his bride.

They sang songs to each other, love songs and school songs and patter songs, songs in French and Flemish, English and Afrikaans, songs they had learned while growing up, and taught them to one another in order to create shared experience. Since, they agreed, it was probably a good idea that each one should know to whom he had pledged his life, they recounted to one another those important events of their lives that they had not already shared in their journey.

Petra decided not to tell Gat, not just yet, that her mother had borne an out-of-wedlock child in Rhodesia or that her father worked for the Special Branch. Gat omitted mentioning various relationships he had enjoyed with women; these did not seem the sort of thing one spoke of driving away from one's wedding. He also declined to reveal that Adriaan Gautier was not the name his parents gave him. It was the name Petra had made real by giving it context. It was the name he intended to keep.

As they drew ever nearer to Johannesburg, Petra began to recite stanzas of Afrikaans poetry that she had memorized for her father as a child. Gat watched her with fascination as sounds not unlike Flemish tumbled from her mouth. He began singing to her a Flemish drinking song, laughing and flicking his eyebrows when the lyrics grew ribald, pounding out the rhythm on the steering wheel.

Suddenly Petra felt a foreboding. She bit her lips and looked away from Gat, out her window. She realized she must telephone her mother. Otherwise, this glorious day, the day of her wedding, was going to end badly.

She put her hand to Gat's mouth to stop his singing and he nibbled at her fingers with his lips. She pulled her hand away. He stopped singing. "Is something wrong?"

"I want to call my parents. To tell them our news."

Gat watched the road. Finally he suggested that it might be best to call from the airport, just before they boarded their flight. He sensed that something had spooked Petra. "You having second thoughts?" he asked. She shook her head. "Will your father try to keep us from leaving the country?"

"He might," she acknowledged. "He'll be furious . . ." After a moment she added, "I'm sure he expected to have some say in the man I married."

Gat realized that her eyes were swimming with tears and pulled off the road.

"What is it? What is it?"

"I can't just flee, can I? As if I hated them? They've been wonderful to me." She began to weep. Gat held her close. "I love them so much. I don't want to hurt them."

Now that he had married, it shook Gat to think that his wife was weeping on her wedding day. He found a petrol station with a restaurant and pulled into it. Petra went inside to make the call. As he waited for her, he also began to feel a foreboding. Perhaps, he thought, when Petra returned, he himself should make a call to her father. Since they had already married, he could hardly ask for Rousseau's blessing. But still, he might call.

"I talked to Elsie," Petra said when she returned. "They're on their way to Joeys. She told me where they're staying."

"Let's call them then," Gat suggested. "We'll invite them to dinner. On our wedding night. Our treat."

"Thank you." Petra smiled gratefully.

Gat said, "Maybe we can get a room in the same hotel. We'll be a family. Do you want to call them from here?"

"Let's get into Joeys first. I need to think about what I'll say."

They drove on. The open veld became increasingly dotted by small Afrikaner dorps with Afrikaner dorp names: Groot-Marico, Swartruggers. Gradually the dorps gave way to towns and small cities—Rustenburg, Krugersdorp, Roodepoort—with African townships dotted about, always sited where South African police or defense forces could isolate them in case of trouble. Finally they saw, looming ahead of them, the tall buildings of the city and the slag heaps from the gold mines that had made it—or at least its white citizenry—wealthy. The mounds of slag seemed to shimmer with a golden sparkle in the sun.

Gat noticed in the rearview mirror a police car following them. Once again he felt a foreboding. He slowed to let the car pass. As it moved beyond them, the officers studied both occupants of the Ford. Gat pulled off the road. He had a very strong sense that something was wrong. Even so, he did not want to alarm Petra.

She regarded him as if she, too, sensed danger. "The police," she said.

"I suspect something's gone wrong. Military instinct."

"You feel it too?"

"I think we should go directly to the airport and take the first plane out to Australia."

Tears rose in Petra's eyes. "It's my father, isn't it?"

Gat did not want to criticize Petra's father on their wedding day. But the man was a high-ranking police official accustomed to protecting his daughter, to having prior approval of the life choices she made. He was certain to be furious that a man unknown to him intended to separate her from the *volk* to whom he had dedicated his life.

They looked at one another. "Can I just leave?" she asked. "We know he's trying to stop us."

She looked away from Gat and stared out the window. Tears ran down her cheeks. Gat handed her a handkerchief. She wiped away her tears. "I don't think he would do anything to hurt me," she told him. "But I'm not sure."

Gat pulled back onto the road. "Here's a plan," he said. "We go to the airport and check what possibilities are for a flight to Australia. If it seems a good idea for you to call your parents from there, you can do it."

Petra leaned closer to him. "Thank you," she said. "This seems crazy since I've just committed myself to you. But I couldn't just leave."

"You're my wife," Gat said. "I trust your judgment."

One thing to say that, Gat told himself, another to believe it. As he drove on, he hoped he believed it.

AT THE Jan Smuts airport, they parked the Ford and sat in it conferring about how to proceed. They took account of what was left of the two thousand American dollars Gat had received as blood money. It would be enough to see them to Australia, to buy them groceries, and get them into some kind of lodging. Gat would need to start earning money almost immediately. The Rousseaus had opened a bank account for Petra's use at Wits; unless it was canceled, they would keep that as reserve. Petra would take two suitcases of clothes and leave the remainder of her belongings in the trunk of the Ford. They would telephone either her parents or Hazel to notify the family as to its whereabouts.

They took their luggage and entered the terminal. Checking a listing of departures, they discovered a flight leaving that evening for Melbourne. They hugged each other with relief.

"It's been awhile since Lobatse," Petra told Gat. "I'm going to spend a penny. Then you can spend one and we'll get our tickets." She headed off toward the ladies' room.

Gat watched his wife walk off across the terminal. How lucky he was, he felt, that such a woman was willing to commit herself to him. Still, that feeling of satisfaction was tinged by a sense of danger. He glanced about, but saw nothing to arouse his suspicions. He paced back and forth before the luggage. Finally a woman and two men approached him. One of them said, "Adriaan Gautier?"

Gat recognized the police. "That's right," he replied.

"We have a warrant for your arrest."

"On what charges?"

"Kidnapping. Corrupting a minor. Car theft. Come with us, please."

"What about my wife? We were married this morning."

"The matron will stay with her and explain everything."

When Petra returned from the ladies' room, she found a woman she had never seen before standing beside her luggage. Gat was gone.

CHAPTER ELEVEN

JOHANNESBURG

Saturday, February 11, 1961

Piet and Margaret Rousseau arrived at Jan Smuts airport in Johannesburg shortly after noon. Rousseau took charge of their luggage. He had brought a single suitcase; Margaret had brought four. Because their relationship had grown strained, he did not question or comment on the difference in the amount of luggage each had brought. He did not expect to spend more than a day or two in the city. He wanted to resolve the matter that had brought them there quickly, get Petra settled into Wits expeditiously, deal with the Belgian officer as befitted his case, and return to his responsibilities in Cape Town.

He assumed that Margaret felt that Petra might need a good deal of mothering while she both returned to earth after the excitement of her adventure and began her new life at varsity. He personally thought it might be best for Petra to return to the Cape and enroll in the University of Cape Town, living at home. That or go out to Stellenbosch where she would be close enough to keep an eye on. When he had mentioned such notions to his wife, she had refused to discuss them. He had decided that, given the circumstances, it was perhaps better to agree to Margaret's staying a week or two near Wits where Petra could reach out to her if need be.

As a taxi drove them to their hotel, they did not speak. In fact, daily conversation between them had become difficult. He knew that Margaret and especially Petra regarded him as having "blacks." But it was Margaret who now seemed to have sunk into one.

Rousseau was known at the hotel and so there was no problem about having to wait for their suite until three P.M., the customary check-in time. They went to the rooms, ordered sandwiches from room service, and had their lunch there. Rousseau moved a lounge chair near a window so that his wife could gaze out over the city and arranged a lamp beside the chair so that she could read. She ensconced herself in the chair, her book unopened in her lap, looked occasionally at the city, but more often at the mirror above the dresser where she could see an image of herself. With her taken care of, Rousseau made phone calls from the adjoining room.

As the afternoon wore on, with Piet busy in the other room, Margaret Rousseau gazed at her image in the glass. She saw past the middle-aged woman reflected there and discerned the child-woman she had once been. In the days since Petra had run off, Margaret had thought time and again of her youth, of the lad and the love they had felt, of her running off to Rhodesia to have their baby and give it to his sister. She realized now that she might have been wiser to reveal the truth to her parents, certainly at least to her mother. She wondered if her parents had understood why she went to Rhodesia. Probably. It was surprising what a little experience of the world taught people. She wondered why they never asked about her time there. Were they honoring her adulthood, letting her take the lead? Since she had not talked to her parents then, she was determined to talk to her daughter now. She was not prepared to let her husband damage something fragile and meaningful to Petra.

In Petra's call to her two days earlier she had seemed carefree and pleased with herself and open about sharing her first-love joy. Margaret wanted to nurture that joy and their relationship and the trust that undergirded it. She was very afraid that Piet was determined to smash it.

If he did, she knew what she would do. She had heard about short-term rentals, small flats designed for business people who needed to camp out in Joburg for a month or two. She would take one of those. She had brought along clothes enough to see her into autumn and even winter. Petra could stay with her until she made a life for herself at Wits.

Once Petra was established at varsity, Margaret would take a trip to Rhodesia. Perhaps even to England. She had long wanted to check on things in both places. Then? Perhaps she would return to Grahamstown, get a job of some kind, perhaps at the varsity there. In her spare time she would take courses, less for the degree she had never received—although she would work for a degree—but for the enrichment that learning and new views on the world would provide.

She wondered if Piet had any inkling that he was threatening a rupture in his marriage that might never be repaired. Probably not, even though it could not have escaped his notice—he was an observant man—that she had brought four suitcases, clothes enough for an extended stay. He was observant, yes, but also what he called principled. One of those principles was that his women behaved as he expected them to. At the moment he saw himself saving both Petra's future and her reputation. Margaret saw him as bent on ruining her happiness.

She understood that he meant well. That was what made it so difficult. After he finished his telephoning, he had nothing to do but wait for the call that might come from Jan Smuts. He had brought reports to read, but he could not focus on them. Instead he paced in his stocking feet. Margaret looked out the window or pretended to read. She did not want to talk.

Finally the telephone rang. Rousseau answered it immediately. He spoke into it in low tones. Margaret continued to sit at the window, her novel in her lap, her eyes still on a page she had hardly looked at all day.

"They've picked them up," Rousseau announced when he hung up the phone. "They're bringing Petra here in the Ford. They'll take the Belgian to headquarters." Margaret heard in the tone of his voice how pleased he was. The police had done their job. His daughter was safe, at least as he saw the matter. "I better get over there."

"What will you do?" she asked.

"Interrogate him."

"Which means what?" She looked at him beseechingly.

"He's an enemy of the state."

"You don't know that."

"I do. He ferried a terrorist across the border."

"Petra was with him," Margaret said. "She loves him—or thinks she does."

Rousseau sat in a companion chair nearby. He shoved his stockinged feet into his shoes and laced them up, preparing to leave. "We need to find out about him. He claimed to be a Belgian army officer. But we really don't know who he is. He could be ANC for all we know."

"Please keep in mind that he's important to Petra."

"The man's a scoundrel," Rousseau said. He rose and stretched to his full height in a gesture of triumph. "As I see it, he kidnapped and corrupted a minor. Showed her things she didn't need to know and put her under a dangerous spell."

"Will you interrogate him yourself?"

"I will. If he doesn't talk, we may have to crush a testicle."

Margaret looked away, aghast. What a barbaric way to talk! Did it not occur to him that Petra would never forgive him? "Excuse me for mentioning it, but Petra may be partial to his—"

Rousseau's expression froze. What his wife was about to suggest appalled him. It shook him to think that his daughter might have been transformed into a slave of— He would not allow that thought to form.

"Pardon my rough talk," he said. "You know I don't mean it."

Margaret stared at her book.

"We are civilized people," he reminded her. "We do not use torture in police interrogations." Margaret would not look at him. To show his annoyance, he added, "We might give him a love pat or two—just so he'll know we're playing by our rules."

"Will he have a lawyer?"

"He won't need a lawyer."

Finally she turned toward him. "Be smart, Piet," she implored. "Smart enough not to hurt him. Hurt him and she'll never get over him." He gave her an exasperated look. It tired Margaret—depressed her, in fact—to see her child's father so ready to hurt her. "If she loves him, she may follow the path of Jan-Christiaan."

This caution stung him. Still he felt forced to reply, "She hardly knows him." He stood, ready to leave.

"You asked me to marry you the second time we were together. You hardly knew me."

"He's one of these fellows who thinks he can take any-thing he can grab. Well, not this time!" He gave his wife a grim smile and was gone.

Margaret sat in her chair, her head bowed, her eyes closed, and thought, "I must scrub this out of my thoughts before Petra arrives."

AT JAN SMUTS, Gat was handcuffed by the police, his hands crossed before him. As if to maximize his humiliation, he was led from the departure terminal, a policeman on either side of him, holding onto his arms. Gat understood the game; he had played it himself with suspects. People watched as he walked by, hatred in some eyes. The police pushed him into a van waiting in the loading zone and drove him away.

The ride to the police station was short. There Gat was photographed, fingerprinted, stripped naked, and given a jumpsuit of cotton ticking and canvas scuffs to wear. On the principle that it was humbling, if not degrading, for a white suspect to be herded by a black warder, the biggest African that Gat had ever seen now appeared. At first sight, he reminded Gat of Zuzu, the vicious and enormous African who preceded Patrice Lumumba off the plane at Elisabethville. The warder stood six and a half feet tall, had shoulders and biceps the size of hams, hands that seemed to hang below his knees, a flat, broken nose, mean, unintelligent eyes, and an odor as strong as his body. His huge fists made the truncheon he carried seem as delicate as a conductor's baton.

By the reckoning of Afrikaner ideology, Gat thought, he would feel more humiliation at being shoved into a holding tank with drunk and smelling kaffirs picked up off the street. But the ideology demanded racial separation. The black Goliath escorted Gat along a corridor. He unlocked the door of a holding tank, administered a sharp karate chop to the back of Gat's head, and gave him a push.

Gat's head rang as he stumbled into the tank and fell among other suspects, all white. He rose quickly, stood to his full height, his feet planted solidly, and threw out his chest. The men appraised him for toughness, sized him up for weaknesses. Gat met their scrutiny with a steady stare of his own. He moved to a wall, stood against it, his head still ringing, and hoped that none of the men ever discovered that he was an army officer.

"What're you in for?" one of the men asked.

"A Special Branch colonel caught me stealing from his house," Gat replied. The men guffawed.

Gat assumed he would remain in the tank until Rousseau arrived. Elsie had told Petra that the Rousseaus had already left Cape Town. So he might meet the colonel again within a matter of hours. How would that interrogation go? He would have seen the documents Gat carried. That meant that he would know that he and Petra were married. Gat wondered if that fact would work in his favor or serve as an affront to Rousseau. Probably the latter. More importantly, Rousseau was unlikely to forgive his helping Garvey across the border. The colonel would regard that as endangering all of South Africa. If he had been thinking like a soldier, Gat mused, instead of a bridegroom, dazzled by his wife, he would have realized they'd have been safer in Rhodesia than in trying to fly out of Johannesburg.

He wondered if he would ever see Petra again. Probably not. Rousseau would put her on a plane to Cape Town and try to keep them apart forever. It depressed him to think that he would never again hold his wife. He realized that, when they faced one another, he must do whatever he could to make Rousseau think well of him.

After what Gat judged to be only a couple of hours, the African warder opened the holding tank and pulled him out.

He walked Gat along a corridor. He gave him directions by hitting him with a truncheon. He did not speak. He led Gat to a door, unlocked and opened it. Gat ducked as the warder sent a karate chop toward his head. The man smiled and whacked the truncheon hard across Gat's back.

Gat stumbled into a small interrogation room furnished with a table, several wooden chairs, and a one-way wall mirror through which he could be observed. The warder pointed at a chair with the truncheon and left, locking the door. Gat sat, rotating his back to ease the pain of the blow. Then he put his arms on the table and folded his hands in a posture that was dignified, patient, even suppliant. He assumed that Rousseau was on the other side of the mirror, watching him. He wanted to appear worthy and cooperative. He thought of words he might say when he and the colonel met.

After a time, the interrogation room door opened. Gat looked up. Colonel Rousseau entered the room, followed by the enormous African. Gat stood as he would for a superior officer. He and Rousseau observed one another without speaking, the colonel tapping Gat's passport lightly in his hands.

"We meet again, Captain Gautier," Rousseau finally said.

"Indeed we do, sir," Gat replied. He intended to show his father-in-law every possible respect.

The colonel studied him and finally instructed, "Please sit."

"I'm standing out of respect for you, sir."

Rousseau, who was shorter than Gat, regarded him coolly.

"Before we start," Gat said, "may I say that when I went to your house for lunch, I didn't know what love was. I know now."

Rousseau observed him scornfully. "Because of my daughter?"

"Yes, sir. She and I were married this morning. So I hope that between us there'll be—" Gat shrugged.

The colonel laughed heartily, but without merriment in his eyes. "My friend," he replied, "that is the most preposterous little speech I've ever heard." He suggested strongly, "Please sit."

Gat remained standing. He gestured that he did so out of respect.

"If you want my respect . . ." Rousseau began. "Then why don't you tell me who you are?" Gat recited as facts information that Rousseau already knew: his name as Adriaan Gautier, his captaincy in the Belgian colonial Force Publique, his service in Katanga, his arrival in South Africa for a vacation. Rousseau listened impatiently, standing to his full height, still forced to look up to Gat.

When Gat finished speaking, the colonel said quietly, "I asked you to sit down." Gat understood now that Rousseau wanted to look down to assert dominance over him.

When Gat did not move quickly, Rousseau nodded to the African. The warder swung his truncheon at Gat's shoulder. It hit with such force that it knocked Gat off his feet. He found himself kneeling before Rousseau, blood throbbing in his brain with periodic flashes of red. He gritted his teeth against the pain in his shoulder.

Rousseau again requested, "Please sit. You will be more comfortable in a chair." As Gat struggled to find his footing, the African lifted him off the floor and tossed him into a chair.

"Who are you?" Rousseau asked mildly. He was trying to be patient for Petra's sake. He looked down at Gat. "Tell me, please, who you are."

Gat repeated that he was Adriaan Gautier. He crossed his legs to suggest that he felt at ease. And also to protect his groin.

"You are trying my goodwill," Rousseau said with the beginnings of impatience. "What we know of you is this: You are carrying a great many American dollars concealed in a money belt."

"I am a visitor, sir."

"You are traveling on a most suspicious passport and with a letter on parchment stationery that instructs simply, 'Disappear.'"

"I will explain—"

Rousseau raised a hand to stop him. "You have corrupted the morals of a young woman, an action for which, I presume, you have a talent. But you have chosen the wrong young woman this time."

"We are married, sir."

"A soldier can dance away from a marriage without difficulty," Rousseau observed. "Perhaps you already have experience at that." Before Gat could reply, Rousseau continued, "You have stolen a car and you have helped a wanted terrorist escape to Bechuanaland. That last makes you an enemy of the state."

The warder made ready to use the truncheon again. Rousseau gestured restraint. "Now," Rousseau repeated, "who are you and why are you in this country?"

"I truly am Adriaan Gautier. I'm here because I needed to get out of Katanga."

"What had you done there that required you to leave?"

Gat looked at Rousseau as if the question baffled him.

Rousseau shouted, "Why? Why did you have to leave?"

As explanation Gat offered, "I told you once before, sir, about the Katangese troops going on a rampage, massacring the Northern Baluba. The UN was going to investigate. I was told to leave Katanga so that I could not testify that politicians fomented the rampage."

"For this they gave you more than fifteen hundred-dollar bills?"

"Twenty of them actually."

Rousseau said, "Tell me about Gabriel Michels."

Gat had not thought of Michels in several days. He had not anticipated the question and was uncertain how much to reveal.

When Gat did not answer, Rousseau said, "I'm sure you know Lieutenant Michels. Tell me about him."

"There's a man called Michels in the Force in Katanga. Is that the man you mean?"

"When we picked him up, he was carrying a letter identical to the one we found in your possession. You must know him."

Gat shrugged. "We were both in Katanga. Not in the same unit. I've met him, that's all."

"We know you were sent here together. For what reason?"

"I didn't know Michels was in South Africa." This was an obvious lie. Both Gat and Rousseau recognized it as such. "Probably like me he needed rest and recuperation," Gat said.

Rousseau nodded to the African warder. The warder brought a blow of the truncheon down on Gat's feet, bare inside canvas scuffs. Gat reeled with pain.

"Michels is in our custody," the colonel said. "He has acknowledged that you were both sent here to contact terrorists. Tell me about him."

"Michels is not a man anyone would send on a secret mission," Gat replied. "He frequents whorehouses and gets into knife fights, often with near fatal consequences."

Gat and Rousseau measured one another, for Gat had just shown the colonel that he had caught him in an interrogator's lie. For this arrogance the colonel nodded again to the African. He brought the truncheon down on Gat's arches. Gat clenched his teeth, trying not to scream.

Rousseau walked about the small room, then turned back toward his subject. "When were you last in Brussels?" he asked.

"It's been some years, sir. Eight or ten."

"Your passport says it was issued in Brussels. Where you haven't been for some years. It must be a forgery."

Gat explained that the passport was valid, issued by the Belgian Consulate in Elisabethville. The consul, he said, had wanted him out of Katanga during the Baluba investigation. It was an oversight that no departure stamp from Belgium appeared in the passport; the consulate was supposed to arrange that. "I suspect, sir, that you know how these things are arranged."

Rousseau nodded. "Invariably with false names. Your birth name?"

Gat hesitated a moment. "Adriaan Gautier."

"You hesitated. In order to remember this name?"

"I wondered if your friend here was going to hit me," Gat replied.

Rousseau nodded to the warder. Once again he brought the truncheon down across Gat's feet.

It took Gat several moments to absorb the blow. Then he asked, "Sir, why would I lie about my name?"

"Why indeed? What is your name?"

"Adriaan Gautier."

Rousseau signaled the warder. The man stepped into the blow he delivered to Gat's shoulder. The shoulder stung with pain. Gat's ears buzzed; his head momentarily swam out of consciousness. He clenched his teeth. Rousseau demanded, "The name you were given at birth."

"Adriaan Gautier."

Rousseau studied Gat, then opened a folder and withdrew a document. He laid it before Gat. "Among your things we found this certificate issued for a marriage done this morning in Lobatse. Because of it, I will do what I have never done. I will explain myself to a suspect."

Gat nodded.

"My people arrived here more than three hundred years ago," Rousseau said. "When they stepped onto these shores, they were empty of people. We did not steal this land from anyone. Ever since people have been trying to steal it from us. Sixty years ago we fought the British over this. We lost the war, but won the peace. We do not intend to lose again."

Gat wondered how this speech related to him. The truncheon kept him from inquiring.

"You have come here to take what is ours. You will not do that. We will not allow you to exploit or compromise our natural resources—in this case our young women—and then cast them aside."

"Sir, I love your daughter."

Rousseau nodded to the African. The man raised his truncheon and brought it swiftly down across Gat's shoulders. His body jolted forward. His head snapped and shook at the end of his neck. His stomach churned. He lunged for the table so that he did not slide to the floor. Rousseau watched him. At last Gat sat back in the chair and held himself with defiant erectness.

Rousseau said, "You are carrying sufficient money to set up a terrorist operation. Our people were on the trail of a known terrorist, a man we very much hoped to arrest, and you snuck him across the border."

Rousseau nodded and once again the African hit Gat, this time across his toes. Despite himself, Gat cried out. Pain shot up through his legs and torso and into his head. His ears rang. His scalp prickled as the pain tried to leave his body.

"You have committed crimes against the state," Rousseau said.

"Let me explain," Gat said. "We decided to take a look at Vic Falls." He related that he and Petra had spent the night with friends of hers called Prinsloo outside Vryberg. Petra had slept on a couch; he had spent the night in the car. "As we left Vryberg, we picked up the man on the road. He was hitchhiking."

Rousseau nodded. The African brought the truncheon down again on Gat's feet, this time across his arches. Gat fainted, fell off his chair. The African picked him up, slapped his face, set him back on the chair. As Gat watched the colonel, moments of blackness obscured his vision. He saw Rousseau set a paper before him on the table. He frowned at it, trying to clear his vision. Finally he realized it was the receipt from the clinic with instructions on the back about where to pick up Garvey.

"Don't play with me," Rousseau warned. "I was doing this when you were a child. I know when a man is lying." Gat said nothing. "Who was he?"

Gat told Rousseau the few details he knew about the man who had called himself Garvey. In doing this he felt no sense of betrayal because Garvey had understood he and Petra might be questioned. He had revealed little about himself. "I think he'd actually been to America," Gat said. "He may have even had a business there. The rest of it I discounted." The two men eyed one another. Gat said, "May I go now?"

Rousseau nodded once again to the African. He hit Gat repeatedly with the truncheon. Gat again fell from the chair. The warder continued to hit him on the floor, especially his feet. At last he lifted him and set him back on the chair.

Rousseau said, "Don't think you are getting this treatment as my revenge for your having taken advantage of my daughter. Although I cannot forgive you for that." He nodded again to the African warder. The man whacked Gat, knocking him off the chair, then pulling him back onto it. Rousseau withdrew the marriage certificate from the documents on the table. "We do not recognize Bechuanaland marriages in this country!" he remarked. He tore the document into small pieces and threw them into Gat's face.

A piece of paper wasn't a marriage, Gat told himself. He said nothing.

"I saw Petra before I came here," Rousseau said. "She fell into my arms crying. She said over and over, 'Father, I've got myself into a terrible mess. Help me get out of it! Get me out of it!'"

Gat said nothing. He did not believe what Rousseau claimed about Petra.

"Once she was away from you, she realized how little she knew about you. How likely it was that she was being used. As a cover for some kind of terrorist mischief. That is why this treatment. She does not even know your real name. Fortunately, she saw these things for herself."

Gat sat slumped in his chair, no longer hearing what the colonel said. All he wanted was that the warder not hit him again.

"You may think me a hard man, Captain—if you are a captain. Even cruel," Rousseau said. "But I am not. I could hold you incommunicado under indefinite detention. But you may actually have some feelings for my daughter—although she no longer has any for you. You will never see her again. But you will be released."

Rousseau moved to the door. He turned back to Gat. "Don't ever see her again. Do you understand me?" He gave Gat a look of fury so intense that it crossed the room with the sound of ice cracking. Rousseau left the room with a nod to the African. Gat smelled the unmistakable odor of the black warder as he advanced on him. He lifted Gat off the chair. He pushed him against the wall, staring fiercely at him. Apprehensively Gat tried to slide to a corner to protect himself. But he could not; he could barely stand. As he sank to the floor, the warder came at him with such speed that Gat had no time to protect himself. The man delivered a sharp blow across Gat's thighs. Then, to the small of his back. He hit him repeatedly. Over and over. Even after Gat lost consciousness, he still seemed to feel the blows raining down on him.

WHEN MARGARET opened the door of the hotel room, her daughter stood on the threshold, a look of outrage on her face. "I married him, Mother!" Petra cried. "He's my husband! Where have they taken him?" Margaret threw her arms about her daughter. Petra burst into tears. "This is my wedding day! What has Father done with him?"

Margaret led her into the room and listened to her rail against her parents, their overprotectiveness, their unwillingness to let her lead her own life. Again and again and at the top of her voice Petra demanded to know what had happened to Gat. When would she see him again? Were the police holding him? Why? Because her father had requested it? Her husband had committed no crime. Were the police questioning him? Were they beating him?

When she grew exhausted from shouting, she embraced her mother. "I really do love him, Mum," she said. "This has been the most wonderful week of my life. What will happen to him?"

"Your father wants to protect you from a mistake."

"I've made no mistake!" Petra cried. She began once more to weep.

"Then everything will be all right," her mother assured her.

"Will it? You know Father! He does what he wants."

Who better than she, Margaret thought, knew the truth of that? She held Petra to her, kissing her blonde hair and patting her shoulder. Because Piet wanted his daughter's happiness—and his own—Margaret hoped that eventually he would do what led to those goals. He might, however, require powerful persuasion. One thing was certain. Shouting at Piet would accomplish nothing; it would only reinforce his righteous conviction that he was acting in Petra's best interest. "Go lie down," Margaret advised. "Getting married is an emotional time for everyone. When your father comes in, you can tell us about your wedding and your husband. With your father, you know, it's best not to yell."

Petra allowed her mother to lead her across the room. She lay down on the bed. Margaret sat beside her quietly stroking her hair. As she drew closer to sleep, Margaret sang her the lullaby she had sung to her daughter when Petra was a child.

WHEN GAT regained consciousness, he was lying on the floor of a cell. The air was moist, as thick as soup, and smelled of urine and bad food. The pressure of the air made his skin burn. His mouth was dry, his tongue a mere charred nub of flesh. A caged and naked light bulb stared down at him. His head and body throbbed with pain. His heart worked only with a struggle. He seemed to feel his blood moving so sluggishly as to cause an aching in his veins. When he moved his feet, he felt he would faint. Each toe seemed to cry out like a baby being tortured. He tried to inspect the cell and passed out.

Later two white warders carried him down a hall. He moved in and out of consciousness. As Gat saw the hallway's fluorescent lights pass overhead, his body silently screamed with pain. He was taken to a small room. He saw clothes

draped over a hanger on a wall hook, the clothes he had worn
driving in from Lobatse. The warders laid him on a gurney.
They pulled the jump suit from his body. Gat lay naked, his
body crying out in pain, but he clenched his teeth so that
neither scream nor whimper escaped from him.

He saw Rousseau enter and gaze at him. Although the
movement caused him pain, he shifted his hands to cover
his groin. He closed his eyes. "Everything is here," he heard
Rousseau tell him. His voice came as if shouted through a
tube of infinite length. "Everything: passport, wallet, watch,
money. You have taken from us, but we have taken nothing
from you." Gat heard a door open and close. His eyes opened
onto the place Rousseau had been. He was gone. Gat cracked
a smile.

The warders dressed him in his clothes. Sometimes he was
conscious, sometimes not. When they fit his socks and shoes
onto his feet, he passed out from the pain.

Since Petra was furious with him, since she could not stop
crying for more than a few minutes, Rousseau suggested to
Margaret that they have dinner sent up to the suite by room
service. Petra sat with her parents at the makeshift table only
because she wanted to know what had happened to her husband. Her father refused to discuss the matter until they had
all had dinner. He insisted that Petra eat.

While she did, Rousseau informed her that Gat had
acknowledged that he was a member of a terrorist conspiracy.

"There was no conspiracy," Petra said. "We gave a man
a ride."

"He admitted that there was a conspiracy. He was carrying
money to fund terrorism."

"That's nonsense, Father. Did you torture him to make him say that?"

"He was not tortured," Rousseau said. "I promised to release him—for your sake. He admitted giving the man money. Were they ever alone?"

"No," Petra told him. "Never." Then she remembered that Gat and Garvey had gone together into the Indian store in the Mafeking township. But it was not possible that Gat had given Garvey money. "Where is Gat now? When can I see him?"

Trying to maintain his patience, Rousseau suggested it would be wise for Petra to return immediately to Cape Town. She, too, had acted as a conspirator. If she got out of the province of the Transvaal, Rousseau thought he could steer the investigation away from the young blonde woman who had made such a vivid impression at the border post. He might also arrange to have the marriage records in Lobatse lost. "I'm trying to protect you, young lady," Rousseau told Petra, "because I love you. I am risking my reputation and my retirement for you."

"You are lying, Father. You have lied to us for years." Petra's tears were gone now, her calm giving emphasis to her rage. "Shall we talk about why Jan-Christiaan does not come home?" At Petra's impertinence Rousseau's face went pale. He stared at her, unable to speak. "Torturer! Did you torture my husband?"

Rousseau took control of himself. He folded his hands and gave his daughter a look of infinite patience. "Pet," he said quietly, "the world is not always the way we want it to be." He reached across the table to take her hand.

She put her arms behind her. "What have you done with him?" she asked. "Did you hit him? Throw him out a window? He's my husband."

"Collect yourself," her father said.

"Let's all calm down," Margaret suggested.

Petra stared at the table, clenching her teeth so she would not scream.

"This isn't easy for me, Pet," her father said. "These aren't easy things to say. What life has taught me, though, is that sometimes the things we most want are the things that hurt us most." He bit his lips. His eyes grew teary. "When I say that, of course, I am thinking of Jan-Christiaan."

Petra glanced at her father. Because she had not heard him mention his son for two years, she knew that he spoke out of deep emotion.

"I talked with Captain Gautier, as he calls himself," he said. "An attractive fellow. I thought so when we met in the Groote Kerk."

"When can I see him?" Petra asked. "Where is he now?"

"He told me he thought it best if he did not see you again," Rousseau said.

"That can't be true," Petra retorted. "You've got him locked up somewhere."

"I am sorry to say that he is acting like a Belgian," Rousseau declared. "The Belgians had to flee the Congo because they wanted only to exploit it, rob it, suck it dry of resources. That's what's happened here."

"What are you talking about?" Margaret asked. "They were married today. How can he not want to see his wife?"

"Pet, he exploited you," Rousseau said. Petra shook her head. "Do you think I enjoy telling you these things?" he asked. "He used you as a cover for contacting terrorists."

"I don't believe that, Father."

Rousseau pushed his dinner plate into the center of the table. He set his hands before him, folded them, and stared at them. Petra and Margaret watched him, knowing that he was wrestling against one of his black moods. Finally he looked up at Petra, an expression of pity in his eyes. "Captain Gautier has a wife in Belgium," Rousseau said.

The blood drained from Petra's face. Her mother pulled her chair beside Petra and put her arm about her. "I don't believe that," Petra managed to blurt out.

"He gave me this." Rousseau took a small photo from his pocket and set it before Petra. It showed a young fair-haired woman holding a child. Petra turned away and burst into tears. "It's been very hard duty in the Congo and Katanga these last six-eight months. He came here for a break from that."

"Why didn't he go home to his family?" Margaret asked.

"He came here to advance a terrorist plot. He saw the wife at Christmas." Rousseau looked carefully at his daughter, his expression pained, to see how she received this difficult news. "While here— I hate to say it—he needed a young woman to mask the plot he was here to promote. And to have a good time as well." Rousseau looked at his folded hands. "And I introduced him into our home," he acknowledged repentantly. "I'll never forgive myself for that."

"A man looking for a good time does not ask his good-time girl to marry him," Petra said. "It was his idea that we marry. I never pressed him for that."

"Darling, I'm sorry," Rousseau said. "Gautier told me that he had concocted a story about himself that would engage a young woman's sympathies. Something that would make her think he needed her."

Petra quietly began to weep. "If this is true," she said, "why didn't you make him come here with you to tell me face-to-face?"

"I suggested that," Rousseau said. "He declined. He said he knew it would break your heart and he couldn't bear to see that."

"So there was some affection on his side," Margaret suggested, reaching for a few scraps of good news for Petra to hold onto.

"I told him where we were staying," Rousseau said. "I invited him to come and do the honorable thing. I refused to hold him out of consideration for you. He's a free man now." The colonel watched his weeping daughter. "I'm so sorry. The cost of our mistakes can be so dreadful!"

Petra stood and made her way uncertainly to the room she would occupy. Margaret hurried after her.

Once in her room Petra lay on her bed. Her mother shut the door and came to her side. "It's not true," Petra said. "He's lying. He would have lied to keep Jan-Christiaan and he's lying to keep me." Her mother embraced her, began to rock her as she would a child. Petra gently removed her mother's arms. "I'm a woman now, Mother," she said. "I'm going to face this like a woman. And I need to be alone." Margaret embraced her and left the room.

When she saw her husband's bent figure still sitting at the table, Margaret shook her head. "You should have made him come with you," she told Rousseau. "If it's true, she needed to hear that from his own lips."

"I wish I had," Rousseau told his wife. "I know you're worried about her. But let me assure you: in two weeks it will all blow over. She will be adjusting to varsity. She'll be meeting men who will seem enormously more interesting and talented and attractive than the Belgian. She will feel immensely proud of herself for being at Wits, for having declared her independence and defied me. She will take secret pleasure in knowing that for a few hours she was a married woman. But it is a secret she is not likely to share with the next man in her life." He took his wife's hand. "Everything will work out, I assure you."

Margaret said nothing, thinking: How little you know of women!

Rousseau glanced at his watch. "Excuse me," he said. "I must make a short telephone call downstairs. I may get a cognac in the bar." Margaret watched him leave, knowing that he was going into the night to meet the black mood that was already trying to find him.

In her room Petra stood at the window, looking into the streets below. Gat had told her about various women he had had. If there truly were a wife and a small child, why did he not also mention them? If he was already married, why did he want to marry her? And that business about Lumumba. Why would he tell her that if it wasn't true? He had insisted on telling her names. She had not known love, except with Gat, but she knew in her heart that Gat loved her.

But her father also loved her. Was he telling the truth? She had to admit that men did take advantage of young women. She had always taken Gat at his word. Maybe that had not been wise. Maybe he married her for whatever reassurance he could derive from the fact that she would actually marry him. Would she ever know? Only if and when she saw him again.

GAT WAS lying on a gurney in a van and the van was going somewhere. He knew strangely that he was wearing his own clothes. Because of that, even though the motion of the van made him wince, the pain and stiffness in his body seemed to have lessened. Because the van was traveling through darkness, he thought—when he was able to think—of the ride out of E'ville that chilly night only four weeks before, the convoy of cars moving toward the lake formed by the Francqui dam where the bird-watching was excellent. The cars had pulled up in a line at the clearing with the large tree and left their headlights on. He wondered if they were taking him there.

Finally the van stopped. The rear doors swung open. Two men in suit coats and ties stood beside the doors, one on each side. "Here are your escorts," a warder told Gat. The two men reached into the van as the gurney was wheeled toward them. "Can you stand, mate?" one of the escorts asked. Suddenly the gurney was turned upright. Gat slid to the ground. When his feet hit the pavement, he emitted a whimper. His knees buckled. The men grabbed him, stood him upright. His feet found footing beneath him. "Sorry we have to do this, mate," the escort said. "Regulations, you know." The escort slipped a pair of cold handcuffs around Gat's wrists. "Tight enough, but not too tight. How does that suit?" The escort tightened the cuffs. "Better to hold your hands this way." He positioned Gat's hands, one clutching the other, before his stomach. "Thumbs under belt. That's it." The escorts took Gat's arms above the elbow. Although he could hardly walk, they steered him through the balmy summer night. "Nice out," observed one of the escorts.

"Can you climb stairs?" asked the other.

When it was clear he could not do this, the two men lifted him off his feet. As they took him up the stairway into the plane, he clenched his teeth against the pain. They bundled him through the cabin, past open-mouthed passengers watching in astonishment. They moved to a row of three unoccupied seats at the rear of the plane. One escort took the seat at the window, the other the seat on the aisle. They maneuvered

Gat into the seat between them. By the time he sat, his body was sweating, his throat panting. He felt his body had never worked harder in any ten-minute period in his life. He lowered his head against the headrest. It throbbed with pain and dizziness. He fainted and revived, fainted and revived, over and over. He was hardly aware of the plane racing down the runway of Jan Smuts airport and lifting into the sky.

CHAPTER TWELVE

LONDON / JOHANNESBURG

February / March 1961

At Heathrow Gat and his escorts waited until all other passengers left the plane. The escorts removed the handcuffs—there was no need to humiliate him here—and Gat asked a stewardess for a pair of crutches. By the time he made his way to the front of the cabin, lurching from one row of seats to the next, gritting his teeth against the pain, one escort in front of him, the other behind, the crutches were waiting for him. The stairway was more than he could manage. The escorts lifted him by his armpits and carried him to the ground. Walking with the crutches was possible, but very slow. There were still moments when pain rushed to Gat's head, dizzying him, moments when he thought he would faint. Inside the terminal the escorts arranged for him to have a wheelchair. Gat was pushed through passport control, holding the crutches upright on a foot pedal, and wheeled into the transit lounge. There he was transferred to a chair, his suitcases placed on the seat beside him.

"What now, gents?" he asked the escorts. "I've never done this before."

The escorts said they would find a loo and see about arrangements with British authorities. He should wait where he was; they would be right back. It struck Gat as strange that the escorts should go off so casually. After all, until then they had all but manacled themselves to him. But he assumed they knew their business. He thought about trying to flee. But he knew he would not get far on crutches and, in any case, from whom was he fleeing? He had not slept well on the plane. He spent the night worrying what Rousseau would tell Petra and wondering how to contact her. Now amid the comings and goings of the transit lounge, he nodded off. He slept fitfully for two hours. When he woke, he was alone. He looked about, wondering what had happened to the escorts.

As he searched for them, turning this way and that in the wheelchair, the woman in charge of the transit lounge approached him. She had seen that he was awake now, she said. She bent beside the wheelchair and explained that, when they'd left, the friends he'd arrived with had asked her to give him his passport and other documents. Gat looked baffled at first, but thanked her and took the documents. He realized that the escorts had dumped him.

At first he felt elation at receiving his freedom, but that emotion quickly passed. He began to experience the same depression that accompanied his first days in Johannesburg. He had no career now. Even if he wanted to return to soldiering, what Rousseau and his black warder had done to his feet made that impossible. He had no connection to family, few friends and none in Europe. Worst of all his wife of a single day must now be repenting her foolhardiness in marrying him. She was half a world away and possibly forever beyond his reach.

What should he do now? Return to Belgium? But what would face him there? He had not seen his parents in a decade. He had not even written them during the worst hysteria over the Congo's collapse to assure them that he was safe and in good health. Could he return to them now, a broken man and a failure? Would they believe him if he revealed to them what happened in Katanga? From a paper he had seen on the plane he knew that Katanga authorities were still insisting that Lumumba had escaped from prison, that he was making his way either to Bukavu in the eastern Congo or to the base of his support in Stanleyville. Could he ask his parents to take him in? No, Gat could not turn to them. He had too much pride for that. Maybe someday he would write them, but he could not contact them now.

And he could not ask for help from his brothers. They had just entered their middle teens when he left. They would not want him around. He'd be a stranger.

If he went to Belgium, could he get treatment in a military hospital? Not without endangering himself. Had he not received strong advice—and a good deal of money—to disappear? If the people at the address in Tervuren knew he had gone to South Africa, would they not know if he turned up in Belgium? Luckily he still had the money they had sent him. He was not without resources.

With the help of a customer service rep Gat found a cheap hotel near the Parsons Green tube station and arranged by phone for a room. The rep got a second wheelchair, took Gat to a cab, and he was on his way. The hotel was simple, but satisfactory, and offered breakfast, the customary fry-up. The room was warm and had a telephone. The hotel owner arranged for Gat to see a doctor, an Indian. His nurse gasped when she saw his bruises, but the doctor assured him in singsong Gujarati-accented English that in no time at all he would be running along the Thames.

PETRA SPENT the day after her wedding wondering what had happened to Gat. Had he really been released from questioning, as her father insisted? If so, why didn't he call? Or come to see her? Did he not come because he knew that her father would have shown her the photo of his wife? But how could that possibly be? Was the child really theirs? For long periods she sat staring out the hotel window, tears streaming down her cheeks, waiting for Gat to call.

At other times she paced the room. Was it possible her father had lied to her? If he had, what had he done to Gat? Was he in jail? Had he been charged with aiding terrorists? How could she find out? She locked her door and called Johannesburg police stations. There was no record of a Captain Gautier in custody. But would the police tell her the truth? Africans need not be told about detainees, but she was white. So was the person about whom she was inquiring. If there was no record of Gat, then it must be that her father had never arrested him. They must simply have talked. After which her father released him. Unless, of course, he had been deported. Or told to leave the country and escorted to the airport.

In the early afternoon her parents had sandwiches brought to the suite. They called her to join them for lunch. She determined that she would confront her father, ask him the questions she had asked herself. But when she emerged from her room and he embraced her, full of paternal compassion for her distress, she knew she did not possess the audacity to accuse him again of lying to her.

As they ate lunch, her father announced that he had made reservations for them on the five o'clock flight to Cape Town. He told her quietly, gently, that he knew she had been waiting for a call. But no call had come. Might it not now be time to place the whole incident in the past and resolve not to look back? Petra glanced at her mother. When she said nothing to support her husband, Petra simply shook her head. She would not leave the hotel, she said. She knew that if Gat were really free he would contact her. She watched her father clench his teeth. He urged her to face the truth: she had spent a week with a scoundrel—and a married one into the bargain! He'd taken advantage of her inexperience and naïveté. He hated to say it, Rousseau declared, but it was an old story. There were plenty of names for men who acted as Gat had: bounder, rascal, cad, louse, heel, rogue. The police dealt almost daily with women who'd been bilked by them. His best advice was to close the books on the regrettable business, return to Cape Town, and move on. Those who loved her would forgive her mistake. "Those who can't forgive it," he said, "well, to hell with them!"

"I will not go back to Cape Town," Petra answered quietly.

"You know, Piet," Margaret interjected, "that going back home is no way to close the accounts on this business. Her friends will gossip. Ours will shake their heads and whisper, 'Oh, shame! How too bad!'"

"I'll start at Wits," Petra declared. "That was the plan. Tell people I've gone to varsity if you're worried about what to say."

"We're worried about you, Pet," her father replied.

"Well, don't be! I am not a fallen woman! Or a ninny! And my husband is not any of those names you called him."

Exasperated at last, Rousseau instructed, "Come home today, Petra. I can't argue with you. Do as I say. I've got duty tomorrow."

But Petra would not leave. And Margaret would not leave her alone in Johannesburg. She proposed that she and Petra move into cheaper quarters and that she stay in Johannesburg until Pet got settled in a dormitory and started her classes at Wits. Accustomed to deciding what happened in the family, Rousseau insisted for two hours that his women do as he suggested. But in the end he took the eight o'clock flight to Cape Town alone.

Margaret found a small apartment near the Wits campus that could be rented by the week. The women moved into it. Petra started classes at the university. She avoided social activities and applied herself to studying with more diligence than she had ever shown at Herschel. Except when the phone rang or when she rushed to get the mail, her manner remained subdued. Margaret had trouble drawing her into conversation. She refused to talk about Gat from whom she had heard not a single word. Occasionally her mother found her at her desk, staring into space, her cheeks wet with tears. "Please talk to me," Margaret would say. Petra would bite her lips and shake her head.

GAT'S DAYS took on an ordered routine: visits to the doctor, slow, cold walks on crutches around Parsons Green followed by resting times on his bed. There he stared at the chipping paint on the ceiling and got warm again. And always the mullings about what next. A neighborhood pub stood at the edge of the green. If he wanted conversation, which he rarely did, habitués of the pub provided it. During his meals there, he kept looking at women, hoping one of them would turn out to be Petra. He did not see the papers that reported that Patrice Lumumba had been discovered in flight from Katanga.

Villagers, it was reported, had killed him and two companions with machetes and secretly buried their bodies.

On his second day in London, Gat tried to telephone Petra in Cape Town. He assumed her father had taken her there. Rousseau's number was not listed. He tried other Rousseaus, but no one offered help in contacting Petra. He could not write to her in Cape Town because he had never known the address of her parents' home. He wrote to her at Wits, at Stellenbosch University, at the University of Cape Town, sending some letters to Miss Petra Rousseau and others to Mrs. Petra Gautier. But the mail was slow. He heard nothing.

The longer he remained in London, the more it seemed a dream that he had ever been with a young woman in South Africa, that they had fallen in love and married. His world shrank to the size of the room, the route to and from the doctor, his circuits on crutches around Parsons Green.

AT THE end of her first week of classes, Petra had a visitor from Cape Town: Kobus Terreblanche. He took her to dinner at an elegant restaurant, intimate with soft lights and music from a piano and violin, beguiling aromas and delicious entrees tastefully presented by tactful waiters. Kobus ordered Cape wine and insisted they share a chateaubriand. He chatted about Stellenbosch and Cape Town and told her that he missed her. Petra ate little. She refused to share the wine and frequently stared off across the dining room as if waiting for someone to enter. Kobus found her more attractive than ever, but as difficult to talk to as her mother said she was. After dessert, as he drank coffee, he took her hand, fearing she might withdraw it. When she did not, he moved his chair close beside her. "I love you," he told her. "You know that. You must know I hoped you'd marry me."

She nodded, staring at the white expanse of tablecloth. "That hasn't changed. Not for me. You know more about the world now than you did the last time I saw you. But so what?" Petra did not reply. Kobus watched her. "You're so beautiful," he said. "More beautiful than ever." Kobus took her hand in both of his, raised and kissed it. "So I'm not the most exciting chap you'll ever know. So what? I can make you happy." After a moment he added, "Happy again."

Petra watched his hands play with her fingers.

"What do you want?" he asked.

She replied, "What do you want?" She thought: What a dumb conversation!

"I want to see you happy," he told her. "Making you happy would give me—" He stopped in midsentence. "We have the same background, Pet. The same religion. Same values. Same approach to life. Basically we want the same things."

"Do we?"

"I can give you those things. I'm going to be a success. Especially if I have your help. We'll have children. We'll live the life of the people of our background. We'll make a contribution to society."

"What contribution?"

"You can decide that." He watched her earnestly. "We've known each other too long for me to sweep you off your feet. You know me so well you may think me a little boring. But five years into a marriage that's the way it'll be with anyone. I know I can make you happy."

"I'm already married," she said.

"Your father can make those records in Lobatse disappear," he assured her. "That's no problem."

"I think my first job is to get through varsity."

"I don't want to wait four years to marry you. Let's do it this year."

"You are very nice to come here, Kobus," Petra said. She realized she must not allow this old friend to spin ever more elaborate dreams for himself that she would only dash. She withdrew her hand and touched his face, then folded her hands in her lap. "But I think marriage has to be between equals."

"Of course," he agreed. "We'd make equal, though different, contributions to our life together."

"What I mean is—" She paused, not wanting to hurt him. "I couldn't be married to a man who thought he'd rescued me from— A terrible mistake." Petra continued, "I don't think I made a mistake."

"But he's a married man! He came after you to seduce you."

"I love him." Petra laid a hand on his hands and gazed at him. "If I have to get over that, it'll take me awhile."

Kobus pursed his mouth. "I can wait if I have to." He hastily added, "Look, I'm not as uninteresting as you think. I've had romances that have gone further—"

She put her hand lightly on his lips. "Don't tell me." She smiled at him. "I guess you better take me home. I have studying to do."

When he left her at the door of the apartment, he leaned down to kiss her. She shook her head and smiled. "Are you intending to kiss a married woman? Shame!" She smiled, turned quickly, and went inside.

At the end of a month Gat was still on crutches. By then he had decided that the only bridge to a future he wanted was Petra. He called for a taxi and went to a jewelry store. He bought a pair of proper wedding rings, simple gold bands. He returned to southern Africa. Not wanting to risk being denied entry at Jan Smuts airport, where Rousseau might have immigration officials watching for him, he traveled to Salisbury, Southern Rhodesia, by air and south from there by train. In Joburg he got a room in the hotel where he'd originally stayed and took a cab to the University of the Witswatersrand. He told the clerk in the registrar's office that he was a cousin of a student and he gave her his most winning smile. Seeing that he was on crutches, the woman felt sorry for him. He told her the cousin's name. There were several Rousseaus enrolled. But no Petra. He suggested they try Gautier. The cousin had recently married. He did not know if she had changed her name. The clerk found a Gautier. Petra. Gat's heart leaped inside him. She had chosen to use her married name! The clerk said it was against varsity rules for her to give Gat Petra Gautier's address, but she told him her schedule. One of her classes was in session right now. The next one was the following morning.

Gat hobbled to the room where Petra's class was being conducted. He waited outside it. When the class period ended, students streamed out the doors. Gat scanned the young men and women. Petra was not among them. He moved to the door of the classroom. Across it, leaving by a door on the opposite side of the room, he spotted her blonde hair, cut as it always had been. He called her name, but she did not hear. She disappeared. He started to hobble after her, shouting her name, but fear paralyzed him, the fear that she would run from him.

He returned to the hotel. He called for new telephone listings in the name of either Gautier or Rousseau. There were several Rousseaus, no Gautiers. He called the Rousseaus. Only one answered, a woman speaking Afrikaans. Gat replied in Flemish. The woman answered angrily in a torrent of Afrikaans. He switched to English. She hung up. He tried walking without crutches back and forth across the room. The doctor had advised him not to rush the healing; it might take several more weeks. If he did not use the crutches, pain shot through his feet, sizzled up his shins, and rang in his head. He kept falling down. It got harder and harder to pick himself up. But because he equated his failure to walk with a possible failure to win back Petra, he kept trying to complete a passage across the room.

He managed it once. Then he collapsed into the room's only chair. He watched out the window. He listened to the radio. He tried to nap. On crutches he went out to a double feature. He entered when the first film was halfway over; he left before the second one finished. He walked back to the hotel to tire himself and in the hope that somehow on the streets he would run into his wife. He kept seeing women who reminded him of her: the set of one's shoulders, the way another placed her feet in walking. But none of the women was Petra. He ate alone at a restaurant near the hotel. He retired early and did not sleep well.

THE NEXT morning he was outside the only door to Petra's classroom half an hour before the class was scheduled to start. He presented a curious, impaired, yet virile figure on crutches, alertly scanning students, nodding to some of them. Petra did not appear. Perhaps she was not much of a student. Perhaps she had other things on her mind. Once the class began, Gat sank down onto a bench. What now? There must be some way to find out where she lived. He would try again at the registrar's office.

As he pulled himself onto his crutches, he saw two students hurrying toward the class, a young man and a girl, both carrying books. The girl was Petra. Gat wondered who the young man was, why they were together. The couple did not look at him until the young man had swung open the classroom door. Petra glanced at Gat. Seeing him, she stumbled, stopped, dropped her books. She turned to the young man and said, "Go on. I'll be right there." The young man glanced at Gat, then back at Petra, and disappeared. Petra stooped to pick up her books. She gathered them, paused to collect herself. Gat watched her, trying to stand erect. She stood, the books on a loose-leaf binder pressed against her chest. They gazed at one another for a long moment, neither knowing what to say.

"I walked into a door," Gat finally said.

Petra shook her head. "That's how you get a black eye." She watched him.

"I fell off a cliff," Gat said. "You look thinner. Are you eating properly?"

"I've been crying a lot."

"Me too." Gat watched her, wanting very much to touch her. But she stood out of reach, seeming uncertain, not wearing the ring he had placed on her finger in Lobatse. Despite the crutches, he held himself erect, fearful that she would see how damaged he was. Finally he asked, "Can we talk sometime?"

She nodded.

"When you don't have class."

"I don't even know what this class is."

He watched her, hoping she would not flee. "History of the Ancient World."

"You're well informed." She released a hand from the books and brushed tears from her eyes. "Are you all right? You look a mess."

"You should have seen me a month ago." He said, "It's lovely to see you."

"There's a milk bar just off campus. We could go there."

They started off. Petra still held the books self-protectively against her body, not yet ready for Gat to touch her. He maneuvered slowly, not wanting to appear damaged, fearful he might fall down because the joy he felt inside made him want to leap. As they walked, Petra said nothing. She watched the path before them to be certain that there was nothing on which Gat might trip. He watched the pathway as well, but kept glancing at her, made joyful by the smell of her, the sweetness of her voice, the smear of her tears on her cheek, the look of uncertainty she was trying to control.

They entered the milk bar and made their way to a table. "Where have you been?" she asked once she had put down her books and they were settled.

"London. Getting repaired from falling off that cliff." She watched him, examining him carefully. He arranged the crutches while she scrutinized him. They looked at each other. "I hate you seeing me this way," Gat told her. But he assured her tenderly, "I love seeing you!"

Tears swam again in Petra's eyes. She turned away and brushed them from her eyes. "I hate it that they hurt you." Again she brushed tears away. "I want so much to touch you."

"Go ahead. I won't break." He put his arms about her. She sat stiffly and did not return his embrace. He released her.

"I guess I should get us something," she said. "What would you like?"

He reached for his wallet. "Coffee, please. Black. Get us a pastry we can share." He gave her the wallet and watched her walk to the counter, delighting in the blondness of her hair, the curve of her chin. As she stood there, she seemed fragile. When she returned, she gave him his wallet, but did not look at him. He wondered what had happened that she was so reluctant to touch him. Once they began to eat, he asked her about it.

"I wasn't sure you would remember my name," she said.

"Gautier. Last time I checked, you were my wife." Petra set down her coffee. Tears ran down her cheeks. Gat wiped them with his handkerchief. "You're not wearing your wedding ring," Gat remarked.

"If I wear it, other students think I'm strange."

She stirred her coffee, looking away from him. To change the subject he asked, "How do you like school? I see you've made some friends."

"I went to primary school with that chap," she said quickly. "We're both feeling lost here and sometimes we—"

"You should have friends," Gat interrupted. "That's good."

She rose and walked away from the table. Gat wondered if she were leaving him. But her books remained. The counterman gave her a sugar dispenser and she returned with it. "This coffee tastes bitter." She poured sugar into it.

Gat reached over to take her hand. She offered him the sugar dispenser. He smiled at this ploy, shook his head, and continued to hold her hand. She regarded him. "Recuperating in that hotel room in London, thinking about you all day—"

She looked surprised and he told her urgently, "Yes, I was thinking about you. You. My wife! I kept trying to see how this made any sense from your point of view."

"That's what I was wondering about you. Why would a man of the world want me? A girl who hasn't been anywhere, knows nothing, and can't even cook his eggs in the morning."

"I wrote you a letter here at Wits," Gat said. "Didn't you get it?"

Petra shook her head. "I didn't think soldiers wrote letters."

"I wrote you at three different universities. I tried to phone you in Cape Town. No listing. I never did know the address."

After a moment he asked, "What did your father tell you that makes you think you shouldn't touch me?"

Petra said nothing for a long moment, drinking her coffee and staring across the milk bar. Finally she said, "My father showed me the photo he took from you of your wife and child." She turned to watch his reaction. Gat frowned, perplexed. "She looks like a nice person and the baby's adorable."

"Petra," Gat said, "you're my wife. The only woman I've ever married."

"He said you told him I was just an adventure. Marrying me was a joke. He said you'd probably gone back to Belgium to be with your family."

"You're my family! I haven't set foot in Belgium for ten years. I've never married anyone but you. I love you. That's why I'm here."

Petra gazed at Gat, her eyes moving up and down his body. Finally she said, "My father did that to you, didn't he? He tried to break you."

"You can hardly blame him. I kept lying."

A smile played at the corners of her mouth.

"I don't want to talk about your father," Gat said. "He loves you very much. Too much, I think." Petra looked at him and drank of her coffee. She pushed the pastry toward Gat. He leaned forward to her. "I love you. I came back for you." She said nothing and did not look at him. "I told you about the African girl in the Equateur. About the secretaries at Union Minière. There is no wife in Belgium."

Finally Petra said, "Why does my father want to hurt me so much?" After a moment she said, "I'll be right back."

Gat watched her move through the tables to a public phone. When she returned, she said, "I called for a taxi. We can go to my flat."

"You're in a flat?" Gat asked. "Who with? You have flatmates?"

"The flat's on the second floor," Petra said. "Can you manage that?"

"I think so. We'll see." He smiled at her, pulling himself upright on the crutches.

ENTERING THE second-floor flat Gat wondered if, in the tiny space, there would be room enough for both Petra and him to sit at the same time. The place included a miniscule living room with a couch, a chair, and a table on which other of Petra's schoolbooks were piled, a kitchen carved out of a hall, and a tiny bedroom, filled by a double bed, a chair, and a vanity off which rose the smell of cosmetics. The living room gave onto a tiny balcony filled with potted plants and two sun chairs. When she saw Gat looking at the double bed, Petra told him, "I sleep out here." She lightly kicked the couch with her foot.

"Who sleeps in there?" Gat asked.

"My mother." Gat looked surprised. "She's in Rhodesia just now," she said. Gat nodded. "She and Father are living separately for a while," Petra said. Gat watched her, but she offered no more explanation. "My mother has a secret son in Rhodesia. So you can understand why I thought you might have a secret wife."

"Has your father had our marriage annulled?"

"Is that what you want?"

"What I want is to kiss you," Gat said. "Would you hold my crutches while I do that?" Gat offered the crutches. She refused to take them. "You don't feel sorry for me, do you? A man who can't grab his wife and kiss her. Can't chase her into the bedroom."

Petra smiled and shook her head.

"Good," Gat said. "I couldn't stand you feeling sorry for me." She nodded, but there were tears in her eyes. "None of that," he said. He reached out for her wrist, seized it, and pulled her toward him. He put his arms around her and kissed her. "I kiss you and you cry!" he complained.

She brushed tears from her eyes, and pulled out of his grasp. "I'll put on a kettle for tea."

"We just had coffee," Gat said. The girl shrugged and went into the kitchen. Gat sat down on the couch. He listened to her putting the kettle to boil. He heard the clinkings of her—his wife, amazing!—setting out cups. He shoved his crutches under the couch and sat back. He was tired, but for the first time in more than a month he was not conscious of pain in his feet. When she returned, she stood watching him.

"I want us to be married," Gat said. "What do you want?"

"What do you want? What do I want? I hate this kind of talk," Petra said. "Kobus came to see me. We talked this way the whole time."

"Did he forgive you for me?"

"He said he wanted me." She stood, her fists clenched, then paced back and forth across the narrow room. Gat smiled inside and made sure to keep the smile off his face.

"God forbid I should talk like Kobus!" he said.

"Yes!" she agreed. She stopped pacing and turned to him, her fists on her hips. "For God's sake what happened to your virility when you fell off the cliff? Was it shaken out of you?"

"It's in very good shape," he assured her. "I'd like to prove that to you, but I'm trying hard not to force you—"

"We're married. Didn't you come here to claim what's yours?"

"You're a feisty woman!"

"You married me. Claim me!"

When she started pacing again, Gat grabbed her by the skirt. He pulled her to him. She fell against him, jarred his legs. Pain surged from his feet, but he did not even wince. He kissed her and her response told him that everything was going to be all right. He pulled the pair of gold rings from his pocket, took her left hand, and slipped the smaller ring onto its third finger. He gave her the larger of the rings. She fitted it onto his left hand. They kissed. And continued to kiss until the teakettle whistled.

WHEN MARGARET walked out of baggage claim, returning from Rhodesia, and saw a waving hand shoot up from a radiant young woman who looked remarkably like Petra, she knew it was not studying that had put the bloom back in her daughter's cheeks. "You don't need to tell me a thing," Margaret assured her as they embraced. "You exude it. Where is he?"

"He's right over there," Petra said, gesturing toward a man standing erect, but tentatively against a wall. He bowed slightly and smiled at Margaret. "I don't want him carrying your bags," Petra said, taking her mother's suitcase. "He's finally gotten off crutches." Gat started toward the two women walking carefully.

"Off crutches?" Margaret asked.

"He won't tell me what happened. When Father deported him to England, I take it, he was hardly able to stand. That business about the other wife? All lies."

As Margaret reached Gat, she opened her arms to him and hailed him, "Hello again, son-in-law!" She grinned and embracing him felt him uncertain on his feet. She did not release him until Petra embraced them both and Margaret shifted his weight to her daughter.

"How was your son?" Petra asked as they started toward the parking lot. Margaret stopped, flummoxed by the words.

"Mum, he's my husband!" Petra reminded her. "He knows a couple of family secrets."

"And who would I tell?" Gat asked. "You're the only people I know here."

Margaret shrugged. "He's fine. Married now. The wife's expecting a child. We went to his farm for an overnight."

"Did you have time with him?"

"He drove me around the farm," Margaret said. "I almost told him. But his mother's not ready for that yet."

As Petra drove away from the airport, she explained to her mother that they had moved her to a hotel. "I'm sure Father will be happy to pay for it."

"It won't be for long," Gat assured her.

Petra broke the news. "We are off to Australia next week. It's all arranged. Gat bought the tickets."

Margaret sat in the rear seat of the car, feeling suddenly old. Her role as a mother had ended. JC was in England; Petra was headed for Australia. She wondered what would become of her now. She wondered if Piet knew about these plans. She did not ask.

"Gat? Do I call you Gat?" Margaret asked as they left her at her hotel.

"Please."

"Is there some time when we could talk? I need to get to know you."

They arranged to have a late breakfast together on a morning when Petra, who was still going to classes, would be at Wits.

THEY ATE in the hotel dining room overlooking a small garden at the rear of the place. Gat expressed his hope that he and Margaret could be friends. Margaret assured him that this was her hope too. Gat told her about his background. He declared that he had never been married before he married Petra. He had heard about a photo of a woman purported to be his wife. He had no wife but Petra. Margaret assured him that she believed him. She was not entirely sure she did, however, for believing him would entail her acknowledging that her husband had lied to her and Petra. She asked if Gat was certain that he must take Petra as far away as Australia. Was there not some place closer where they could make a good life for themselves? Gat replied that Petra seemed really to want to go to America. "I've promised her a visit there once we've put aside some money."

Having finished her scrambled eggs, leaving a portion of bacon untouched on her plate, the "polite bite" that her mother had always counseled her to leave, Margaret set her knife and fork tightly beside each other, pointed from the center of the plate toward six o'clock. Gat watched her. He detected in the precision of her orderliness a disquiet about the disorderliness with which he and Petra had found and committed themselves to one another. "You must be a little uneasy about the way Petra and I behaved," he said. "I want you to be as happy for her as we are for ourselves." Gat gazed at her a moment. "So let's speak frankly to each other," he said. "You must have things you want to say to me."

Margaret reset the knife and fork although they had not moved since she placed them carefully on the plate. She wondered what exactly this young man meant. She looked up to watch him carefully.

He said, "Please, say them."

A little shyly, glancing at him only occasionally, Margaret told him of her long-ago romance with the lad and of its outcome. She explained that her son was now farming, happily enough as far as she could tell, living the sort of life his father had offered her when he told her he would leave the university so that they could be married. "Of course, I wish we had not made our mistake," she acknowledged. "But, given the situation, I'm sure I did the right thing. I would not have been happy living on a farm, even with a man I loved."

Gat nodded, fairly certain that he understood the point she was trying to make. He wished she would relax. Margaret kept playing with her utensils, straightening them. Finally Gat said, "What are you trying to tell me?"

"I know that being young and in love can be wonderful."

"I'm not quite that young," Gat told her with a smile.

"It can be wonderful even when you're not as young as Petra. I know being in bed together when you're young and in love can be beautiful." Gat watched her. "You and Petra had a lovely, wonder-filled week together. Is that enough for a marriage?"

"Yes."

"Because if it's not, do yourselves the favor of not staying married. It's romantic flying off to Australia, but it will not be easy. You will know no one but each other. Neither of you will have jobs. You'll have no family to fall back on and no network of friends. It may be that the best thing you two can do is to thank each other for the week you had together and move on in your separate lives."

"I love her," Gat said simply. "She rescued me from—" He shrugged. "We really have talked about this. The love is strong enough to last."

Margaret smiled, a little ruefully. "I accept you at your word," she said. After a moment she added, "I want to apologize for what my husband—"

"Don't," Gat interrupted her. "You had nothing to do with it."

"He must have done to you what I try not to think about him doing to others. And he did it to his son-in-law."

"I don't feel any animosity toward him," Gat said. "Really. I understand why he acted as he did. He loves his daughter and I stole her from him when he wasn't looking. He had a right to be upset."

"I won't defend him to you."

"He and I have something in common. We both love Petra. She loves him. I won't do anything that damages that love. So I haven't told her what happened when he interrogated me. I don't want to do anything to make her feel that loving me means she can't love him. She'll love me less if she does."

"He would not be so generous to you."

"Why should he be?" asked Gat. "He loved her first."

As THEIR departure drew closer, Petra began curiously to feel a yearning for the homeland she had not yet left. One morning as they stood together in the small kitchen, she told Gat, "I don't know what to do about my father."

"Go see him," Gat urged.

"But how?" she asked. "I don't have the money to fly to Cape Town. And I can't ask you for it."

He nodded over his cereal bowl. "We'll need all the money I've got to keep us afloat in Australia." They stared separately into their cups of coffee. Finally Gat said, "Let me see what I can do."

Once Petra left the apartment, Gat called his mother-in-law. He asked to see her. They had tea together and he put the proposition to her. "I can arrange that," Margaret said. "Her father will buy her the ticket as well he should."

When Petra went to thank her mother, Margaret gave her a check and asked that she telephone her father to set up the visit. Petra made the call from her mother's hotel room. Colonel Rousseau's secretary chatted in a friendly way and said she would put Petra right through. Then she returned to say that her father was in a meeting and could not be disturbed. Petra called twice more that day, but failed to reach her father. When she called that evening, knowing that he almost never went out at night, there was no answer at home. When she called his office the next day and again received evasive replies, she understood that he would not speak to her. She flew to Cape Town that afternoon.

Hazel picked her up at the airport and dropped her off at home. She embraced Elsie, told her about Gat and Joeys and Wits and implored her not to tell her father that she was in the house. Then in the gathering darkness she went to wait for her father in the small parlor where he always went through the day's mail.

Petra heard him enter the house and call a greeting to Elsie. Soon the colonel entered the small parlor. Petra did not know what to do. She could not jump up and hug him. Nor would she make accusations against him. She sat without moving and observed him. He took a chair, turned on a lamp, and began to sort through letters and bills. After a moment he stopped. She watched him sense that something was amiss. He took control of himself, listened without moving, his policeman's instincts all on alert. He glanced about the room, ready to confront whatever danger might await him. Then he saw her. Involuntarily he gasped. He peered at her. He raised a hand before his face, the palm outward, so that she could not look at him. He turned away.

Finally Petra said, "I didn't want to leave South Africa without seeing you."

Rousseau kept his hand before his face. In the silence between them Petra heard a flutter of breath escape from his throat. She wondered if he were crying. She had never seen him cry. She wondered: Should I go to him? When she sat forward in her chair, as if to rise, he stood abruptly. He hurried from the room. She sat back in her chair, wondering what to do. She rose and followed him, only to hear his Buick backing out of the driveway. She ran onto the front stoep and watched the car drive off down the street.

Petra waited in the small parlor for her father to return. Finally Elsie came in to inquire what she wished to do about dinner. Petra went to the kitchen and ate with Elsie at the small table covered with oilcloth as she and JC had sometimes done when they were children. Then, after thanking Elsie for the meal, she returned to the small parlor. She sat in the darkness, waiting for her father. She thought about the family's life together, all the good things they had done over the years, the love they had shared.

When she realized that her father would not return that night, she walked through each room of the dark house. In the formal parlor she bid good-bye to the large portraits of burgher forebears who had come to the Cape from Europe three centuries before and to the piano on which JC had often played. In the dining room she swept her hand across the table at which she had dined her entire life. In the kitchen she touched the stove; she wished now that she had not spurned Elsie's efforts to teach her to cook. Upstairs she sat for a moment on the bed in her parents' room where she was conceived. Her mother's perfume was still embedded in the pillows. In JC's room she opened the closet where he had stowed his cricket gear. It retained the odor of that gear, the scent of her brother. She had thought to spend her last night in the house in her own room. But when it came time to sleep she chose instead the bed where she and Gat had first been together.

MARGARET PICKED her up the next day at Jan Smuts airport. "You know how hard it is for your father to admit he's wrong," she remarked when Petra told her what happened. Petra remembered how strong her father had always seemed, how confident, a veritable rock. "You know who he is now," her mother said. "That he's lied to you for years. Your knowing that humiliates him. But because of the *volk* he will never change."

As they drove through the streets of Johannesburg, Petra's nostalgia for her homeland, for the Cape, for the comfortable childhood she and JC had shared: all that drained away.

THAT NIGHT as they lay together in bed, holding one another and not yet ready for sleep, Petra told Gat that she was ready now to depart. For a long moment he said nothing. Finally she asked, "Did you hear what I said?" Gat kissed her hair and made no reply. "What is it?"

Finally he said, "I've been as stupid as your friend Kobus might have been."

"What?" she exclaimed with a laugh. "Impossible!"

Gat told her that he had had dinner with her mother the previous evening. They had talked about the things Petra would most like to do in her new life. "And I said, 'She wants to find a job that makes enough money to support me.'"

"Of course!" Petra agreed. "That's my top priority. What else?"

"You want to rent me a house where I can bring my mates—they're called 'mates,' I believe, in Australia—for meals that you'll make and beer you'll provide."

"Really. And what did she say?"

"She said, 'Petra wants to ride an elevator to the top of the Empire State Building. And climb up inside the Statue of Liberty.'" Gat turned toward his wife and put his arms around her. "'She wants to bicycle across the Golden Gate bridge.'" Petra lay quiet in his arms. He pressed her closer to him. "'She wants to walk down Hollywood Boulevard and watch movie stars pass in golden convertibles on the street.'"

"My mother sees too many movies," Petra said.

"She said, 'Petra wants to see Half Dome in Yosemite Valley and hike to the bottom of the Grand Canyon.'" They stared into the darkness. Gat kissed her hair.

"I don't really want that," she said.

"You want kangaroos jumping through your backyard, do you?" Neither of them spoke. "And duck-billed platypuses in your—" Gat paused. "What do duck-billed platypuses get into anyway?"

"Your bathtub."

"Your mother says you want to go to American drive-ins and order gallons of American ice cream." He added, "I wouldn't mind doing that myself."

Petra reached up to touch his cheek.

"She says you want to finish your studies at UCLA. Or Harvard. Or Yale. Or 'the University of New York.'" They were quiet for a time. Finally Gat said, "You can't do any of those things in Australia."

"I want to be with you," Petra told him. "And you're going to Australia."

They talked for a while and Petra swore that she wanted to do whatever Gat wanted. After all, the goal of her life was to please him. Which made him burst into laughter. "Oh, do you?" he asked. "You who are not a dishrag?" Anyway, he said, she already pleased him more than he could tell her. She suggested then that he might give her proof of that fact. He declined, saying they must first straighten out their destiny. Then he would provide all the proof she needed.

They talked on. Each assured the other—repeatedly!—that whatever the other wanted was fine. Not only fine, but super. What was really important was being together. They finally agreed that this kind of talk was not only stupid but, in fact, almost infuriating. They ended up deciding to go to America. And while Petra slept peacefully in his arms, Gat worried about how to get her there and how to provide for her once they arrived.

Getting the proper papers for entering America was no simple matter. It took Gat several months to trace his sister and her American husband through his parents to their new home in Tucson, Arizona, a place neither Gat nor Petra had ever heard of. Neither could they pronounce it. Since the sister had not heard from him in a decade, it required a number of expensive phone calls to explain what had become of him and to secure her and her husband's agreement to sponsor his and Petra's immigration. Then visits to Pretoria were needed to push the papers through the American Embassy.

As their departure drew near, Petra sent her father an overnight telegram. She announced that she and Gat would leave shortly for America. She urged her father to come to Joeys to see them off. He could collect Margaret at that time and take her back to the Cape. But Petra heard nothing from him. He did not appear at the airport.

By the time they left, Gat had fully recovered his strength. So fully, in fact, that as he and Petra walked across the tarmac, he picked her up in his arms, trotted up the movable stairway and onto the plane.

FOUR MONTHS after they arrived in America, Petra wrote her father a letter on his fiftieth birthday. She included their phone number, hoping that he would call her. A week later she received a telephone call from Cape Town. "It's so good to hear your voice!" she kept telling him. When she asked how he was, he said he was fifty. He insisted he had called to find out how she was.

She told him that the first weeks in their new homeland had been difficult. Neither she nor Gat wanted to stay in Tucson. It was a small city in a desert and saguaro cactuses frightened her. They had moved on to San Diego, a place slightly reminiscent of Cape Town, where they had rented a small house. She was looking for a position; Gat had found a job. She would not have gotten through all the trying times, she said, had she not been with someone she loved. Her father did not react to that declaration. When she asked again how things were with him, he told her what she already knew: that her mother was still in Johannesburg. "She's waiting up there for me to beg her to come home."

"You can do that, Father," Petra assured him. "She's worth it."

"She wants to humiliate me," her father complained. "Even though she knows I was only doing what I thought best for the family." He sounded older, feebler. Confidence had gone from his voice. As she said good-bye, Petra urged him to call again. They did not have the money right now, she explained, for her to call him. But she wanted to stay in touch. When she hung up, she wondered if he would ever actually go to Joeys for her mother.

At Christmas Gat sent his parents a photo of himself, the first image they had seen of him in many years. The photo showed him sitting on the fender of a used Chevrolet coupe before a small house—a "ranch," he called it. Beside him stood quite a beautiful young woman. The photo, he explained, would serve to introduce them to his wife, Petra, whom he had met at church in Cape Town. She had taken him, not only to America, but to a country he had never known before, the undiscovered country of love. He explained that he now managed properties for a real estate company that developed housing tracts. Petra worked as a receptionist for a firm of attorneys. In the coming year she would be resuming her university studies. They planned to have children, but not until they had framed her college diploma and hung it over their mantel.

He wrote that he had taken a new name for a new country. He was now called Adriaan Gautier. In San Diego the name was pronounced "Gow-tire." His "buddies" at work were beginning to call him Ty. Now and then even Petra used that name. He wrote that the man he had been when they last saw him had disappeared. The man he was now could not be happier in this new country he and Petra had discovered together.

ACKNOWLEDGMENT

For information about the execution of Patrice Lumumba, I am indebted to Ludo De Witte and his book *The Assassination of Lumumba*. London and New York: Verso Books, 2001.